I0645473

SYLVAN DREAMS

MAPLE HILL CHRONICLES
BOOK TWO

ELIZABETH R. ALIX

Copyright © 2022 Elizabeth G. Wilmerding

All rights reserved.

This is a work of fiction. Names, places and events are products of the author's imagination or used in a fictitious manner. Any resemblance to actual persons living or dead or actual events is coincidental.

No part of this book may be reproduced in any form or by any electronic or mechanical means, including information storage and retrieval systems, without written permission from the author, except for the use of brief quotations in a book review.

Printing History: First Edition, November 2106, ISBN-13 978-0-9985243-1-3

Second Edition, September 2022, print: ISBN 978-0-9985243-4-4

E-book: ISBN 978-0-9985243-5-1

Cover illustration and layout by 100 Covers https://100covers.com/

Supported by Palouse Digital Press, Pullman, WA USA: http://palousedigitalpress.com/

Distributed by IngramSpark

✿ Created with Vellum

*To Raphael who told me stories about
picking up hitchhikers in Jamaica.
To Austin, always.*

CHAPTER 1

$\mathcal{R}$uari closed his eyes and ran his fingers over the surface of the lazy Susan, feeling for any roughness. The faint scent of fresh wood rose in their wake. He smiled. The dark Celtic knot inlay over the honey maple background was smooth as the proverbial baby's bottom. He examined the design critically one last time. It had taken weeks to get it right, but the result was worth it. Now when a potential client called to ask if he could do inlay, he could in all confidence say yes. He couldn't get the last client back, but maybe he could catch the next one.

Aye, it's a braw job, laddie.

He glanced at the photo of a craggy-faced man with a wild shock of salt and pepper hair and stubbled cheeks staring out with a fierce glare. Around the magazine clippings, a dozen photos of a tree arched like a cathedral window. It was the same huge, old, copper beech tree from different angles, in different seasons. Ruari had taken them from his grandfather's barn studio in Scotland when he'd gone for the funeral.

A braw job.

He turned the piece over and fastened the metal hardware onto the blank back and checked the results for a smooth action.

He then wrapped it carefully in a towel to protect the finish on the way over to his parents' place later.

He got out a broom and swept up his former carriage house studio. What was Marianne doing today? Their simple coffee date at the Maple Hill Co-op had been way more eventful than he'd expected when her ex had shown up. Ruari's knuckles whitened on the handle of the broom remembering how Marianne had shrunk in her seat as the arrogant bastard had berated her. Ruari had been an inch away from escorting the guy by the shirt front out of the sidewalk cafe' when Marianne had spoken up. She didn't throw a single punch, but her words had leveled the guy better than any fist.

Afterwards, they'd gone for a long walk and talked about lots of things and nothing at all. It was the nicest date he'd had since he and Jenny had split.

The stale remnants of shame and guilt washed over him. Jenny had been a wonderful woman, but he'd gotten cold feet and backed out shortly before their wedding. His parents had been confused and embarrassed. He'd fielded furious calls from her friends and family before it was over. His sister Erin had been the only one to say, *I don't get it, but you must've had a reason.* Since then, he'd hunkered down, focused on his job, his craft, and avoided any entanglements.

Marianne had upended his routine with her broken windows and strange stories about ghosts and remembered fires. She made him tongue-tied and shy. She was beautiful and odd and painfully honest. She seemed to like him. *Can I trust myself not to hurt her?* When he thought back, he couldn't remember clearly why he'd gotten cold feet with Jenny. *I must've had a reason.*

I should call Marianne and ask her out again. Panic warred with the flush of pleasure at that thought. *But maybe give it a couple days. I have to survive the family Labor Day barbecue first.*

He pushed the sawdust into the pan and dumped it in the trash. His eyes fell on the cloth-wrapped bundle on a shelf below the pictures. Another wash of feelings, these more on the anger and sorrow end of the scale. One of these days, he'd have the time to try piecing that together again. He hadn't had the heart in three years.

Three years ago, Ruari had made a box for Granda. He poured all his love and skill into it as a kind of masterpiece to give his mentor as a gift. Made of European beech, it was twelve inches long, perfect for keepsakes or Granda's collection of small carving chisels. Ruari had carved an elaborate spray of beech leaves and seeds on the fitted lid. It was one of the most detailed pieces he'd ever done, and he'd been very proud of it. When he finished it, he imagined the old man's words in his thick Scots brogue. "Aye, it's a braw job ye done."

Ruari brought it with him on the next family trip to the farm in Scotland. Nana was gone by then, and his crusty old grandfather rattled around the farmhouse and grounds by himself. While Mom, Dad, and Erin got the rental car unloaded, he went hunting for Granda. He finally found him in the barn studio.

"Granda? We're here."

The interior was dim but for a single pool of light and a hunched figure on a stool. "Granda?" Ruari heard the scratching of a chisel on wood. His grandfather wasn't hard of hearing. He should have looked up by now. Ruari shivered a little in the damp chill. Maybe he was in one of his trances.

When Ruari was small, it was his job to retrieve Granda at dinner time. Sometimes the old man was so deeply absorbed in his work that he was oblivious to anything else. When he was six, Ruari had peeked at what held his attention. A startlingly lifelike, stern face emerged from a block of wood, and he half expected the eyes to snap open and glare at him. In contrast, Granda's face was curiously blank. Goosebumps prickled Ruari's arms the longer he watched. It was as though someone else stared out of his beloved grandfather's eyes.

"Granda?" He whispered tentatively, touching the old man's leg. It took several tries.

At last the old man came back from wherever he'd been, his shoulders relaxed, and he sighed. "Ach, Ruari, I didn't see you there. Tatties and neeps is it?"

He nodded. "Nana says it's hot. Who is that?"

The carver looked at the piece in his hands as if for the first time. He scratched his stubbly jaw with the blunt end of his chisel. "Ach well, this is The Old Man of the Forest, you see. He was a fierce fellow."

Young Ruari shivered. "He looks scary."

"He was. You didn't want to cross him."

Granda's focus and concentration on his work remained legendary throughout his life.

Ruari now approached the hunched figure on the stool. He was close enough to see over Granda's shoulder at the table in front of him. A shock coursed through his system like lightning, raising the hairs on his arms. The chisel's handle had been wrapped with leather so it was oddly bulbous. Granda's hands, beautiful strong things that had picked Ruari up as a child, were twisted and the knuckles were swollen. The tendons and muscles stood out on his right forearm as he guided the chisel over the surface of the wood. A simple pattern was developing, but the lines were wavy from irregular pressure. As he watched, the old man's hand spasmed and the tool slipped, digging too deeply into the grain. It looked like something Ruari had made in grade school. Ruari's own hands suddenly tightened.

He cleared his constricted throat. "Granda?" He touched the old man's shoulder.

Coll Allen startled and looked up. He put the tool down. "Hey, Ruari lad. Here already are you?"

"Yeah, Dad and the others are in the house."

"Tatties and neeps time is it?" He asked, recalling their familiar exchange.

"Aye. Erin's got her heart set on going to the little tearoom in the village."

"Best not disappoint her then." He got up stiffly and moved toward the door slowly.

Ruari came alongside him and offered his arm. The old man pushed him away.

"Haud your wheesht. I'm not so feeble as that."

Ruari dropped his arm and relaxed, following him out the door.

Later over lunch, Ruari couldn't contain his excitement any longer. They'd all eaten a good meal, and the jet lag and lingering sense of Americanness had fallen away. They were in Scotland for the entire week.

"Granda, I wanted to give you something." He pulled a brown paper-wrapped parcel out of his backpack.

"What's this now?"

"It's a late Christmas and birthday present for you."

"There's no cause to be doing anything like that." But Granda undid the string anyway and folded back the paper to reveal the pale wood box.

Erin peered past his arm. "Ruari, you didn't show me this!"

"I meant it to be a surprise." Erin was the only one in his family who came by his studio. She usually demanded to see what he was working on, but he'd kept this one under wraps. She couldn't keep a secret.

She scowled and stuck her tongue out at him.

"Ruari, it's beautiful," his mom murmured, but Ruari hardly heard her. All his attention was focused on the old man.

Granda turn the box over, examining all the corners and edges, automatically checking the joints. He ran a finger over the beech leaves on top, his face pensive. Ruari waited for the words, *it's a braw job, laddie*. Finally, Granda looked up and smiled gently. "Thank you, Ruari." He set the box aside and wrapped the paper around it again for the trip home.

Rauri felt his chest slowly implode. He waited for something more, but Granda just looked away. Rauri's eyes flicked to the box and the beginning of the design where he hadn't been as confident with the interwoven leaves. Or perhaps he'd chosen the wrong design altogether. He should've done a face. His grandfather would have been impressed by a face.

As he looked away, he caught sight of his father's expression. Flushed with emotion, Dad pressed his downturned lips together angrily. Ruari couldn't recall seeing such a look of bitterness and anger on his father's face before and couldn't fathom what it meant.

Six months later they were all back in Scotland again. It was the wrong season, and they were there for the wrong reason. Granda had died in his sleep, and the family was gathering for the funeral. During the long weekend of family meals and conversations, meeting people who had been friends and admirers of both Granda and Nana during their lifetime, Ruari found time to slip away to the barn studio.

He'd seen Dad disappear earlier and return, stamping snow off his boots at the back door and assumed he'd gone to have a little quiet. The need for peace and quiet after too many people was one of the few things he shared with his father. Feeling the sharp hollow of grief in his chest, Ruari followed the trail of footprints through the snowy backyard and pushed aside the barn door enough to slip inside. He flipped the lights on and closed the door behind him. Without a fire in the wood stove, it was as cold inside as out. He drew into his lungs the faint aromas of wood shavings, oil, stain, and fainter than that, animal dung and hay. It smelled peaceful and familiar. He relaxed enough to feel the ache in the back of his throat.

Walking along the benches lining the walls, he touched the tools hanging on the pegboard. Granda's shop was always immaculate and orderly. "A tidy shop helps you think clearly." On one wall, Granda had pinned a series of tree photos around the black and white pages of a magazine. Rows of carved faces looked down from the shelf. Life-sized portraits, their expressions were by turns fierce, wild, stern, sorrowful, and all of them slightly alien.

"What are we going to do with those awful carvings of Granda's?" Cousin Mary had said not ten minutes ago in the heat of the crowded living room. She was talking with her mother and Aunt Maggie.

"I don't think anyone'll want to buy them," Maura replied. "They're too eldritch."

"Aye, like evil fairies or something!" Maggie agreed. "I wouldn't want one of them staring down at me! Though I would never have told Coll that." They all laughed.

"I suppose we could try Ebay or Etsy. There's plenty of strange people in this world who might like them," Mary suggested.

That conversation had pushed Ruari out the door. No one understood Granda's work. As he looked along the row of wooden faces, he felt a lump rise in his throat. It was the end of part of his own life. He trailed a hand along the shelf.

In one corner of the shop, a couple of dust covered broken chairs bearing tags tied on with string waited for repairs. One chair stood askew with something on the seat. Curious, he stepped closer to see better.

It was his box. Ruari's heart dropped into his shoes. The lid had been smashed into pieces, the sides split by the force. Someone had put the remains in this out of the way spot. He could see where the dust on the floor had been disturbed. Nearby on a bench lay Granda's ancient wood mallet. Flecks of pale wood were embedded in the head, and small fragments lay on the tabletop. Who would do this? Why?

It had to have been Dad. He'd just come from the studio maybe half an hour ago. The look of rage on his face that day at the tearoom flooded Ruari's mind. That jealous, selfish bastard. It was fortunate his father was nowhere near as Ruari's world focused down to thirty hours of painstaking work lying in splinters. His fists curled, and his breath came in short puffs.

He crouched and touched the fragments. A single, savage blow had struck the center of the lid, radiating cracks in several directions and shattering the sides. He might repair it with a lot of glue and patience, but it would never be the same. Hot tears spilled down his cheeks, and his hands shook as he gently gathered the pieces together. He found an old blue cotton apron of Nana's and wrapped them up.

He thought of returning to the house, the mangled body of the box in his hands, to see the look on his father's face when he realized Ruari knew. He thought of how good it would feel to throw the first punch. Instead, he held his breath for three counts and looked over Granda's life arrayed in the shop, waiting for decay to claim it. Memories filled his mind.

A wave of dizziness rolled over him, and his knees hit the floor painfully. He shook his head, panting.

What just happened?

Maybe he'd caught his foot on something and stumbled. He stood, bracing himself on the workbench for a moment.

He'd come out here to be away from the crowded house and found the remains of his beautiful gift smashed to splinters. Dad. He remembered feeling incandescently angry, but now he just felt a dull, empty ache. He thought someone had spoken to him. Had it been the ghost of Granda himself? Something about continuing to teach Ruari if he just let him in.

Get a grip, Ruari. The old man is gone. Nothing you can do about that.

He took a deep breath. He wasn't ready to go back to the house just yet.

Erin found him nearly two hours later covered in sweat and a powdering of sawdust, loading the last of Granda's wood into the storage loft. The time had passed in a blur, and he felt much better.

"Ruari, you in here? It's been ages," she called as she stamped the snow off her boots.

He wiped his face on his sleeves, smearing the tracks of tears, sweat, and grime across clean skin. "Over here."

"You okay?"

"Fine."

"Funeral tea's breaking up," she said. "You can come back now."

"Just a minute. Almost done." He put up the last piece of wood and followed her out, turning the lights off as he left. He didn't say anything to Dad. There was no point.

Before they left, he collected the bundle and took down all the pictures, tucking them into his luggage.

He hadn't been back to Scotland since that day.

Marianne curled up on her couch immersed in a copy of *The Illustrated Victoriana* for a bit of light reading. She'd picked it up at the antiques shop on Main after falling in love with the old photographs, postcards, and period posters. Occasionally, she made a note in her trusty journal for future research. Oscar stretched out in a sunbeam on the other end of the couch, rumbling an occasional dreamy purr. She smiled and rubbed his orange and white belly with her toes.

This is the way life should always be. Peaceful. No more ghosts in my house. No more crazy dreams about the house burning down. No ex stalking me online or in town. And a handsome, sweet handyman who wants to go out with me.

Her cell phone interrupted her reverie with an old-fashioned ring. She pushed back her brown hair and put the phone to her ear.

"Hey, Marianne, how's it going?"

"Hey Gillian! I'm good. How about you?" She hadn't heard from Gillian in a couple of weeks. No surprises. Her friend was busy juggling responsibilities as a young professor in the history department at Park University in New York.

"That's great—it's about to get better!" Her voice filled with suppressed excitement. "How would you like to teach a course with me in January?"

Marianne swung her feet to the floor as she sat up. "Yes, please!"

"The department liked your idea about Victorian influences in America. If we pitch it right, they'll pick it up, and we can run it spring semester."

"That's great!"

"The only drawback is that I'm absolutely booked this semester. I'm teaching four courses, advising three grad students, and on a committee. You're going to have to carry the ball on this one."

"Oh." She'd never taught an entire class on her own. She'd been hoping to learn how from a more seasoned teacher like Gillian before she had to do one by herself. "You won't be able to help at all?"

"Like I said, I've got a full load. You know I'm trying to get tenure. I have to get a peer reviewed article out the door by November on top of everything else."

"Can you at least look things over?" She felt a queasy slosh of dismay.

"Sure. You can handle this! You don't have any other jobs right now, right?"

"I guess." *But I've never done a whole class. I was hoping to work with you!* She wanted to add.

Gillian lowered her voice a little. "So, I let Dr. Plank know about our plans, but because you haven't taught your own class yet, he wants to see a syllabus and three complete lectures before he's sold on the idea."

Dr. Plank? She knew his work in the history journals, of course. It was unassailable, and people quoted him all the time. *I have to impress him? Yikes.* Well, she could come up with lots of good stuff by Thanksgiving, for sure. "As long as you're willing to look over my shoulder and check my work. What's the deadline?"

"That's the other kicker. They need to put their course offerings together by the end of October, so you're going to have to submit everything by the middle of October."

That's not a lot of time, but I really need this job. "I guess don't have a ton on my plate at the moment. I should be able to do that."

"Great! I knew I could count on you! I'll send you the details in an email this weekend."

"I'll look for it. Um, do you have any idea how much they'd pay me to do the class?"

"They usually pay about five thousand a class."

That wasn't too bad. It would certainly pay the rent for a semester and keep her and Oscar in food.

"By the way, Dr. Plank is a stodgy old so and so who's not very forgiving. If you impress him, you're in. If you don't, he'll never change his mind."

Marianne made up her mind. She needed his support if she was going to teach anywhere in the city. "No problem, Gillian, I got this!"

"Perfect!"

Gillian hung up, and the phone sank into Marianne's lap. She pulled out a calendar. That would be at least thirteen lectures. How many students? What level would they be at? Probably freshmen and sophomores, but maybe a few upper classmen. She was going to have to teach basics but still try to engage the more advanced students. It was going to be a challenge, but it was doable. She could do this. Her excitement welled up. If she got this, it meant income and would be a gateway to more teaching opportunities.

She dialed her grandmother to share the good news. Grandma Selene had been a lifeline throughout Marianne's awful divorce and recently revealed that she, too, had a touch of clairvoyance.

"Hello?"

"Grandma, it's me!"

"Marianne, I've been meaning to call you. Thank you for a

wonderful time at your housewarming party." Her voice was tinged with a British accent, like a rich cup of Earl Gray tea with cream and sugar.

"I'm so glad you came. Remember, we talked about my teaching? My friend at Park University called a few minutes ago to offer me a chance to teach there next semester!"

"That's wonderful news! You love teaching, and your students will no doubt learn a lot."

"I hope so. I have to put together a syllabus and outline the first few classes before they accept me, but I have till the middle of October to do that."

"Sounds like you have it well in hand. Would you like to come for a visit sometime?"

"I'd love that."

"Perhaps next week. Just give me a call."

"I will," she promised and hung up. Still brimming with good news, she scrolled through her contact list. It was a holiday; Ruari should be around. A vision of his lightly tanned, freckled face under a fringe of reddish blond hair came to mind. The shy smile that lit up his blue-gray eyes. She hugged herself and dialed.

Ruari's cellphone rang, breaking his painful reverie. His old flip phone displayed the caller's name, scrolling it across the tiny blue screen. His heart did a little stutter.

"Marianne!"

"Hi Ruari! Happy Labor Day!"

"Same to you."

"I called to share some good news. A friend in the history department at Park University offered me a chance to teach a class with her!"

Ruari didn't know much about the inner workings of colleges, but he appreciated the best teachers he'd had in college and bet she'd be a good one. He would have spent too much time staring at her to pass the class, though. He smiled. "That's great!"

"Thanks! I'm worried about having to write most of the lectures since Gillian is so busy. But it's my one shot to get into teaching."

"I'm sure you'll do great." He groaned inwardly. *What dumb thing to say.* It had been so much easier to talk to her when he was fixing her dishwasher or her windows. "You still doing okay? After the other day, I mean?" *Way to go, bringing up her ex. It's probably the last thing she wants to remember.* He needed to ask her out again.

"I'm actually okay. I was scared at the time, but I needed to do it. It helped that you were there."

He felt his fist curl reflexively. "I just wanted to pound the guy when he was picking on you."

Her voice sounded warm. "I appreciate that. I'm glad you didn't, though. He would have found some way to get back at you or me, more likely. This way he left on his own, and his new girlfriend will take up all his time. With any luck, he'll forget all about me and move on."

"I hope you're right. If he bothers you again, tell me, and I'll back you up." *With my fists, if I'm lucky.*

"Thanks."

Suddenly his phone buzzed with another call. "Shoot, I'm sorry. I have another call coming in."

"That's okay. Talk to you later. 'Bye."

" 'Bye." He pressed the button and answered, "Ruari Allen."

"Mr. Allen?" The woman's voice sounded impatient and unfamiliar. "I'm calling from two-twenty-one Oak Street. You were here a couple of days ago for an overflowing toilet? It's broken. Again. You have to come fix it."

He suppressed a sigh. "Certainly, ma'am. Give me twenty minutes."

"Twenty?! We have people here! They can't hold it forever!"

"Yes, ma'am, I'll be there as soon as I can."

"You'd better be or your office'll hear about it." She cut the connection.

He groaned. There went the rest of his free day. Plumbing was either a five-minute fix or five hours. Mom and Dad were expecting him at four for their annual family picnic.

And he had to find a time to call Marianne back. Why hadn't he asked her out again? Coffee, dinner, something. His sister and cousins had the gift of gab, but, like Granda, he wasn't good with words when it came to women.

CHAPTER 2

*R*uari threw on his Kelly green polo shirt with the Gloria's Valley Homes and Properties logo on the left breast pocket, and got into his battered white pickup. Agency rules stated he had twenty-four hours to respond to crises, but Mr. Carter had been through so much that Ruari was willing to come out on a holiday. He straightened his shirt reflexively and got out his box of plumbing gear.

A woman with long, wavy blonde hair and dark red lipstick opened the door. Attractive in a sharp sort of way, she gave him a piercing once over and sniffed. The light from down the hall gave her an odd green corona, and he blinked. He wondered who this woman was to Mr. Carter. She acted like she owned the place.

"Mr. Allen? Please come in. It's the bathroom on the first floor back by the kitchen."

He entered and followed her down the hall. Her dress fit her curves and was short enough to show her shapely calves.

She gestured toward the bathroom with one hand and stood aside with her arms folded as if she planned to watch his every move. *Geez lady, I'm not going to steal the soap.*

His family had taught him to be polite and respectful to

women, regardless. He gave her a brief smile and stepped inside. This was the bathroom below the one that had flooded a couple of days ago. The ruined lath and plaster on the ceiling and the bare floor below belied the cleanliness of the rest of the room. An open window and a plug-in canister of air freshener were gamely trying to overcome the odors of damp wood, plaster, and an unhappy toilet. Various things floated in an overly full bowl like a drunk about to throw up. He set down his plumbing bucket and got to work.

I'm so tired of doing this. I just want to be in my studio and call Marianne back and ask her out.

Twenty minutes later he cleared the blockage, most likely a wad of paper or feminine product. He washed his hands and grabbed his tool bucket. Out in the empty hall, he followed the sound of voices into the kitchen. Several people were milling about eating dip and vegetables, and the smell of grilled meat cut through the bathroom smell lingering in his nostrils.

Mr. Carter separated himself from the others and walked over. He wore a tweed driving cap over his bald head, and his clothes hung loosely on his thin frame. Was he even thinner than the last time? Ruari wasn't sure.

"I'm sorry to bring you out on a holiday, Ruari," he said apologetically, his voice reedy. "Thank you for coming."

"No trouble. It's all clear. Please remind your guests: the pipes are old, so only flush toilet paper and human waste."

"Of course."

The blonde woman bustled up and put her arm around his shoulders. "Dad, it's his job to fix things. You don't have to thank him. Go enjoy your party. I can take care of this." Mr. Carter tottered off. Now that Ruari saw them side by side, he saw the resemblance.

Her voice sharpened again. "Mr. Allen, if there are any further problems, direct them to me, please."

"Certainly. Leave your number with the agency, and Mrs. Talmadge can take care of it." She was backlit by the kitchen windows, and for a brief second she was outlined in a dark green flash again. He squeezed his eyes shut and opened them. *What was that?*

She stiffened. "Is there a problem, Mr. Allen?"

"No, ma'am. Have a good evening." He turned and walked out.

When Ruari got home, he had time for a quick shower, and a change of clothes, before heading over to Mom and Dad's place. Trying to salvage the remnants of his good mood earlier, he dialed Marianne's number before he could chicken out. She answered on the third ring.

"Hi Ruari, what's up?"

"Would you like to try having coffee again?"

"I'd really like that! Do you have time now?"

"I have a family thing I have to go to tonight. Maybe next weekend?"

"That sounds good. Where would you like to go? I'm kind of over the Co-op."

His phone buzzed with another incoming call. "Sorry, I have another call."

"That's okay. I'll look into a few places and get back to you." She sounded happy.

"Great!" His phone buzzed again. " 'Bye."

" 'Bye."

He looked at the little screen. Caller ID read "Talmadge."

"Ruari Allen," he answered with a sinking feeling.

"Allen, I pay you to respond to rental emergencies quickly and professionally." Her voice sounded pinched and nasal when she was angry. "I just got a call from Staci Carter Greaves at two-twenty-one Oak Street. She told me you had taken overly long to respond to her father's emergency plumbing issue, and you were unprofessional in your manner."

He bristled. "No, I got there fifteen minutes after she called, fixed the problem in twenty, and was out of there ten minutes after that. I was absolutely professional. Mr. Carter was very happy with my work." Ruari felt his jaw muscles clench. Although he was Talmadge's only handyman and was more or less on call 24/7, she always made him feel like an errant college student.

"Perhaps, but his daughter was up for the weekend. She's a very successful real estate broker in Scarsdale. She was concerned for her father's well being."

"That plumbing is over fifty years old," he said tightly. "If you want to stop having plumbing issues, you'll have to replace it all."

"Well, then you'd better get on it this week, Allen. We don't want to be viewed as a substandard housing agency, since Staci Carter Greaves sends clients our way."

He couldn't restrain his outrage at her casual suggestion. "It would take weeks to pull out all the old pipes, replace them, and then do the wall repairs! He'd have to move out. You know that."

She paused and made a little noise of frustration. "Fine. Come up with something that looks good then."

He clenched the fist not holding the phone and said stiffly, "I have a family gathering to go to. I'm late."

"See you tomorrow, Allen. With a solution." She hung up.

Still fuming, he threw on a button-up shirt and his one pair of khaki pants for the occasion. He tucked the wrapped lazy Susan under one arm and set out. Walking to his parents' place would help clear his head. Maple Hill took about ten to fifteen minutes to cross, depending on where you were going and what you were carrying.

What was Staci Carter Greaves' problem? Now he had a load more work on his plate for the week, and his boss was going to be breathing down his neck until he fixed the plumbing. It figured Talmadge would demand a solution that appeared to solve the problem without actually addressing it.

It was deeply against his nature to do a bad or half-assed job. Granda had instilled in him the idea that if a job was worth doing, it was worth doing properly. How could he do the best job possible without compromising his work schedule? Maybe he could change out all the valves and make sure the shut off in the basement was working properly if there was another flood? That would take a day or two to implement, but would probably be enough. That would push his usual schedule of maintenance and repairs only by a day or so. He needed an assistant, but SueAnn Talmadge was too cheap to hire one. Maybe he could advertise for a good plumber, electrician, or even a general contractor who wanted side work and didn't mind doing odd jobs. Then he could interview them and present them to Talmadge in a positive light.

Yeah, that would work.

Ruari walked up the pavement to his childhood home, a light blue, two-story clapboard house with a small front yard. It had been a couple of weeks since he'd been there last. Spending more than half an hour in his Dad's company sent his blood pressure into dangerous territory. Last time, it had taken only five minutes before Dad tried to convince him to apply for a job in sanitation with the town of Maple Hill. The man still thought he needed to direct his son's life and didn't care how he did it.

Ruari had kept his cool and declined the offer, but he'd been on edge since then, wondering if the job issue would rear its ugly head again. The memory of the shattered box no longer throbbed like a fresh wound, but it festered quietly, making everything else with his dad hurt more.

It would be a relief to have a peaceful family picnic.

He went in the side door, straight into the kitchen. Mom stood at the counter putting the finishing touches on a red velvet cake, her contribution to the annual tradition. She looked up with a warm smile. "Ruari, glad you made it."

He pushed aside his brooding thoughts, mustered a smile, and gave her a peck on the cheek. "Good to see you, Mom." He put his package on the counter.

"What's this?" She asked.

"A little something I've been working on. I'll show you later."

She gazed at him for a long moment, and frowned. "You look a little harried. Everything okay?"

Ruari shrugged. "I had an emergency call at a rental just before this."

She patted his arm. "You're a good man, going to the rescue on a holiday. Your father's out in back by the barbecue. I think Erin's in her room."

He nodded, cutting through the dining room to the back, and stopped. Turning, he said, "Can I take anything out for you, Mom?"

She loaded him up with bowls of chips, cut veggies, and dip. "Erin," she called, "come help your brother."

A moment later Erin appeared in the doorway. She came up to Ruari's chin, had a rose and cream complexion that took after their mother's side of the family, and a shock of short red hair straight out of the Allen family tree. Today, she'd gelled it back into a crest that swooped out from the back of her head. She looked like a cockatoo with attitude. Her short tartan skirt showed off sturdy legs and black Doc Martins. She'd dressed like that in high school and still did a decade later.

"Hey, big brother," she greeted him. "You look like you got that." She gestured to his full hands balancing an extra bowl between his forearms.

He gave her a wry look. "So get the door, doofus."

She grinned and opened the sliding door to the deck with a flourish. "Any time I can be of help." She followed him out and shut the screen behind them. "I'll get the croquet set up. You ready to have your ass whupped?"

"You wish!"

"Hello, son!" Dad called. He stood with a long-handled spatula in one hand and a wicked looking, two-pronged fork in the other. His apron read, "City engineer by day, barbecue beast by night." A Christmas gift from Erin a couple of years back.

"Hi, Dad." Ruari put the food on the picnic table and got a beer from the cooler.

"How's work?"

Such a simple question, loaded with an entire circus caravan of freight. Ruari took a deep breath and let it out. He was determined to make this be a nice family picnic. If it went south, it wouldn't be his fault. "It's okay." Ruari had a sip of the cold, bitter beer and felt it glide down his throat and explode in his stomach. "You?"

"Busy." He turned and opened the grill to turn the marinated chicken pieces. Dad was proud of his special barbecue sauce. It was a family favorite. Raw steaks and burgers lay on a platter off to the side, ready to go.

"I'll go help Erin set up." Ruari stepped off the deck before the conversation could drift into dangerous waters.

He joined Erin on the grass.

"Nice evasion tactic," she murmured.

"Thanks. I thought you outgrew the Goth stuff," he replied.

"As if! I got sick of corporate-wear. I'm hoping my next job will think this is my uniform."

He laughed. "Well, Goth Girl, prepare to lose!"

The annual croquet match had been going since they were old enough to wield a mallet without braining someone else. He and Erin usually had their own match before the meal, and their parents joined in afterwards. The game brought the competitiveness out in all of them, and they had a running tally. Their yard was not big enough for a full sized court, so they went around twice to make up for it. The flower beds were out of bounds.

Trying to change his mood, he thought, *I wonder if Marianne plays croquet? Would she survive the family tournament? Maybe not; she's so polite and unassuming.*

"Hey, are you taking green like always?" Erin cut into his thoughts. She tossed her favorite orange ball up and down in one hand.

"Of course."

"Let's go then!"

They did rock-paper-scissors, and Ruari won the right to start first. If he got a decent head start, he stood a good chance of winning. He struck his ball through the first wicket, but it bounced off the second one and stopped. He took a second shot to set himself up for the second wicket. The disadvantage of getting in front of his sister was that she was now behind him.

"Hah!" Erin crowed. She set her ball down and gave it a sharp smack, bumping into Ruari's ball and coming to a stop resting against his. With a wicked grin she placed her Doc Martin on top of her ball and gave it a wallop, sending the green ball bouncing through the grass with the transmitted force while her ball remained stationary. Ruari's ball stopped ten feet away.

Ruari suppressed a groan. That was going to take some time to recover from. She leaned on her mallet and sipped her iced tea with casual nonchalance.

He got the green ball realigned with the second wicket two shots later and just barely bounced through, but Erin was already past the third wicket, headed for the center.

He didn't think Marianne would enjoy his family's version of killer croquet very much and would probably sit on the sidelines. If Marianne played, Erin would probably destroy her.

Ruari rallied and caught up as Erin reached the starting point for the second half of their shortened course. He sent her ball into the bushes long enough to get out of the starting gate without her breathing down his neck. But his ball bounced the second wicket again.

"This wicket isn't straight!" He protested.

"There's nothing wrong with the wicket. You're just a bad shot!" Erin retorted. She came back with a lucky hit and dinked his ball out of the way enough to get through.

"Come on, son, don't just let her win! You got to wear her down for me!" Dad called.

"I'm working on it!" Nothing like pressure from the peanut gallery. In the family game, Erin and Dad always tried to demolish each other, and anyone who got in their way was collateral damage.

They were neck and neck all the way around a second time, and Erin won by the simple expedient of whacking his ball into the bushes where it hit the fence with a resounding thud. She knocked her ball through the last two wickets, and it fetched up against the stake.

Ruari scowled.

"Sore loser!" She teased. "That's two years in a row for me!"

He retrieved his ball, dropped it with the others, and tried not to add losing to his pile of troubles for the day.

Food filled the picnic table, and Ruari piled his plate with chicken, strips of steak, chips, and some token carrots. The family arranged themselves in a ragged arc of folding chairs upwind from the grill. For a few minutes, everyone concentrated on the excellent meal.

Erin finished her chicken leg and wiped her fingers on a paper napkin. "So Dad, what did Scotland want?"

Ruari looked up. "Scotland called?" Their Scots relatives didn't call very often, less so now that Granda and Nana were gone.

Dad made a non-committal noise and ate a few more bites of steak.

"Yeah, Uncle Fergus, I think. Did he say how Mary was?" Erin asked. Of all the cousins, Mary was closest to her in age, only a couple of years older. They'd been great friends when they were younger but lost touch.

"Mary's fine. She's due with her first child this winter," he said tersely.

"Babies already? Geez!"

"Erin, don't be rude," Mom interjected. "Mary and Tomas are excited for their baby."

"Yeah, but I'd rather work than be a mom!"

"Speaking of which," Dad cut in. "How's your job search going?"

Erin's expression closed up. "It's going. All my long-term applications are out. I'm waiting to hear back. I thought I'd look for something local in the meantime."

"Good idea," he said. He dug into his potato salad.

They managed to navigate the remainder of the meal without any more landmines. Erin helped clear the plates, and Ruari offered to bring out the cake. Once in the kitchen, he unwrapped his gift and placed the cake on it.

"Ooo, that's pretty!" Erin said.

"Thanks, would you open the door for me?"

She obliged and cleared a space for him on the picnic table. The honey maple glowed in the sun and the grain of the darker wood took on reddish highlights.

"Oh, Ruari!" Mom said. "That's gorgeous! I didn't know you did this kind of work."

He smiled. "I was just messing around. You can keep it. It's for you."

She gave him a hug and kissed his cheek. "Thank you. I love it. Who's for cake?"

Dad hadn't moved from his seat and gave the lazy Susan only a cursory glance. Was he going to say nothing? Like Ruari hadn't just made something beautiful? *Don't say anything. Peaceful family picnic.* His mouth opened anyway. "What do you think, Dad?"

Dad pinched his lips and twisted them in distaste. "Son, when are you going to give up this obsession? I thought you might let it go after your grandfather died. Wood might be a hobby, but it's not enough to make a living at. You'd be better using your head for math and design working for someone else."

"Douglas, that's hardly fair," Mom said. They ignored her. Erin sat back, watching the unfolding argument warily.

Stung, Ruari said, "Dad, I'd rather fail at woodworking than keep fixing plugged toilets!"

"I offered you a perfectly good job with the town, and you turned it down. You're lucky you don't have a family to support and distract you." His tone held a note of bitterness as his Scots accent emerged.

"Granda managed his farm and his woodworking successfully."

"There's a reason he died alone, " Dad snapped, his face turning pink. He was just getting started. "He left his bloody family to twist in the wind!"

"No he didn't!" Ruari retorted and saw a strange dark yellow light flicker around his father's head and shoulders for a split second.

"Ruari, that's enough." Mom's quiet voice went unheard.

A flush crept up Dad's neck and jawline, obliterating the odd flicker. "Aye, he did. You think he was some kind of saint! He brought in the money, but Mam was the one who clothed us, fed us, got us through school, ran the house and the farm while Da sat in his damn workshop being famous and carving fucking wood! He might as well have been on the moon for all he cared about us!"

"Did you ever go into his shop? Or be a part of my life?" Ruari shot back. His frayed temper unraveled into a fierce heat. "He taught me everything he knew about wood!"

"Aye, you were a piece of wood to be made into whatever likeness he wanted! You weren't a real person to him! You didn't have to deal with him more than two weeks in a year!"

"Douglas, stop." Mom put her hand on his arm, and he ignored it.

Ruari felt his own face heat as his pent up frustration burst its dam. "I would have gone to live with him all summer if you'd let me!"

"I saved you from him!" The tendons in Dad's neck stood out.

"Saved?! He was the only person who understood me!" The image of broken wood, hours of loving craftsmanship smashed in an instant, blazed across Ruari's vision.

Dad's face was nearly purple with apoplexy. "Your sainted Granda thought you'd never amount to anything! Stop wasting your life trying to impress someone who's dead and didn't care, anyway." The words emerged like a cloud of smoke.

"That's a lie! Just because you hated him, doesn't mean I have to!"

"I didn't hate him!" More smoke fouled his words.

"Then why did you destroy the box I gave him?!" That just slipped out. He hadn't meant to, but he couldn't stop.

Dad paused and gaped. "I did no such thing!"

"It was the last thing I made for him, and you smashed it into pieces!"

"What the hell are you talking about?" The flash of pain and guilt across his features said it all.

"You were the last person in there at the funeral!" Shaking with rage and grief, Ruari rose out of his chair, his fists balled.

"Get out of this house." Dad stood, knocking his chair over. He raised a shaking finger and pointed toward the street.

"Don't mind if I do." Ruari felt like a coiled spring ready to hit his father. It took all his effort to turn his back and keep walking, while the blood thundered in his ears.

"Ruari!" Dad roared.

Ruari's hand whipped up of its own accord and flipped a bird over his shoulder.

"Ruari!"

"Let him go, Douglas," Mom said, sounding weary.

"Way to go, Dad," Erin chimed in.

Ruari strode blindly through the narrow weedy passage between the house and the neighbor's fence and turned onto the sidewalk. Thrusting his shaking hands into his pockets, he let his feet propel him away from the house.

Granda thought I wouldn't amount to anything. What bullshit!

He handed me my first tools, showed me how to hold them. He smiled whenever I made something, no matter how bad it was. Every summer he showed me what he'd been working on and taught me new things.

But he was always quick to point out the flaws.

That was to help me improve.

Wasn't it?

He never said the box was a braw job, though, did he?

"Ruari, wait up!"

It figured Erin had come after him. He wished she would just go away.

Erin caught up with him, jostling his shoulder.

He pulled away. "I'm not in the mood, Erin."

"What did you mean when you said Dad broke your box? You mean that pretty little box you made for Granda?"

"Yeah."

"Are you sure? It could've been someone else."

He snorted. "He was the last person in the barn before me. The box was freshly broken, the pieces dumped in the corner. He didn't want me to find them, but I did."

"Shit." She was silent for a couple of paces. "Can you fix it?"

"It was matchsticks."

"That's horrible. Well, at least Granda didn't know about it."

"Yeah."

They kept walking, but his furious pace had slowed so she could keep up without running. Erin followed like a determined terrier. They turned onto Main Street, where Labor Day weekend visitors filled the sidewalks.

"What are you going to do?" Erin asked.

"I don't know." He shrugged.

"You won't do something stupid, will you? Like throw away everything you've ever done just because Dad thinks you shouldn't be a carpenter."

He glanced at her, irritated. "No."

"Good. That would be a shame." She stopped abruptly, forcing him to halt. She stared at him intently. " 'Cause you're the best wood carver and furniture maker I've ever known."

He snorted and rolled his eyes. "You obviously never looked at Granda's stuff."

"Yeah, well, he's dead. You're the best. Bar none." And she turned and walked back up the street toward home, leaving him to be buffeted by tourists on the busy walkway.

CHAPTER 3

*P*ost holiday, the library was as quiet as a tomb. Only a few other patrons hunkered down at nearby tables or comfy armchairs, reading. Marianne sat in the farthest corner surrounded by books, papers and her laptop. It felt good to be up to her eyeballs in a new project, though she kept getting sidetracked by looking through online menus of local cafe's and restaurants with a smile.

You'll never get this done if you don't focus!

She worked in peace until she noticed whispering and giggling in the shelving area behind her. Having been a grad student, she had great respect for the rules of quietude among books. You never knew who was trying to make a deadline or puzzle out a difficult passage. There was a special circle of hell dedicated to people who disrupted the peace of the library.

She ignored it, hoping that a librarian would pass by and take care of the offenders, but no one did. No one else seemed to be disturbed, but at least one person had headphones on and another looked like they could read through a twelve piece marching band.

After a few more minutes of whispering on the edge of her

hearing, she could almost make out the words, but not quite. It sounded like two little boys.

Come on, take it outside, you two. Where're your parents? She thought in irritation.

After reading the same paragraph five times and not taking it in, she laid her pen on the table and got up. She'd told more than a few people to be quiet in the past. She pressed her lips together and followed the voices, ready to tell them off. She pictured two boys staying just out of sight. They got louder as she rounded the last bookcase for the second time. The voices cut off. No one was there. She felt a little shiver.

+*Stupid head.*+ A suppressed snicker followed the muttered words.

The hairs rose on Marianne's arms. She steadied herself with one hand on a bookshelf and closed her eyes. Turning her head from side to side, she scanned the aisle. Less than two feet away, two boys crouched. They held still, watching her, hands over their mouths as if she couldn't see them. Her eyes flew open in surprise. The aisle was once again empty.

She backed slowly away from the apparition, her heart suddenly beating faster. She saw spirits more clearly with her eyes closed than open. Something to do with filtering out unnecessary visual chatter.

"Go home, you two!" She whispered, making a shooing motion. She blinked again, and they were gone.

One reader glanced curiously in her direction before sliding their eyes back to their book. Still half listening for the whispering, she sat back at the table and tried to soothe her ruffled nerves.

I thought I was done with ghosts after Anne and George left. Should I call Sarah? She thought of the stern, unsmiling features of her mentor, and remembered she was a very busy local family lawyer. *No need to bother her. I can handle this.*

The silence stretched, and her mind settled back into research. Those class lectures weren't going to write themselves.

She finished at five and called Ruari on her way home. He didn't pick up, so she left a message asking if he wanted to go out for a bite to eat.

The day after Labor Day, Ruari went into the office after waking with a pounding headache and a queasy stomach from an unscheduled visit to The Dutch. At his favorite watering hole, Trevor and his friends had bought him enough drinks to obliterate the ugly argument. Trevor had given him a lift home. He'd done his usual hangover remedy of drinking lots of water and taking several ibuprofen before crawling into bed. He dreaded the thought of how bad the morning would have been if he hadn't. More water and ibuprofen chased with a couple of pop tarts was the best he could manage this morning.

On the way in, he bought a large black coffee, hoping to drag his brain to work. He also vaguely remembered a drunken impulse to call Marianne and tell her not to go out with him. In a moment of panic, he checked his phone to make sure he hadn't drunk texted her. Nothing in or out since yesterday afternoon. He breathed a sigh of relief. In the calm light of day, he was relieved he hadn't embarrassed himself like that.

"Hi, Ruari!" Alyssa, the receptionist for Gloria's Valley Homes and Properties, greeted him when he arrived. A single mom, raising two kids, she somehow put up with SueAnn's caustic personality. He'd fixed her washer and dryer for the cost of parts a year or so ago, and she always had a kind word for him. She lowered her voice. "Ooh, Ruari, did you have a rough weekend?"

He forced a smile. "Just tired. How was yours?"

She smiled. "We went to my parents' place in Woodstock. They took the kids for a day, and I got to read a book!"

"That sounds nice." His face relaxed into an easier smile, though his temples still throbbed dully. "You have the work orders for the day?"

"Yup." She printed it out and put it on the clipboard for him.

He took it and sat down to fill out an Emergency Response form for the weekend's work.

A few minutes later, SueAnn Talmadge's strident voice cut across the morning quiet. She stood in her doorway. "Allen, fill that out later. I need to speak with you in my office."

Alyssa darted him a sympathetic gaze sideways, picked up the phone to make a call and stay out of trouble. Ruari set the clipboard aside and followed the squat figure into the office and shut the door.

Talmadge was almost wider than she was tall. Her fluffy black hair on top and spike heels on her feet did their best to make her seem taller. The overall effect was that of a very expensive, ill-tempered poodle. It didn't help that her clothes were so intensely red they positively glowed. He winced and looked at the beige wall past her head.

Without any preamble, Talmadge sat behind her desk and looked at him, folding her hands and pursing her lips. "So, what's your solution for two-twenty-one Oak Street?"

He herded his thoughts like reluctant sheep. "I can replace the valves for the sinks and toilets and install a new shut-off valve for the entire house. That'll keep the plumbing running for another few years."

She nodded, her teeth bared in a crocodile's smile. "That sounds good. Besides, doesn't 'poor' Mr. Carter have advanced liver cancer or something? We can replace the pipes and raise the rent when he's gone." As she spoke, a thin line of smoke escaped her lips and curled into wisps, but Ruari couldn't see any cigarette. Curious. He'd never known smoking was one of her vices. Then again, she was as secretive as she was stingy, and he wouldn't put an undercover cigarette habit past her.

Ruari's headache pulsed in time with the red glow around his boss's head. *This is the last time I have nitro stout on a half empty stomach.* As she droned on, he amended, *and the last time I mix hangovers with a ghoul like Talmadge.*

Clients like Mr. Carter had kept him at Gloria's for one more year and one more year. He couldn't leave them to her tender mercies. She stopped talking, and he hoped he hadn't missed anything critical. He kept his expression neutral. "Okay," he said into the silence and turned to leave.

"Oh, and Allen?" she called as he exited. "Tuck your shirt in. We have standards to maintain."

Ruari had worked for Gloria's Valley Homes and Properties for almost ten years, and he and SueAnn Talmadge had developed a functional relationship. He could repair a wide variety of things from carpentry to mechanicals, so she didn't have to hire expensive specialists at every turn. When it came to replacing a roof, driveway, or anything more complicated, she grudgingly hired it out to a bigger company. In exchange, she paid him a living wage plus overtime for emergencies, and she reluctantly acknowledged that he was good at his job. Her casual insults were free, and mostly he ignored them. Some days, he wanted to put her "Clients are our number one concern" plaque through the wall, and let her snap her fake nails off as she figured out how to do drywall. Those days were coming more frequently. But quitting wouldn't fix Mr. Carter's pipes, and the poor man didn't need plumbing issues on top of terminal cancer.

Gritting his teeth, Ruari finished the paperwork, picked up the list of work orders, and headed for his truck.

Ruari spent the day replacing old, frozen valves at the Oak Street property. Staci Carter Greaves greeted him at the door when he arrived. He made an effort to smile blandly and ignored her narrowed eyes that said, "Don't blow it. I know how to torque your wrench, Mr. Handyman." She hovered over him until she was sure he was handling the job effectively, then she kissed her father's cheek and bid him goodbye.

"I'll be up next weekend, Daddy," she said as she left.

Mr. Carter stood in the doorway to the bathroom watching him, looking tired and gray.

"Mr. Carter, I've got this," Ruari said. "You look like you need a rest. I'll take care of it."

He nodded and shuffled back to a recliner in the living room and pulled an afghan over himself.

As the day progressed from one sink to the next, Ruari's vision blurred unexpectedly. It reminded him of going to the optometrist and having his vision deliberately doubled as he looked through the little lenses. He dropped screws, stabbed his hand with a screwdriver, and struggled to thread the new valves into place.

Maybe I'm getting sick. His crazy vision had been most intense when he was talking to Mr. Carter. The second, slightly offset outline of the man had been a sickly gray brown. Ruari had to squint and blink hard to return his vision to normal. When his vision wasn't doubled, he kept imagining he saw faint clouds of smoke around Mr. Carter's head. His head ached after fighting it all afternoon. But the relieved smile of the elderly tenant as Ruari told him his plumbing was as good as new was worth everything.

As he pulled into his parking spot next to his shop after seven, he got Marianne's message from a couple of hours earlier. He was sweaty and tired and felt awful. Just great: the leftovers of a monster hangover and the flu. He texted her, *Sorry, I think I'm coming down with something.*

Oh no! Get some rest. Hope you feel better tomorrow.

Will do.

Chicken soup steadied his stomach. He took himself to bed early. His dreaming mind showed him valves and pipes and tools all night interrupted by a brief dream of someone at the alley door to the studio. When he opened it, a tall, red-headed woman stood outside. She wanted to see his work. He knew he could use her business, but he couldn't form the words to invite her inside.

He surfaced from sleep feeling feverish. His head still pounded. He drank a glass of water and fell asleep again.

. . .

The rest of the week passed in a blur. Still unsettled by the blow up with Dad, Ruari found it hard to concentrate. Stray fragments floated through when he least expected it.

...Stop wasting your time trying to impress someone who's dead and didn't care anyway...

"Shut up, Dad," he muttered when this thought floated by.

If he was in the studio when he had that thought, he looked at Granda's craggy face pinned up on the board. "I know you cared."

He tried to keep the momentum of success from his inlay project by starting something new. Maybe he could build up a catalog of projects to show people as evidence of his skill. Too bad he didn't have much storage space. Maybe a portfolio? Too bad he wasn't much of a photographer. He'd have to hire out. Too much to think about now. Make something new. That was the ticket.

He spent some time sketching out designs for different pieces of furniture and did a little research into inlay with stone and colored resins. They all looked intriguing. His spartan lifestyle and a lot of overtime had left him a pretty good cushion, but he was careful with his spending.

Gloria's had grown significantly since he'd started and now had over thirty properties. It was very hard to keep up. It was becoming critical to ask Talmadge to hire another full-time handyman, or at least an assistant. He wished he had time to look for someone. If he could vet a few people, he might put a short list on her desk and save her some time. That might put her in a good enough mood to actually hire someone.

On a lunch break, Ruari saw that Dad had tried calling, but hadn't left a message. His thumb hovered over the call button. Unless Dad was going to apologize, they had nothing to talk about. Ruari felt a little guilty for flipping a bird where Mom could see it, but not enough to call back. Dad deserved it and more.

His eyesight continued to be flaky, showing him weird haloes and smoke around people in bright light and blurring his vision.

The headache returned with a vengeance, feeling like someone had jammed a screwdriver in his temple. He gulped down more ibuprofen with an afternoon cup of coffee from the drive-thru and went to the next address.

He wasn't prone to migraines, but weren't they preceded by halos and sparkly lights? What if he had a brain tumor? That gave him an icy spike of fear. Cancer didn't run in his family as far as he knew. Granda had died of a heart attack in his sleep and lain there for a day before someone had found him. That's what Dad told him, anyway. What if he'd died of an undiagnosed brain tumor? Would Mom and Dad know? *Should I go to the ER?* He couldn't bring himself to go. If he just waited long enough, it would probably go away.

Marianne called on Thursday. "Hey, how are you feeling?"

"I'm okay."

"Are you better?"

"More or less."

"Sounds like less," she said shrewdly. "Did you take a day off, get some rest?"

"It's been pretty busy, so, uh, no."

"Hmm. Well, let me know if we have to postpone our date."

He'd been holding onto the prospect of being in her company like a lifeline in a snowstorm. "Not if I can help it!"

"How does Hudson River Trading Company sound? They have an in-house bakery for pastries that sounded amazing."

His stomach lurched with a new anxiety, but he acknowledged, "Yeah, they have good food."

"Are you sure?"

"Absolutely! Their food is really good." He'd make it be okay.

"Nine o'clock Saturday, then?"

"See you there." The Trading Company would never again be his first choice, but he could cope if she wanted to go.

"Take care of yourself. 'Bye."

. . .

Marianne worked like a fiend all week. By Friday she'd written the introductory lecture and made a short list of essential readings for the students to follow the course. She felt good about striking just the right tone. She shipped it with a brief note to Gillian asking her to look it over and give her feedback as soon as possible.

Ready for a break, she called her grandmother. "I promised to visit you this week. Is today a good day?"

"How about coming for tea?"

"Perfect! I'd love that."

Oscar lolled on the couch in a sunbeam, and she picked him up and gave his densely muscled body a snuggle. "Okay, Mister, we got the first one done. Just got to do two more, submit them, and I'm in to teach!" He purred and butted his head against her chin enthusiastically.

After a quick change of clothes, she grabbed her purse and got into the Flea, her mother's old Ford Escort. She passed through town and drove farther up into the hills.

Grandma Selene lived in Vandenberg, a small community with one gas station and a tiny post office that served scattered houses in the woods along a winding road. Grandpa Clair had passed away many years ago, and Grandma continued to live on her own in the huge old Victorian that had been a judge's house when it was first built.

Marianne bumped down the long drive through the trees and parked next to the old carriage house that was now the garage. The door was open, and she glimpsed the old Lincoln Continental Mark II. The black spare wheel housing reflected the humble Ford Escort in its polished surface. She grinned. Grandma had driven it to car shows a few times and not only turned heads but gotten offers for purchase that beggared the imagination. It had been Grandpa Clair's pride and joy, and she wouldn't part with it for anything.

Marianne walked up the flagstones to the big front porch and mounted the stairs. She knocked on the door. A few moments later the wooden door opened, and Grandma appeared in a blue cotton dress with a gray cashmere sweater, her iron gray hair gathered at her neck.

"Come in, come in! I just put the kettle on."

"Grandma!" She embraced her favorite relative.

Grandma Selene was in her eighties. After her son, Marianne's father, had died from pneumonia many years ago, she'd stayed in contact with Marianne and her mother. "I felt I owed it to Charles to be part of your life," she'd told Marianne once. When Grandma had recently confessed to being clairvoyant, Marianne wondered if her grandmother had watched over her for other reasons as well.

Marianne followed her through the formal dining room with its polished walnut table and family portraits down a narrow corridor into a small kitchen at the back of the house. Victorian standards dictated that the servants were separated from the master and his guests. The kitchen was much more lived in. A six-burner white ceramic stove with a double oven gleamed on one side, and the counters were spotless. A vase of gladiolas provided an accent of color.

The kettle whistled, and Selene poured boiling water into a large, dark green teapot. "Would you look in the cupboard? There's a tin of fancy biscuits in there."

Marianne put some on a plate, got out a pair of china cups and saucers, and put them on the table. They sat down across from each other and poured strong tea into each cup, filtering the loose leaves through a small strainer. They passed cream and sugar, and the ritual was complete.

"How is your research going?" Grandma asked as she took a couple of cookies.

"It's taking longer than I thought to organize my ideas. I have to make it accessible to everyone and not bore the ones who have several other history classes under their belts."

"That sounds challenging. Hopefully, you'll gather momentum, and the others will be easier to write."

Marianne sighed her agreement.

"How is your young man?"

She smiled. "He seems kind of shy, but we've talked a bit and have a coffee date on Saturday."

Grandma watched her intently over the rim of her cup.

Marianne elaborated. "He works a lot. And he's been sick this week."

"Hmm." Grandma put her tea down and said, "Please don't be upset with me, but I made a few inquiries with friends about Mr. Allen."

Marianne's eyebrows lifted in surprise. Grandma was connected to the matriarchs of Maple Hill society through a complex web of bridge, mahjong, and the quiet assistance of worthy causes.

"I worry about you, dear," Grandma said. "I just don't want to see you hurt again."

Marianne held her breath, feeling like something momentous was coming.

"My sources tell me that he had a serious relationship with a woman a couple of years ago. They were engaged to be married, but he called it off."

A chill passed through her. "Did they say why it was called off?"

"No." Grandma gave her an anxious smile. "Just be careful, Lovie."

Marianne nodded, glad of the warning. She did not need another manipulative man in her life. She would have to tread cautiously until she figured out more.

Grandma cleared her throat. "That being said, I enjoyed talking to him at your party, even though it was only briefly. I will say that he couldn't keep his eyes off you, my dear."

Marianne felt her face grow warm. "Really? Well, that's something."

Grandma patted her on the knee. "Courage, Lovie." She

pronounced it as though it rhymed with 'mirage,' an affectation Marianne loved. "Only time will tell."

They poured a second cup of tea, and Marianne said, "You told me you have clairvoyant dreams. Do you also see ghosts?"

Grandma took her time adding cream and a teaspoon of sugar. "Ghosts? You mean the spirits of the departed?" Marianne nodded. The older woman kept her gaze on her teaspoon as it swirled the cream into the tea. "Not really. Your grandfather keeps me company from time to time, and we have a chat when I'm feeling down. Other than that, no. I have the odd dream that comes true, but that's not really the same."

"I've been seeing ghosts in odd places. Sometimes I just see them. Other times, they seem to know I can see them and come up to me. I just wondered what to do about it."

"Have you talked to Sarah?"

"Not yet. She's busy, and I don't want to bother her and Kelly too much. They put me up when I was dealing with Anne and George, and I don't want to be a bother."

Grandma raised her eyebrows. "I had a long conversation with Sarah as well. She might be strong minded, but I think she would be glad to help you. Don't let her demeanor get in your way."

Marianne chuckled. "She is a little scary. Okay, I'll call her."

Grandma offered her the plate of cookies and took another for herself. "How is your mother?"

Marianne shrugged. "We don't talk very often. She's uncomfortable with my dreams and my 'ghost stories,' so we don't have a lot to talk about."

"I understand. She always avoided talking to me about that as well."

Marianne felt a familiar pang. "Did you ever get any… messages from my father after he died?" She sometimes wondered what it would have been like to grow up with a father. Mom had always had a weariness about her when Marianne was young. Life as a solo parent had been hard on her. She might have been a happier person if Dad had been alive.

Grandma shook her head. Her eyes held an old sadness. "No. Most people move on when they die. Only those who still have business to take care of here on earth or people they love who they're waiting for remain. Your father's life ended too soon, but he must have made peace with it." She smiled gently. "I know he would be proud of you and all you've accomplished."

"Thanks. I hope he would. I don't have a lot of memories of him. They're like old photos and faint recordings. Half the time I'm not sure I remember him at all." Mom had done her best, but there was still a Dad-shaped hole in her life. "You ever think about calling for him? You know, just to see if he'd talk to you?"

Grandma Selene frowned. "You mean hold a seance? No, it's not a good idea to disturb the dead. Very few people know how to focus their 'calling.' Unless you know exactly what you're doing, it's a bit like opening a dark room and shouting for attention. You never know who or what will answer."

Marianne nodded. *That would be stupid.* Sarah would tell her the same thing, no doubt. She mustered a smile. "Don't worry. I won't do any yelling, I promise."

"Good. I'm sure your father is fine where he is. I know he loved you."

They continued to talk until the shadows lengthened outside.

"I should get back. Oscar will be hungry. Thanks for the tea, Grandma." She gave her grandmother a one-armed hug as they sat together.

"My pleasure, Lovie. Let me know how your class work goes. Come visit your old grandmother again."

As she approached the bridge over the Schukill Creek, a mile or so before the first buildings of Maple Hill, Marianne caught sight of a familiar figure on the side of the road. He half turned and stuck out his thumb, hoping for a ride. It looked like the same person in a hoody she'd seen a couple of times before at this hour. Why would he be wearing the same thing and be hitching in the same place every time?

On impulse, she slowed her car, passed him, and pulled over. She had a hunch. Looking in the rearview, she saw no one. Feeling a bit foolish, she threw the car into park and got out. Twilight had turned into night, and it was dark between the streetlights this far from town.

If he was a ghostly hitchhiker rather than a live one, she should be safe, right? She'd read a few accounts online of people giving ghostly hitchhikers a lift to their destination. She peered into the darkness, trying to see a form and get an emotional reading, but nothing revealed itself. Cautiously, she walked around, putting The Flea between her and any oncoming traffic. The vegetation here was fairly dense and smelled like the end of summer with a faint autumn spiciness.

She cleared her throat. "Um, 'scuse me? If you want a ride, I can give you a lift into town as far as I'm going." She opened her door to the empty roadside, and waited briefly. Nothing happened. No one got into the car. No one jumped out of the bushes yelling 'boo!'

Regretting her Good Samaritan impulse, she muttered, "Right," slammed the door, and returned to the driver's seat.

Belting herself back in, she looked in the rearview to check the road behind her. A car coming from the opposite direction flashed its headlights through the windshield as it passed, and she glimpsed a hooded form sitting in the backseat. She jerked involuntarily as her heart jumped a mile. Looking over her shoulder, she glanced in the backseat and saw no one there. A second look in the rearview showed a shadowy form.

Okay, I've just successfully picked up a ghostly hitchhiker. I hope this isn't the dumbest thing I've ever done. He can't hurt me, right? This isn't an episode of "Supernatural," and I'm not named Winchester.

She extended her senses, trying to feel if there was any emanation of ill will and felt only a sense of presence. *I'm just doing a good deed for someone who is stuck here and maybe needs to move on. Surely Sarah does this all the time?*

"Hi." It came out as a squeak. She cleared her throat and said in a slightly shaky voice, "I didn't know if you'd gotten in or not. Where do you need to go?"

+I need to go to Beacon.+ The words formed in her head. He sounded like a young man.

"Oh. I'm not going that far tonight. But I could take you to the center of Maple Hill, and maybe someone else could take you the rest of the way."

+Okay. Thanks for picking me up. I've been waiting for, like, forever.+

"Sure. No problem."

She looked in the side mirror, then pulled into the road again. Her heart had slowed to an almost normal rate now that she'd "heard" his voice. "So what's in Beacon?"

+I was headed home from a concert in the city, and my ride ditched me here.+

"Oh, bummer. Who did you see?"

+The Melvins. They played at Williamsburg.+

Marianne was mystified. She knew the venue but had never heard of the band. "What kind of music do they play?"

+Sludge metal. Punk. They had a new drummer and were totally awesome. Napalm Death and BananaMelt opened for them. They were amazing!+ He sounded happy.

"Sounds like it was a good concert." They were approaching the better lit edge of town, and she drove towards the center along Main Street. Surreptitiously, she looked at her passenger in the rearview. He was still wearing his hoody, but she could see a bit of his profile. He appeared to be in his late teens, maybe early twenties. She wondered how he'd died but thought it might be rude to ask.

Pulling up in front of the Silver Penny Inn in the center of town, she stopped the car. "This is as far as I can take you. I hope you find a ride to Beacon."

She got out and opened the back door for him. Once again, she saw no one there, but she pretended he got out and shut the door after him. "Good luck," she murmured and got into the driver's seat again.

A few passersby gave her odd looks. "The door wasn't shut properly," she said, feeling awkward. Pulling away from the curb, she reflected on how strange her life had become. Once she was home, she ate dinner and surfed the net until she couldn't keep her eyes open anymore.

CHAPTER 4

y Friday Ruari's headache had faded and the feared migraine had not materialized. Now it felt more like eyestrain. He'd gotten better at making the disturbing haloes around people go away, but if he unfocused his eyes while he was thinking about something else, they reappeared. The weird smoke appeared erratically, but if he tried hard enough, he could ignore it. After feeling out of sorts all week, he hadn't had the energy or desire to go down and work in the studio.

While he searched his limited pantry of food for something vaguely suitable for dinner, his phone beeped with an incoming text. For a hot second he thought about joining Trevor and the others at The Dutch for a drink, but the memory of his last hangover made him text Trevor, *Thanks, but not tonight.*

His date with Marianne was tomorrow morning, and it loomed with a mix of pleasure and dread. He'd survived the week with the shining thought of spending time in her company, but the Trading Company would always be haunted by memories of all the time he'd spent there with Jenny. He should have told Marianne they had to go somewhere else, but she'd sounded so excited about wanting to try it he couldn't say no.

He swallowed. He was going to have to face those demons

one of these days. She'd felt better having him by her side when she faced her ex. Maybe he'd be okay with her by his side when he faced the memories of his ex.

He heated a couple of leftover slices of pizza in the microwave and sat at his desk to eat. Broken bits and pieces from rentals he'd emptied out of his pockets were scattered among papers and receipts. A pang of loneliness struck him as he chewed and swallowed the stale crust and sauce. *I hate this.*

His phone rang. "Now what?" He muttered irritably, fully intending to let it go to voicemail at least long enough to let him eat dinner. The number made his heart lift.

"Marianne, hi!"

"Hey Ruari. How are you feeling?"

"The headache's almost gone. I think I dodged the bullet."

"Glad to hear it. I'm looking forward to seeing you tomorrow!"

"Me too. What are you doing tonight?"

"Just watching some TV. You want to come over sometime and watch a movie?"

"What kind of movies do you like?"

"I only own a couple. Do you like *Lord of the Rings, Galaxy Quest,* or *Princess Bride?*"

"*Fellowship* is my favorite," he said with a grin.

"Mine too! Though I love watching Eowyn fight the Witch King of Angmar."

"I don't know *Galaxy Quest.*"

"Hah! You have to see it. Okay, it's a date."

They talked for a few more minutes. When she hung up, he let out a deep breath. Her call had lifted a weight from his chest. He hadn't realized how much he needed to hear her voice. He still didn't trust himself to get romantically involved with her, but maybe they could just be friends. *Yeah, sure.*

The cold pizza was about as appetizing as sawdust, and it thudded as it hit the trash can. His eyes traveled over his room. A weeks' worth of dirty clothes lay on the floor in heaps, his desk looked like a packrat's den, and food-crusted dishes filled the bathroom sink and the floor next to it. No proper kitchen, meant no proper sink. It had never really bothered him before that the bathroom had to double as kitchen sink. Abruptly, he couldn't stand it. The place had a distinctly lived in odor. If Erin got up here, she'd rag on him for days. Marianne being up here didn't bear thinking about. Feeling a burst of energy, he opened the window and puttered until the place at least looked tidy and smelled better.

Ruari woke to the steady drumming of rain on the roof. The air was chillier than it had been all summer, and he lay feeling warm and comfortable in bed. It was Saturday, and fatigue weighed his body down. He drifted in and out of sleep.

He woke again and rolled over to look at his clock. Eight-thirty.

Coffee with Marianne!

He dressed in his last pair of clean jeans and a blue T-shirt (anything but Gloria's sickening Kelly green). He zipped his gray 'Edinburgh' sweatshirt over it and dashed out the door. The rain had lightened to a drizzle. He couldn't face sliding his butt into the worn seat of his pickup if he didn't have to. He pulled the hood up and hurried up to Main Street on foot.

Main was the north-south centerline for Maple Hill. Streets to the east were considered uphill, and those to the west angled down towards the Hudson. Those that cut across were mostly in a grid at the center of town and the rest bent around natural forms like the occasional glacial boulder. Sturdy brick buildings lined most of Main, punctuated by 'painted lady' Victorian homes and smaller wood-framed buildings of more modest means. He passed the library and the Avery Theater. They looked like grumpy old men hunkered down in the rain.

Hudson River Trading Company was a couple of doors down a side street off Main on the uphill side. The bell jangled overhead as he stepped inside, slipped his damp hood off, and shook the droplets from his hair. The warm, intoxicating scents of cinnamon, brown sugar, and coffee filled the air underscored by the rush and gurgle of the espresso machine. There were only a few people reading the newspaper and sipping drinks. He'd made such good time he'd gotten there before Marianne. Hands in pockets, he stared at the chalkboard menu over the counter trying to calm his suddenly racing heart.

The last time he'd been here was with Jenny, his almost-wife. The Trading Company was one of her favorite places, and they'd had coffee and a pastry every other weekend for over a year. They'd met in a New York gallery looking at sculpture and hit it off. She loved painting Hudson Valley scenery, and her beauty and talent dazzled him. They'd made plans to create a studio space for her in his shop and talked about art. They'd organized their wedding over coffee here. He closed his eyes and tried to swallow down his combined sadness and shame. He didn't regret not marrying Jenny, only that he hadn't figured out he wasn't ready before they'd gone so far down the road that withdrawing guaranteed a complete train wreck.

The bell jangled behind him again, and he turned. Marianne closed her drippy umbrella and unzipped her rain jacket. When she looked up and saw him, her face lit up with a huge smile as if the sun had come out. She was short where Jenny had been tall. She was dark-haired and olive-skinned where Jenny had been fair and blonde. He swallowed his sadness.

"Hi, sorry I'm late," she said. "Pretty soggy out there."

He smiled back. "No trouble at all. I just got here."

They ordered drinks. He got a dark roast with cream, no sugar and a breakfast burrito, and she got a London Fog tea with an almond croissant. He steered them away from Jenny's favorite perch overlooking the front steps. Instead, they sat at a small table along the side street and settled in.

She sipped her tea and smiled. "They do this just right, not too sweet."

He watched her nibble at the croissant as if she was savoring every bite. Jenny only drank soy lattes, and when she gave in and ate a muffin, she always looked guilty. *Stop thinking about your ex, dude.* Under cover of eating, he racked his brain for something to say. Talk about work? Talk about headaches and funky vision? Ugh. *Ask her about her class, dummy.* He cleared his throat. "How's your class going?"

She brightened. "I sent the first lecture to my colleague, but she's taking forever to get back to me. I've never been in charge of an entire class from start to finish before, so I'm a little nervous about doing a good job."

"What's it about?"

She described the sweep of Victorian Britain's influence on American life, and he did his best to follow. She watched him closely. "What do you think?" she said as she finished.

"Honestly, I was more of an art and architecture kind of guy," he replied, feeling bad about disappointing her. "But that sounds really interesting. I'm a pretty visual person. Maybe you could add some pictures?"

She didn't scoff. Instead, she tilted her head to one side, considering his suggestion seriously. Her amber eyes took on a faraway look before she focused on him again. She flashed him a smile, making his belly do a few flips. "That's a great idea. I could make a full slide show. You're right. Different people learn in different ways."

She sipped her tea. Her hands were soft, the nails unpainted. Another difference with Jenny. She'd liked makeup and mani-cures. Marianne was beautiful without all of that.

"You took art and architecture in college?" She asked. "Is that how you got into woodworking?"

"No, I've been carving ever since I was little."

"That's really unusual. Most guys are into sports or computer games. How did that happen?"

"My family has roots in Scotland, and we spent summers in a small village outside Edinburgh when I was a kid. My grandparents lived on a farm with cows and goats, a big garden, chickens, the whole nine yards. I loved it. My grandfather was a carpenter and a carver, and watching him work always fascinated me. When I was about five, I picked up his scraps and tried to carve them, and he decided to teach me. I didn't know until I was in my late teens that he was famous in certain circles. People came from all over to buy his furniture and sculpture. They even begged him to teach them, which he sometimes did. I had no idea. He was just my grandfather."

"He sounds really special."

"He was. He taught me about the properties of wood, how to choose the right piece for the job." He smiled. "Right down to the taste and smell of different species."

"You're making that up!" She teased.

"Nope, Dad had a fit when he found me licking different pieces of wood!"

She laughed, making her eyes crinkle at the corners.

"Granda was right: they do taste, smell, and feel different. When I step into my studio, all the crap from work goes away. My favorite thing is starting a new project. After I measure and draw it out on a plank, I love watching the saw dissolve that line when it cuts." He closed one eye and sighted down an imaginary board. "When you're done, you've built something that wasn't there before."

"Is that how you carve too?"

He shook his head. "Not exactly. Those ideas come in odd moments. Sometimes I dream about them. I just let my hands find the right piece in the scrap box. By the grain, the hardness, the color, the scent. I picked the cherry wood for *Sleeping Lady* because of the smell and color."

"It sounds a little mystical, or maybe like meditation."

"I guess it is. Even when I come across a flaw in the wood, I work around it." He chuckled. "I used to get so pissed off when a piece broke after all the work I put into it. Now if it's really bad, I just chuck it and start again. Either way, I learn something." He looked up. She was staring at him with a rapt expression, chin in hand. He felt a flush rise in his cheeks. He'd said too much. "Sorry."

She sat up and touched the back of his hand with her fingertips. They were warm on his rain cool skin. "Don't apologize for loving what you do! I can go on and on about something I just learned and bore the pants off whoever I'm with. You're lucky you had a grandfather who taught you."

"He really was something else." *...Your sainted Granda thought you'd never amount to anything.*

"What's wrong?" She asked.

"Nothing."

"You look sad all of a sudden."

He sighed. "Granda eventually stopped showing me things. I guess he got old, his hands got arthritis, and he couldn't carve anymore." He looked down and found his fingers folding the napkin into a compact wad of tree pulp and stopped. "I don't know. I thought he liked my work, but now I'm not sure."

"Why do you say that?"

He hunched his shoulders. "I made him a box, but he didn't really like it. And then," he swallowed, "my dad smashed it to pieces after Granda died and told me the old man didn't think I was any good."

Her warm hands slipped over his cold fingers. "Oh, Ruari, I'm so sorry. That's awful."

"I can't believe I'm telling you all this." He looked down and pulled his hands away.

She reached out and took them again, prompting him to look up. Her expression was full of sympathy. "It's okay. I don't mind. Your father and your mentor aren't the only people in the world to judge your work. You have talent, even if they can't see it."

She caught his half-hearted nod of assent and leaned forward. "My ex and his family are ridiculously wealthy. They can buy anything. I got to tag along for ten years to all the places they liked to go. Trust me when I say I've seen carving not nearly as good as yours being sold for thousands of dollars. You're good enough." Her face was suffused with a passionate glow.

He took a deeper breath past a jumble of feelings. "Thank you, Mahri." With the light from the street behind her, she positively glowed with a pink aura. He flushed, realizing he'd just called her a sweet pet name. But she didn't seem to mind.

She slipped her hands out of his and sat back, draining the last of her tea. "Anyway, I don't think you should let your father or anyone stop you from doing something you love to do."

"You're right." Their food was gone and cups were empty. He glanced out the window. "The rain seems to have let up. Do you want to walk for a bit?"

She wrestled with something internally for a minute before she broke into a mischievous smile. "You know what? I have a ton of work to do at home, but the heck with that. I'd love to walk with you."

He grinned. "I know this amazing place, the Camford Estate. Have you ever been there?"

"No."

"You're in for a treat. It's got a huge, beautiful old mansion with a lake and gardens."

"Let's go!" Her eyes shone with happiness.

On the way there, they chatted, leaping from one thing to the next like bees going from blossom to blossom. She spoke animatedly about her life in the city and finding Oscar in a pet shelter. He told stories of the renters and his summers in Scotland just to hear her laugh.

The parking lot was nearly deserted when they arrived, so they had the place to themselves. Ruari took her to all his favorite spots. They reveled in the late summer greenery and blooms. The house was closed for tours that day, so they walked around the whole lake through woods and little wild gardens. The Camford family had a penchant for odd little garden decorations, and there was always a miniature stone house or path leading into the undergrowth. He took her to a ring of birch trees. The branches had been carefully cut so that the canopy started about eight feet up. Each cut branch had left a scar that looked like an eye. She walked around it, trailing her hand over the trunks.

"It looks like a fairy ring," she said in a hushed voice.

"The precursor to the garden gnome craze maybe?"

"The house dates to the late 1800s. Fairies were a big thing in the Victorian era," she suggested.

They returned in the early afternoon, just before the rain resumed with a steady downpour. Before they parted, they made a tentative dinner date for the next week.

Maybe things would work out better this time. He'd known Jenny for eight months before he'd taken her to Camford.

Back in the studio, Ruari felt light and happy. He whistled a little as he pulled out pieces from the wood bin to start a new project, an inlaid table top. The rain drummed steadily on the tin roof overhead as he got his drawings out, and sharpened his tools before starting. He'd keep this one to show her before he put it away. Maybe she needed a new table, and he could give it to her.

He came across the blue apron-wrapped bundle of broken wood bits. His good mood deflated a bit, like snagging a splinter in his hand.

...stop wasting your life tryin' to impress someone who's dead and didn't care anyway...

Damn you, Dad. Why did you break my last gift to the old man? What made you so angry at him?

He looked at Coll Allen's black and white photo on the cork board. "I know you cared. You wouldn't have taught me if you hadn't."

He moved the pieces of the broken box to another shelf where they wouldn't get knocked off or lost.

When his cellphone rang, he hoped it was Marianne. Instead, it was an unfamiliar number. "Ruari Allen," he answered.

A younger woman's voice said, "Mr. Allen? I'm sorry to

bother you, but my dog was just down in the basement, and I heard splashing. I think the basement is flooded. Could you come look?"

"Sure. What's the address?" Disappointed but resigned, he said, "Got it. Be there in about ten minutes."

He spent an hour splashing through ankle deep water before it receded. His phone rang again, and he was back in his truck on another rain-related call. By early evening, he was thoroughly damp and disheveled. His headache returned accompanied by strange halos around people and occasional smoky words.

Sunday brought more rain and more calls. He was exhausted by nightfall. He plugged his phone into the charger and showered while a bowl of canned chili spun in the microwave. *That's it. I get an assistant or I quit, regardless of Mr. Carter and the others.*

His mind fogged over.

He dreamed of water leaking through the roof, filling an enormous pool in the basement below him. Ruari tried to channel the water away from the pool, but it continued to drip. A voice said angrily, "We had a deal! You work for me!" He scrambled down the steep roof and landed in the backyard of the little farm in Scotland. He stood staring at the barn workshop, longing to go into it, but Talmadge's voice said, "We have standards, Allen." He turned and saw her chunky form in a fire engine red bathing suit lying on a deck chair. She stared at him through enormous black sunglasses and snapped her fingers, holding up an empty margarita glass.

He turned back to the workshop. The barn door was open, and he could hear the belt sander working. *Granda must be starting a new piece. I wonder what it is.* He started forward, but a red taloned hand clamped on his wrist, and he felt a tepid, gritty glass being shoved into his hand. "Allen, we have standards."

He woke with a cry of frustration.

CHAPTER 5

*R*uari sat at the accountant's desk before the office opened the next morning, trying to fill out the over-time forms. A sixteen-ounce coffee and cream with no sugar barely inched him into awareness. Alyssa arrived and shot worried, motherly glances at him when she thought he wasn't looking. He'd given her a terse greeting when he sat down, and she'd had the courtesy not to intrude.

The back entrance to the parking lot banged closed, and he heard angry, three-inch heels striding down the hall. One did not work for Talmadge for ten years without knowing what she sounded like in all her moods. She must have gotten more phone calls from the weekend run-around. Yippee.

She rounded the corner and said, "Allen, my office, now."

Lack of sleep made her voice sound like steel furniture scratching a hardwood floor. He gritted his teeth and followed her in. She let him cool his jets while she put her trench coat on the coat rack and opened the blinds to let in the watery Monday sunlight. Finally, she sat at her desk and regarded him.

"You had a busy weekend. I got two calls! Both of them were from tenants upset that you made them call a septic company instead of dealing with the problem yourself." Her poofy hair quivered with indignation, and he pictured a small black poodle yapping. "Why do I employ you, if all you're going to do is refer our renters to other people?" A small cloud of black swarmed out of her mouth, accompanying her words.

He clenched his jaw before replying, "For your information, I got nine emergency calls this weekend and dealt with seven of them myself. The two who called you were beyond me. One needs a backhoe and a complete overhaul of the septic. The other was a furnace repair that would have taken hours of time I did not have."

"How do you know the septic needs digging? You could have just reamed it out or whatever it is you do."

"Ten years of experience," he ground out between clenched teeth.

She pressed her lips together and chewed her tongue. "You could have taken the time on the furnace then."

"Not with the call volume I was getting."

"If you just managed your time better, you wouldn't get into trouble."

His own anger rose, and he saw red. At first he thought he was getting angry enough to want to break something, but then realized it was her. A dark red, angry glow crackled with energy like a corona around her. Smoky vapor poured from her lips every time she opened her mouth.

He smelled no cigarettes. Not even stale smoke. What was going on? He blinked and sharpened his focus, eliminating the disturbing extra vision.

"What are you staring at?" she added sharply.

Something in him snapped. Glaring at her, he said in clipped tones, "I worked overtime every night last week and spent my entire weekend responding to emergencies. You need to hire another guy to help me! Gloria's has way too many units for me to do alone anymore, especially if there are multiple emergencies. Get me an assistant, or I quit."

Talmadge sat open-mouthed, momentarily speechless.

"I have work to do," he added before she could respond, and left.

Alyssa gave him a furtive, admiring look as he plucked the list of work orders off her desk and stalked out of the office. He would finish his paperwork later. By the time he reached his truck, he was shaking, his head pounding. He sat in the driver's seat and took a few deep breaths to calm himself. Knowing Talmadge, she would make him regret his outburst, but he'd stand firm. He had to.

Damn this headache and screwy vision. This has been going on for almost two weeks. If he had a medical issue, it should have cleared up by now. Gloria's Valley Homes and Properties' insurance plan was only the most basic, but he couldn't afford to let this go. He dialed his family doctor's office and made an appointment. They promised to put him on a waiting list and get him in as soon as possible. That done, he put the key in the ignition and headed out to the first appointment of the day.

Marianne had spent the rest of Saturday in a happy haze. Walking and talking with Ruari had been fabulous, nothing like the anxious, unhappy years she'd spent with Geoffrey. Ruari was so open and genuine and really listened to her even when she babbled on about things historical. He was smart and funny too. Geoffrey had always found a way to turn every conversation to himself or his family and their money. It still surprised her how much her ex had been a drag on her life. She was lucky to be rid of him. *Good riddance, girl,* as Kelly would say. Grandma's warning about Ruari's prior relationship seemed unfounded. There would be time for it to come up naturally in conversation, but it wasn't worth worrying about yet.

There was still no word from Gillian by Monday morning. Marianne had mailed a synopsis of the images she'd chosen to accompany the introductory material to her partner by way of nudging her to respond. She looked at her calendar and counted the days till she had to turn in three winning, exciting lectures to Dr. Plank so she could get this job. She couldn't wait any longer to get going on the second lecture.

She'd laid out the threads of the course. Now it was time to organize the subjects she needed to cover in the following twelve lectures. She also laid out the term paper topic, an adaptation of one she'd done as an undergrad and remembered liking. The midterm would come after she'd composed more of the lectures. Then she sat down and began reading.

Oscar kept her company for a time, lying in the weak morning sunlight on the sofa. Although the rain had let up, he wasn't excited about going outside. Her tea got cold while she turned the pages and made notes.

When the words stopped making sense, she set the book atop the precarious stack on the coffee table. The *Sleeping Lady* sculpture Ruari had given her was awash in papers. She ruffled the fur on the cat's head to wake him. "Oscar, my brain is full. I can't do this anymore. Let's go out."

The orange and white tabby stretched his front paws, then each back leg, elongating and compressing his stripes as he did so. She gave him an affectionate scratch under the chin and reached for her phone.

"I wonder how Ruari's doing?" Coffee together had been their first real date. His nickname of 'Mahri' gave her a pleasant glow in her belly. Maybe it was a sign he was getting over his shyness. She dialed his number. Disappointingly, it went to voice mail, and she left a message reminding him about their dinner date later that week.

Marianne dreamed she was sitting on her sofa reading for class. Oscar paced the floor, lashing his crooked tipped tail.

Living room window, front door, window, front hall.

"You're making me nervous," she told him. "Come up here and settle down." She patted the cushion next to her.

"Food Goddess, come look at this," he said. His voice was orange and white, wrapped around a purring center.

"No, I have to finish this reading," she replied, turning a page.

He leapt up on the arm of the sofa and peered into the twilight beyond the glass. "This is not good," he said.

"What?" She put the book down and knelt on the couch to look out the window next to him.

In the twilight, several shadowy figures milled around out on the cul-de-sac.

"Who are they?"

"I don't like them," he stated flatly. "Shut the curtains." He jumped down and resumed his pacing.

She rose and checked the front door. It was locked. Returning to the window, she knelt on the seat and watched the figures outside. More of them were gathering by the second. Nervously, she checked the side door in the dining room. She went to each window and made sure they were shut and locked.

By the time she returned to the living room window, the shadowy, ghostly figures were in the front yard. They didn't interact with each other, apparently locked in their own private worlds. Then, as if by a prearranged signal, they stopped, turned, and stared at the house.

Marianne shrank back from the window, yanking the curtains across.

Someone knocked on the door.

"Don't worry, Oscar, the doors and windows are locked. Just don't let them in."

The knock was more insistent.

"Food Goddess, that's not going to work!" he yowled and dashed up the stairs to the second floor.

Something white oozed under the door and around the cracks between the door and the frame. It pulsed with an eerie glow.

Someone pounded heavily on the door.

Marianne woke with a gasp. Her heart was beating like she'd

escaped from a feral dog. The bedroom was quiet and dark around her. She reached down automatically and touched Oscar's fur where he lay against her thigh. He looked up sleepily, and she half expected him to say, "What? I'm sleeping here," but he just lay his head down again.

Oscar, are you trying to tell me we have burglars?

Frightened, she turned on the light, pulled out her phone, and brought up 911 on speed dial just in case there was a human intruder. She armed herself with the heavy metal flashlight she kept near the bed in case of a power outage and cautiously walked through the house. She checked all the doors and windows and steeled herself to look out the front window. The yard was dark and empty, lit only faintly by the streetlights. Satisfied that she was secure, she climbed back into bed.

No burglars. That left a random nightmare. Or a premonition of an impending ghost apocalypse. Did picking up one hitchhiker mean somehow she was available to every other ghost in town for help? *Is this somehow my new mission in life?*

No more waiting. Time to call Sarah.

After a fitful sleep, Marianne called Sarah as early as she dared. The phone rang, and Marianne muttered, "Come on, please pick up."

On the fifth ring she heard, "Hey, Marianne, you're up early. What's going on?"

She breathed a sigh of relief at the blunt, matter-of-fact voice. "Hi Sarah. I need your advice."

Sarah's voice sharpened. "Sounds important. What's going on?"

"Last night, I dreamed that ghostly people were pressed around my house, looking in the windows! It was one of *those* dreams. The true ones."

"Okay, slow down. I've been wondering when this would happen."

"What? Tell me this isn't normal!"

"Hate to tell you, but it is kind of normal for people like us. Spirits who linger often have unfinished business. They get impatient when no one can hear them. When they find one of us, they often demand help."

"So spirits are going to come up to me and ask me to do stuff for them? Do you do that?"

She snorted. "Not since I learned to 'screen my calls' so to speak. I highly recommend you develop a thick skin and some serious boundaries or you'll be inundated from both sides."

"You mean people wanting me to do seances or something?"

"Exactly. It's not great when both parties expect you to carry on some kind of conversation like you're their telephone."

"Oh." *Thick skin? I'm not really that kind of person.* "So, I just have to be rude?"

Sarah sighed. "If you want, I can show you how to turn off your 'hey I can see you, just ask me' signals. It'll take some practice, but it helps a lot."

"Yes! What about my dream?"

"That's a little different. We can reinforce the protection on your house so you feel safer. I could come by this weekend and help you do that."

"Please. Tell me what I need."

Sarah gave her a list of items to get from DreamTime, the New Age store on Main, and gave her a time on Saturday. "Oh, Kelly wants to say hi."

"Hey, girl! How are you?" Kelly always sounded like she'd just come from a fabulous party. It wasn't fair so early in the morning.

"I'm okay!" Sarah was good for quelling unease about the supernatural, but talking to Kelly made her happy. "How's Hair Magic these days?" Kelly ran a small beauty salon off Main and had been her link to Sarah.

"Business is picking up," she replied. "Plus, I'm doing more photography and getting my portfolio together. You never know when the economy is going to tank again, and people always want their photos taken, so I'm setting up a side hustle."

"I didn't know you were a photographer. I'd love to see your work sometime."

"There's an album in the waiting area at the salon."

"I'll come by."

They talked a little longer before she hung up the phone feeling much better. She waited until nine-thirty and walked into town to get Sarah's list. Saturday couldn't come too soon. At least she could feel like she'd done everything she could to deal with her ghost problems. Later, she would have to buckle down and keep working on her lectures.

Marianne had been in DreamTime a couple of times before to get crystals and incense for one of Sarah's rituals. The store was full of beautiful things that veered between cute and campy and materials for the serious practitioner. She browsed for a bit, looking over the Tarot decks, incense, and little statues of fairies and gnomes. After picking up a box of white, unscented tea lights, she headed to the bins of semi-precious stones.

The vivid colors of tiger eye, malachite, and lapis lazuli drew her eye, but they weren't on her list, and she regretfully passed them by. Instead, she read the chart about the abilities of the stones Sarah had mentioned. She selected several finger-sized crystals of white selenite which supposedly cleaned the energies of her other stones, her house, and her body all at the same time. She added polished pebbles of goldstone and red jasper for each window and a handful of lumpy turquoise fragments. Purportedly, they deflected negative energy and protected her home from the spirit world. Obsidian she already had.

She was a little skeptical that these would accomplish all they advertised, but she was desperate to protect her house from hordes of anxious, needy spirits. Maybe if she carried a little bag of stones with her, they would help protect her when she was out and about? She picked up a piece of turquoise, selenite, lapis lazuli, and hematite and added a little gauze bag to carry them in. It would be her own personal protection charm.

The next morning Ruari was in and out early to evade Talmadge and headed out on his daily list of calls. He steered his battered white Ford pickup to an empty house currently between renters. Sitting in the driver's seat, he took a moment to scan through his list. The cleaning crew had spent all of last Friday scrubbing, and they had noted all the needed repairs. Emerging from the cab, he got some tools from the big box in the truck bed.

As he unlocked the front door, he noticed two young men coming out of the house next door. It was also one of Gloria's properties, and he'd been there a couple of months ago to deal with a dryer problem. They were pretty chill guys and reminded him of himself and his college buddies. He smiled and raised a hand in greeting. They looked at him with furtive glances and sketched only a bare wave in return. That was odd. *What's with that?*

He entered the empty premises and got to work. His eyes blurred unexpectedly a few times, but not as badly as before. Blinking and rubbing them seemed to clear them. The ice pick headache behind his temples had shrunk to the occasional zing. The worry that he had a tumor pressing on his optic nerve gnawed at his peace of mind, but the doc had promised to call.

After dealing with the kitchen appliances, he went upstairs to deal with a drippy faucet. The bathroom window had an unob-structed view of the neighboring lawn. Under the occupation of the three young men, it was not in great shape.

Thank heavens I don't have to do yards.

An impressive scatter of beer cans and red disposable cups littered the back patio, and a grill lay on its side. There had clearly been an epic party over Labor Day weekend. The longer he looked, the more he saw. A blackened patch of grass peppered with briquettes surrounded the fallen grill, and his eyes followed it straight to the side of the house. A scorched and burned section of cedar shake siding attested to the wildness of the bacchanal.

Crap. It wasn't on his work order list, so there was a good chance the renters hadn't called it in. That explained the lack of a friendly greeting earlier. He couldn't ignore it. The recent rain was only the beginning of fall and winter weather. He mentally added it to his list, knowing he would have to fill out the paperwork when he got back to the office.

He finished replacing the cartridge on the faucet and tightened it, satisfied that the house was ready for the next tenants. While stowing his tools, he decided to bite the bullet and step next door.

I'm here. I should get a better look at that damage. Otherwise, I just have to come back again.

When he knocked, a tall, heavyset young man opened the door. Ruari remembered his face, but not his name and smiled.

"Hi, I'm Ruari Allen from Gloria's Valley Homes and Properties. I was here last spring to fix the dryer. Are you Chad?"

"No, I'm Marcus. I remember you," he said with a fleeting smile.

Ruari gave him a friendly, we're-all-buds-here smile. "I was working next door and couldn't help noticing the damage on your siding."

Marcus's smile vanished, and he looked wary. "We had some friends over is all." As the young man spoke, a dark vapor trickled out of his mouth like cigarette smoke.

What's with all the smoking? Ruari blinked, and it was gone. Suppressing a sigh, he said patiently, "I saw the scorch marks on the side of the house. I'm sure it was an accident, and you were going to call Gloria's and let them know."

Marcus's eyes darted this way and that, looking hunted. "Yeah, we've just been really busy." The smoke rolled like a furnace out of his mouth.

He's lying. "Look," Ruari continued in his most companionable tone, "winter's coming on, and that really needs to be repaired.

Could I take a look at it? If you wait, it'll just get worse and cost more to fix."

Ruari could see the wheels turning in Marcus's head before he relented and stepped outside, leading Ruari around to the back. As he followed, Ruari watched the burly figure blur into a double image. The second image was limned in a muddy yellow light, and he blinked hard to clear it. *Not this again. Come on, eyes, clear up. I can't do my job if I can't see properly.*

His vision steadied as he stared at the siding. Seen up close, the damage was worse than it had looked from afar, and Ruari winced. He was going to have to pull the shakes and replace at least a four-foot section. "Must've been some party," he muttered as he examined the scorch.

Behind him Marcus said, "Yeah. We had some guys over. I don't really know what happened. I was inside at the time."

That sounded like so much bullshit. *I wonder...* He turned to ask, "Any guesses what happened? How did it get put out?"

The twenty-something dude thrust his hands into his pockets and said hesitantly, "Well, Hunter and Chad were out here. I was inside getting more burgers out of the freezer."

Ruari watched more black wisps drift out of his mouth with every word. *You're lying your ass off. That's what it means.*

Marcus gained momentum. "Yeah, then I heard a commotion, you know? I rushed outside, and the grill had flamed up and caught the side of the house on fire. The rest of the dudes were just laughing and throwing beer cans at it to put it out. Hunter knocked the grill aside, but I found the hose and turned it on. One of the neighbors called the fire department on us. When they came, they turned their big ass hose on our food, man! They ruined it!"

As Marcus told his story, his confidence improved, and he concluded with righteous indignation. A faint black haze encircled his head like phantom midges just for a moment before it dissipated and vanished. Marcus had been in the middle of it, Ruari was sure of it.

He schooled his expression into something neutral. "Okay, thanks for explaining things. I'll be back when I can to fix it. Like I said, Mrs. Talmadge won't be happy, but she'll go easier on you if you call it in and request the repair." Privately, he knew she'd rant about idiots, but it meant more money for the agency, and Talmadge wouldn't really care how much time Ruari would have to spend fixing it.

Marcus looked relieved that his story was being accepted. "Okay, thanks, man. And, um, sorry." To Ruari's surprise, he looked contrite, and there was no smoke at all.

The bigger the lie, the greater the smoke. Bizarre. He supposed if he worked at it, he could fine tune it. *How come I never noticed this before? Why now? Where did it come from?* He had a vague memory of some of his Scots family talking about second sight and wondered if this was it. *But weren't you born with it? Or got it if you were hit by lightning or something?*

It was a mystery.

That night Ruari dreamed he was walking through his grandparents' backyard in Scotland. The low, one-story house of fieldstone stood behind him, and the big gray barn with its vertical siding loomed in front of him. Animals occupied one side, and Granda's wood shop filled the other. Nana's garden and chicken run filled the space between the two buildings. But there had been no flowers or animals here since Nana died.

"You should go inside," someone said behind him. The voice was musical, feminine and, if not exactly warm, sounded encouraging.

"Granda's gone. He doesn't want me there."

"I have a commission for you."

"I'm done with that. He said I'm no good."

"You are the best of all of them. You can do things your grandfather never could. He was jealous of your skill. That's why he stopped trying to teach you. You exceeded his abilities long ago, and he was jealous."

He felt a lift of hope.

"It's true," the voice said.

The door to the barn slowly rolled aside of its own accord. "Go inside. I have a wonderful surprise for you. We have so much to do."

He approached the old building and smelled the familiar, heady mix of wood shavings, hay, and animals. Granda's tools were laid out on his worktable, sharp and ready to use. A block of wood almost two feet square sat expectantly. By the look and the faint lemon polish odor, it was a fine piece of black walnut. As he stared at it, the grain twisted and rearranged itself into shapes. Fantastically detailed and like nothing he'd ever made before, it intrigued him. A floodgate opened inside him. He groped for a pencil to sketch the design before he forgot it. He drew it from several angles in his dream, hoping he'd remember when he awoke.

CHAPTER 6

After work the next day, Ruari sharpened all his tools and laid them out on a workbench. An inkling of an idea for a new sculpture had tickled the back of his mind all day. He might have dreamed about it but couldn't exactly remember. He inhaled the smells of sawdust, Tung oil, and shellac tinged with the scent of machinery oil and relaxed.

His muse must be rested and getting back on track again. Even if he would never be as good as Granda, he could still make things for himself. Dad be damned. He raised his mug of coffee in salute to the stern black and white visage on the wall under its arch of tree photos and set to work. The bone pile along the wall contained scrap lumber, spare planks, and blocks. He combed through it, looking for just the right piece when there came a rap on the door to the alley.

The knob rattled, and he went to open it. Some people in Maple Hill still left their doors unlocked, trusting in the politeness and good will of their neighbors. Ruari locked his studio every time he left because of the equipment. It also kept Erin out, though he wouldn't put it past her to secretly make a key just so she could get in when she wanted. She'd never respected his shut door when they were growing up.

Dressed in a black jeans with a blousy top and a dark green fitted vest, she'd swapped out the Doc Martens for high heeled brown leather boots. She'd spiked her copper red hair up in a cockatoo's crest. She looked like a pirate. It was funny, he thought, she'd found the Goth vibe as a teenager, and now she owned it. He smiled, picturing her as a badass old lady.

"Hey, big brother, how're you doing?" Her boots clicked on the cement floor as she strode past the equipment.

"Okay. You?"

"I came by earlier, but you've been out a lot."

"Work's been hell." Work and one emergency doctor's appointment. He didn't want her to find out and blab to Mom and Dad. The doc had checked him thoroughly, drawn blood for analysis as a back up, but told him he was most likely suffering from stress and poor diet. He'd recommended Ruari to eat better, get some rest, and try to exercise more. The office promised to call him with the results as soon as they were in.

She stopped herself from running her hands through her gelled hair and balled her fists instead. "Mom and Dad are driving me crazy. I feel like I'm twelve again."

He was sympathetic. "How's your job search going?"

Erin had been top of her class in B-school and hired at a big accounting firm in Arizona right after graduation. Unfortunately, she'd been downsized when the economy went bust. She'd done what many of her peers had done: gone home to mom and dad. She'd been applying for jobs like mad since then.

She made a face.

"No luck, huh? Have you considered applying to the FBI? I think you'd make a good spy." He was only half joking.

"Hilarious." She stuck her tongue out. "Besides, the FBI and CIA call them agents. Only some CIA agents are spies. I checked."

He grinned. "See. You'd make a great cop."

"Too much physical stuff." She shrugged. A trickle of vapor escaped her maroon painted lips. She was lying, or maybe she was worried about something else.

"I bet they have forensic accounting agents. You'd be great at that."

That teased a smile out of her. "I'll think about it." She nodded at the tools on the table. "Must be thinking about a new project."

"I am."

"Good. How's your girlfriend?"

"What?" Erin's lightning speed change of subjects often caught him off guard.

"Your girlfriend. Word on the street says you were with a woman a couple of weekends ago at the Co-op. She got into a fight with a city guy and a busty blonde. Who is she?"

Ruari hadn't given the confrontation much more thought. Erin's network of gossipy friends must have spotted them. "Her name is Marianne, and she's renting a house through Gloria's."

She gave him a sly smile. "Have you been on a date since then?"

"Coffee a couple of times."

"Taken her out for dinner yet?"

"Maybe sometime this week, nosy pants."

She grinned, hands on her hips. "Good. Don't let that thing with Jenny hold you back forever."

His tentative good mood deflated, leaving him irritated. "Thanks for the reminder."

"Just looking out for you, big brother." Another trickle of black smoke emerged.

Erin, why just can't leave it alone? "Are you dating anyone?" He shot back, nettled.

"Pat Whelan and I are seeing each other for now." She spoke airily but seemed pleased. More vapor accompanied her words. *So, maybe you're not entirely happy about it?*

Ruari vaguely remembered a high school football jock from Erin's class. He thought the guy worked for the chamber of commerce now. "Isn't he kind of boring?"

She flared. "No, he's lovely and polite, and he likes me." A small cloud of black smoke.

Something was definitely up, but he didn't want to deal with her touchiness. He put his hands up. "Okay. You can make your own decisions."

She paced restlessly between the tables, the heels of her boots clicking on the floor.

"Now what?"

"I've got to find an apartment or something." She stopped and stared at him, looking like a thought had struck her.

With the light behind her, he saw a flash of green and orange around her head and shoulders. He couldn't miss it. *If the smoke means people are lying, what do the colors mean? If I had to guess, I'd say super energetic.*

"You could find me a place to live! Gloria's has to have something."

He tried to keep up with her. "I don't know if there're any openings, but I can ask Alyssa tomorrow."

She put her palms on the table between them and pleaded, "Could you keep your eyes open for me, please?"

"Sure."

She stepped around the table and gave him a quick hug, squeezing him hard for just a second. "Thanks. If you find something, I'll owe you."

He hugged her back. "That'll be a first."

After she left, he shook his head with a bemused smile before resuming his search for the right piece of wood. Finally, he found a chunk of black walnut left over from a bowl making project he'd tried a while ago. It was bigger than he remembered, about eighteen inches across and about as tall. It was a hard wood, and he'd have to sharpen his tools regularly, or he'd be fighting it. But it would take fine details really well, and it felt right. It smelled faintly like lemony wood polish.

He set it on the workbench, cleared his mind, and examined the grain from all sides. He wasn't sure what this new sculpture would be, but gave his imagination and his subconscious free rein. After a while, he picked up a tool and drifted into the zone.

. . .

They'd agreed upon No Bones Barbecue as the place for their first dinner together. Marianne had looked at the menu on a walk through town. It offered a pan-regional selection of barbecued meats and some unusual things like barbecued watermelon slice. She and her mom used to get barbecue when she was little, but she hadn't had it in ages. Her ex, Geoffrey, had not been into the smoky, spicy sauces of Creole, Sweet Baby Ray's, or any other tradition. Her mouth watered just thinking about it. She needed a good night out.

Gillian had finally gotten back to her by email. "M, this is a good beginning, but it's too dense. The pictures are okay. Can you tone it down? Undergrads don't want to work too hard these days. Got a big review coming up. Don't send me stuff till after the twentieth. Thx."

She'd had to recalibrate. She'd been an undergrad herself not so long ago, and remembered her hunger to learn, and her scorn when professors didn't deliver. But some students she'd encountered as a TA had been more interested in the grade than the knowledge. Maybe Gillian was right.

A dinner date was the perfect antidote to her dream scare and her work disappointment. Maybe she could get Ruari to come out of his shell a little more. Geoffrey had done nothing but talk about himself and his work, and it was refreshing to have to tease details out of Ruari. Especially since woodworking was so much more interesting than dubious advertising schemes.

She indulged in a luxurious shower and pampered herself with a blow dry and light makeup. Lingering in front of her closet, she took her time choosing an outfit and settled on a batik print button up blouse the color of honey over a pair of jeans. A black sweater would keep her from getting chilly later. It was so nice not to have to dress fancy. It wasn't New York City, and Geoffrey wasn't there to stress about whether or not they looked hot as a couple. Not that they'd ever had to worry about paparazzi, but he'd aspired. Marianne snorted: her ex's new fiancee Sandra fit that role so much better. Thank goodness Sandra was a jealous woman. She would claim Geoffrey's attention for a very long time.

She checked her look in the mirror, fluffed her hair a last time, grabbed her purse, and went out. It was early, but strolling along Main Street and window shopping would be a good way to work off some of her energy from sitting all day.

Ruari knocked off at five for the first time in ages. He went home and straight into the workshop. He was excited and a little nervous about dinner with Marianne later that evening. Doing a little work on the new carving project would help him relax. He pulled the cloth off the work in progress and turned on the table lamp. He turned it this way and that, picked up a small gouge, and started working.

Some time later there was a distant, persistent ringing noise, and it took Ruari a few moments to realize it was his cellphone. He laid his chisel down and searched on the tabletop until he found it buried under a small pile of wood chips.

As he recognized the number, he also noticed the light level in the rest of the studio. It was dark outside his little circle. Marianne. Dinner. *Oh shit.*

"Marianne!"

"Hi Ruari." She sounded tentative. "Did I misunderstand the time for dinner?"

His stomach twisted. "No. I got caught up working on a new piece in the studio and lost track of the time."

"It's a little after seven."

He closed his eyes and said in a small voice, "I'm so sorry. I could shower and join you in about twenty minutes if you still want to?"

"If you're not too busy?"

"No, I want to be there!"

"I'll get us another table."

"Be there as soon as I can." Galvanized, he turned off the work light, set his tools aside to sharpen later, and jetted up the stairs two at a time. He didn't even let the shower get warm before flinging himself through a perfunctory soap and rinse. He donned a brown, collared shirt over khaki slacks, and ran a comb through his hair in record time. He debated whether it was faster to drive up to Main or go on foot and opted for the latter so he wouldn't have to park.

I can't believe I totally blew past the time. What is wrong with me? I've been looking forward to this for days. She's going to be so pissed. When he'd missed a date with Jenny, she'd spent half the time finding ways to remind him what a schmuck he was.

Why is this happening again?

The tiny white lights around the windows and doors along Main Street twinkled invitingly. Usually they reminded Ruari of Christmas time or a postcard village, but tonight he utterly failed to appreciate it as he jogged along the sidewalk. A stitch grew in his side as he crossed the last street. He stopped outside the restaurant to catch his breath and thought ruefully how little aerobic exercise he got. A quick look at his watch showed that eighteen minutes had transpired since he'd hung up.

No Bones was full of people and loud conversation. Subdued country music played in the background. He scanned the room and saw a booth with a single, dark-haired woman seated at it. Bypassing the cluster of people waiting at the door for a table, he made his way over.

"Marianne?" His stomach was tight with anxiety. She looked up from the menu and gave him a tentative smile. Better to get it over with. "I feel terrible for being late. May I join you?"

Her smile relaxed a little, and she nodded. "I had to give up the first table because it got so busy. I just got seated again."

Her hair framed her sweet, oval face in brown waves. She

looked disappointed but not accusing. He searched for her aura. Her usual glow clung in a narrow band around her head and shoulders. It was like she didn't want to let herself out.

I've got to make up for being late.

"So, do you recommend anything in particular?" Her voice sounded carefully neutral.

He cleared his throat. "They have a fantastic house barbecue sauce. It's a little sweet, a little smoky, not too spicy. I like it on ribs or pulled pork."

"How is it on barbecued salmon? That looks tasty."

Jenny liked that too. "I'm not much of a fish eater, but I've heard it's good." *Crap. Stop thinking about the ex.*

When their server came, Ruari ordered an Oktoberfest lager and Marianne, a hard cider. They also put in their dinner order, assuming it would take a while to be served.

"You said you'd started working on a new piece," she began. "Must be pretty intense. What is it?"

"Well, so far it looks like a tree stump, but I think it's going to have some animals in it."

She gave him a quizzical look. "How can you not know what it's going to be when you're done?"

"I sort of give my creative muse free rein and enjoy the process of discovery."

"That sounds very free-spirited." Her smile reached her eyes.

"How's the class going?"

She told him about her research and false starts. "Gillian thought it was too advanced. She's probably right. So I've been simplifying things. I added images, like you suggested, and think it looks pretty good now. I'm working on the second lecture."

He raised his glass in a silent toast and took the excuse to look at her more closely. Her glow had opened up a little.

"Is there something in my hair?" She reached up and patted her hair self-consciously.

"I thought I saw something, but it's gone." *Keep it under control,*

Ruari. She doesn't want you staring at her. "How's your house? Are the ghosts still gone?"

Her smile broadened. "It's just me and Oscar now. I don't think I said it, but thank you for believing me. It means a lot."

He nodded and looked away. When she'd mentioned ghosts at first, he'd thought she was making excuses for causing the damage herself. When she insisted on blaming ghostly doings, he'd wondered if she was a pathological liar.

She watched his face and chuckled. "Well, you gave me a chance, anyway. Not many people in my life believe me on that subject."

"Have you always been able to see ghosts?"

"No! It's new and kind of freaky, honestly. I've started seeing them in other places besides my house."

"Really? Like where?" He'd scoffed at spirits and ghosts being real before he met her. He knew his parents and sister outright denied them as figments of a hysterical or manipulative imagination. But when he watched a logical, grounded person like Marianne talk about them earnestly, he found himself opening his mind.

She leaned a little closer. "Don't laugh, but at the cemetery the previous caretaker still lives in the tool shed."

A smile tugged at his mouth in spite of himself.

"It's true, I've talked to him. There's also been a ghostly hitchhiker outside of town. I picked him up the other night."

He widened his eyes in alarm.

"Don't worry, I let him off in town. He didn't give me any trouble."

He shook his head. He'd picked up a few hitchers in his life, but not recently. "You know that's dangerous, right?"

"Yeah, but it turned out okay. I just thought he could move on if I took him down the road. Sarah says most people who stick around as spirits have unfinished business."

"Sarah Landsman?"

She nodded. "She's helping me protect my house from pushy ghosts and is teaching me how to cope with this new ability."

"I went to school with Sarah."

"Really?" She sounded interested.

He hesitated, then plunged on. "She's always had a reputation for being odd. People teased her for being weird."

Marianne narrowed her eyes a little. "Not just gay, but also weird?"

He looked down, embarrassed. "Well, that too. She and Kelly have been together forever, since grade school. I'm okay with them," he added hastily.

She nodded firmly. "They're good people."

Their food came, and they dug into steaming ribs, salmon, corn bread, and salad. As they ate, Ruari stole looks at his date. It was nice to eat dinner with a woman who enjoyed eating and wasn't focused on her weight. Jenny always ordered salad, making him feel obscurely guilty for eating well.

They finished. When the check came to the table, he claimed it. "My treat. I made you wait. The least I can do is pick up dinner. It's gotten really noisy in here. Would you like to go for a walk?"

"Sure."

The little white lights around the shop windows looked festive now. Ruari held her sweater while she slipped her arms in, and they strolled along for a couple of blocks in amiable silence, close enough to bump but not quite holding hands. Feeling daring, he did a bad Groucho Marx impression, complete with waggling eyebrows and air cigar. "You wanna come up and see my carvings?"

She burst out laughing. "Sure. Is it far?"

Boldly, he reached out and took her hand, leading the way down the darker side streets. An electric spark had jumped between them the first time they'd shaken hands. There was no spark this time, but her fingers were warm in his, and he felt a little tingling thrill echo through him. Half a block away from Main, the streets were quiet and mostly residential. Insects collected in little clouds around the streetlights. He nodded to the people he knew sitting out on their porches and enjoying the cooler air. The dark green foliage of the maples and oaks made shadowy pools between the splashes of light. It was the most peaceful he'd felt all week, and he quelled the restlessness that so often drove him to the workbench. He relished the sense of her body next to his.

As they turned onto the street before his alley, she looked over her shoulder behind them and across the way several times. She'd said her ex had hounded her for months. Maybe he hadn't given up yet. Ruari cast his gaze in the same direction, ready for action if they were being followed. There was no one there.

"You okay?" He asked. "Are you looking for someone?"

She straightened up. "I'm fine. Is it much farther?"

"Another block and we'll be there." There was something else, but clearly she wasn't ready to share. If they'd been in stronger light, he wondered if he'd see smoke with her words.

They arrived at the alley entrance to his studio, a pair of old barn doors illuminated by a single bulb under an old, dish-shaped metal lamp. Ruari got out his keys, and they entered through a smaller door to one side. He flipped the switches, and the first floor lights came on, illuminating the workshop tables and woodworking equipment.

"Wow," she said appreciatively, "what a great space."

"It started out as an old livery stable."

He gave her a tour of all the different tools from the big band saw down to the small jig saw, the lathe, drill presses, worktables, and neatly arranged hand tools. It was a motley collection of equipment. He'd bought the biggest pieces for peanuts when the high school had updated its wood shop and filled in with things gotten at yard sales and store closeouts. Marianne seemed genuinely interested in everything. Even Jenny hadn't taken that much interest in his passion.

She strolled, hands in her pockets, just looking at things. He watched her for a few moments, then to keep from staring at her like a guy with his first crush, he got a broom and began idly digging in the corners for sawdust. He kept an eye on her progress.

She stopped at the table with his muse project nestling amid a collection of carving chisels and wood shavings. "Is this your new piece?"

He leaned the broom against a pile of wood along the wall and joined her. "Do you want to see it?"

"May I?" She sounded hesitant, as if he were inviting her to look at something intensely personal.

Pleased by her consideration, he turned on the lamp as she bent close to examine it. She made no move to touch it, only leaned closer to see his pencil sketching on the wood.

"Is this going to be a hedgehog?" He nodded. She examined it for a few moments more then said, "I look forward to seeing it when it's done."

She passed the cork board and took in his homage to Granda as if it were a museum exhibit. "Is that your grandfather?" She gestured at the magazine pages. The craggy face stared out, the crow's feet around his eyes, the deep crease between his brows, the gray stubble across his cheeks and chin sharply delineated.

"Coll Allen."

She stared at him with her head tilted to one side. "He looks so sad," she murmured. Stepping back, she looked at the archway of tree photos. "He must have really loved that tree. It looks like the same one in every picture."

"I think it is. He called it his muse or inspiration."

"Huh." She made her way back to the foot of the stairs. "Is there more upstairs?"

"Just my apartment. It's a mess," he said, embarrassed. He

crossed to join her. Her dark hair framed her face as she stared at him. All he wanted to do was lean down and kiss her.

As if she'd read his mind, she stepped up onto the lowest step, raising herself to head height with him. Hardly daring to believe his luck, he leaned forward and felt her breath on his face as she brought her lips to his. Their kiss was warm and gentle, her lips full and soft on his. His body reacted to her with an intense ache, and he hoped she wouldn't shy away.

After a moment, she withdrew. "Will you walk me home, Ruari Allen?" she asked softly.

Feeling slightly dizzy, he nodded. He really wanted another kiss, but maybe there was time.

She stepped down again and took his hand in her smaller one and looked up at him inquiringly. Senses singing with the sweetness of her lips, he fumbled in his pocket for the keys with his free hand. He didn't want to let go of her even long enough to open the door, but she slipped from his grasp and out through the opening ahead of him. Her hand was right there when he reached for it. Their palms fit together perfectly.

They walked in companionable silence along the quiet streets. The warm darkness was the perfect temperature and smelled of late summer leaves with a hint of autumn earth and spice. He steered them down another side street lined with houses for two blocks, passing from one pool of light to another. All normal points of reference were gone, lending a surreal quality to the familiar places around them. The porches were empty now, and there seemed to be no other foot traffic. Perhaps because of their kiss, the night had a dreamlike, transcendent quality to it. It was like walking in an ocean of air. The air currents and eddies slid over his skin like a whisper. His awareness expanded as if the night were a huge creature that lived and breathed on its own, and he was a connected organism within it. It wouldn't have surprised him if they'd risen off the pavement and flown.

Wondering if this hyper awareness was related to his weird double vision, he hazarded a look at Marianne. An unconscious squeeze of his hand on hers made her look up. Her shining eyes and look of wonder suggested that she was feeling the same thing. They passed through the ether between his house and hers, and he felt like an invisible thread had been drawn between their places as surely as the string through the Minotaur's maze.

At her doorstep she turned and said, "Thank you for an amazing evening, Ruari."

"My pleasure," he whispered. "Thanks for coming to see my studio."

The touch of her lips on his felt as light as the brush of a bird's wing. "Goodnight, Ruari."

"Goodnight, Mahri," he breathed. He walked home in the velvety darkness.

Marianne lay in bed mulling over the evening. How could a simple dinner date feel so complicated? Ruari had stood her up and then told her a story about getting caught up in work. She certainly had done that herself, but that was what alarms were for.

Maybe he wasn't that interested after all. When Geoffrey had pulled away from her, he'd been involved with someone else. It had taken her months to figure that out, but when she looked back, that was her clue. Maybe Ruari had other women in his life? Maybe she should just let him go.

And yet, he seemed to be completely focused on her when they were together. Grandma Selene had said, "He couldn't take his eyes off you, dear." That meant something. She relived their kiss on the stairs. His mouth had been firm, just the right amount of moist, a little brush of his tongue, not too demanding. On the whole, a first rate kiss.

And their walk home had been so ethereal. It had been a long time since she'd felt that sort of magical, living, breathing sense of the moment. It had to be a good omen.

Sarah arrived on Saturday in her old Volvo station wagon. Dressed in khaki slacks and a polo shirt, she wore her chestnut brown hair pulled back firmly with barrettes. Her face was angular with an arched Roman nose and piercing brown eyes. Although Sarah didn't smile much, Marianne was grateful she'd been taken under her wing. She also admitted that the lawyer still overawed her. Sarah had been ruthless when she'd expelled the angry ghost of the previous owner, George Rutherford.

"Thanks for coming," Marianne told her.

Sarah looked at the freshly painted living room. Marianne had done it in stages when she couldn't concentrate on research anymore. "I see you're repainting. Good. Making the place look different will help keep George out. Let's do what we can to prevent every restless spirit and their sister from knocking on your door."

She looked over Marianne's purchases and nodded her approval. "I've done this protection thing for several other people. So here's the spiel. We want to prevent unwanted negative energy or influences from invading your home and keep out spirits or entities you don't want. This will make your home a safe space and hopefully keep you balanced, happy, and healthy."

When Marianne had lived in New York City, protecting her house against unwanted intrusions had always involved alarm systems, locks on the doors, and bars on the windows. Now, it seemed, potential invaders could pass through solid walls if they wanted to. If smoke, pretty stones, and chanting was the way to go, she was ready to try it.

"We purged your space of negative energy with a smudge after George left. Today, we'll reinforce that and then make it longer term. Strengthen your wards at least once a month. If you're dealing with something actively, you'll have to redo them more often. How many windows do you have in your house?"

Marianne turned slowly in place, her finger twitching toward each one as she counted silently. "Thirteen, I think? Ten down here and three upstairs."

"Basement?"

"Oh! I'll have to look."

"While you're at it, disconnect your smoke alarms."

"Right." She went downstairs and added another five windows, including the big one in the old coal bin. The others were small and let in only weak, dusty light.

"They count too," Sarah said when she returned to the kitchen. "Put a little tea light in each window." She looked at the packaging. "Hey, cool, these are floaters. Do you have eighteen containers? We'll float each one in a little water, and then we won't have to watch them all the time."

"As long as they don't have to match and don't have to be fancy," Marianne replied with a grin. She went to the recycling box. "I've got lots of empty cat food tins!"

Sarah barked a laugh. "It would be nice if they were a little classier. You're trying to construct a formal barrier and presentation does matter. On the other hand," she considered, "Oscar is an important member of your family and part of your alert system, if what you told me about him being able to detect George and Anne is true."

"I'll start with cat food tins and keep my eye out for something nicer."

She rinsed out a dozen, then rummaged in her cupboard and found six cups and saucers to hold the remainder. The first-floor windows got the pretty ones, and tins sat in the rest of the window spaces.

"Good," Sarah said when they reconvened in the kitchen. "You'll also want to put a separate container in each window with one of each of the stones. You can just make a little pile of them on the sill for now, but it'll be easier to keep track of them if they're in a cup or something."

Marianne quickly realized she didn't have enough stones. Every window could have something, but not all windows could have one of each. She added to her mental shopping list for the future. "Okay, we've protected the windows. Do we have to do doors too?"

Sarah produced three sprigs of dried herbs and flowers tied round with a black satin ribbon. "I made a little herb charm for each door to the outside." Marianne found some thumbtacks, and the doors looked rather festive with a little dried bouquet hanging over each one.

"If you can find a used horseshoe to nail above your front door, that would be an additional protective charm."

"Why used?"

"A horseshoe becomes infused with the energy of the horse that wears it even as it protects the animal. That energy will help your house. It's also associated with good luck. Hang it with the ends pointing up."

Before they started the smudge, they took a few deep breaths to ground themselves. Marianne felt a little calmer now that she was being proactive. Sarah lit a bundle of dried sage twigs, and they began at the front door. As they walked around the house, Marianne lit each candle. Sarah kept up a steady murmur, invoking the protection of the elements of earth and air, fire, and water and expelling negative forces. She reinforced the notion that George Rutherford was no longer allowed in this house, but Anne, if she wished to visit, was welcome.

Marianne asked what she could do as they walked, and Sarah told her to think about her little cottage enveloped in a warm, protective, white light, embodied by the little candles, imagining it as a haven of safety. Marianne did her best. The sage smoke, slightly sweet and acrid, hung in the air, making her cough. Sarah waved the tendrils everywhere, inside cupboards and closets, even opening the dishwasher, stove, and refrigerator.

Partway through the house, Marianne suddenly asked, "Sarah, will I still be able to dream true dreams?" Clairvoyant dreams might be scary, but she wanted to keep that line of communication open.

"Yes. If you want to block them, put the tourmaline and river stones around your bed after you charge them in the sunlight for a day."

Marianne felt surprisingly tired after they finished. They sat together in the living room, drinking herbal tea and munching cookies.

"It's a lot of work to put out that much energy to protect your place." Sarah leaned back against the sofa and closed her eyes, looking as tired as Marianne felt. Her hair wisped out of its clips and frizzed around her sweaty face. "But it's totally worth it if you're as sensitive as we are."

"Is your house protected like this?"

"Yup."

Marianne sat opposite Sarah in the easy chair, her bare feet propped up on the coffee table, a warm mug of tea cradled in her hands. "How do I keep spirits from asking me to do things for them?"

"That takes some practice. Mostly it's will power. It's like being really firm with an annoying person in a bar or on the subway. Tell them to piss off, you're not interested, and they will generally go away."

"If they don't?"

Sarah bobbed her head to one side in a tired, half shrug. "Mostly they just want to be heard. If they're obnoxious about it, call me. We can work something out, and maybe resolve their issues, or get them to back off."

"The equivalent of a restraining order for ghosts?"

Sarah smiled faintly. "Something like that."

"Can I use some of the stones I got as personal protection?"

Sarah nodded. "Tourmaline is a good focus stone. You can wear it in a pouch or as jewelry. There are also herbal charms that might help."

Marianne let out a deep breath. "Thank you so much for all of this. I don't know how I'd manage without you."

Sarah's expression softened. "I had a good teacher and mentor when I was growing up. It's time to pass it along. I also had a fair amount of denial and bigotry to deal with. You'll encounter that too."

Marianne shrugged. "Geoffrey thought I was crazy and still does. And my mom is not very sympathetic. I spent a lot of the last ten years ignoring my dreams."

The light glinted off Sarah's spectacles as she looked up, making her look stern and owlish. "You can't afford to do that anymore. You're going to need all of your abilities available to you, if you continue down this path."

Marianne gulped and nodded.

After another night of vague dreams hinting of danger, Marianne woke with the covers bunched in her hands. Oscar looked up sleepily from her side.

"What's the point of having clairvoyant dreams if they're so cryptic you can't do anything about them?" She grumbled.

He yawned, baring his sharp fangs, stretched, and jumped off the bed. "At least you're sleeping well."

When Anne and George had haunted her house, she'd interacted with them multiple times in her dreams, allowing her to understand their problems. But ghostly hitchhiker guy was not in her house, so maybe that put him out of reach. Anyway, she had work to do.

After breakfast, she sat down with her class material and reread her notes, trying to get back into the flow. After half an hour, she gave up. Thinking about being followed by the hitchhiker reminded her of the kiss she'd shared with Ruari and their wonderful walk home in the dark. She was not an impulsive person by nature, and her ex had made her overthink everything. But that sizzling kiss had made her want to abandon all caution. She smiled. It had taken a lot of self-control to just walk home and say good night at the door. Part of her still wasn't sure about Ruari. They hadn't known each other that long, and she'd promised herself to go slowly with her next relationship.

She opened her eyes, and Victorian economics stared her in the face. *I can't do this right now. If I find out more about the hitchhiker, maybe I can get back to working on the class.*

Washing dishes and tidying up helped her think. If someone had died out on the road near Maple Hill, surely that would have hit the local news. The Maple Hill Library might have something.

Oscar finished his morning wash and meowed to be let out. Marianne stroked his sturdy back before she opened the door. "Looks like it might rain, so be back before it gets dark, okay? Be careful, Mister, there's spooky stuff going on." He flirted his crooked tail tip and headed off into the yard to check out the fresh smells.

Marianne pulled her research material together, grabbed her umbrella and rain jacket, and headed out to the library. She patted the bulge of stones in their gauze bag where they rested in her pants pocket. Maybe she wouldn't be distracted by ghosts if she satisfied her curiosity.

She entered the fieldstone building that housed the Maple Hill Library. She descended the steps into the basement where the local history resources were housed. So far, she had encountered no ghosts down here. The only difficult spirit was that of the librarian.

Mrs. Caldwell looked up from her desk and peered over her spectacles. In spite of watching over her collection like a she-dragon over a clutch of eggs, she'd been very helpful with the Rutherford project. She wore her her iron gray hair in a severe bun, and she had a habitual expression of disapproval. Marianne had a private goal to get the older woman to smile, but had so far been unsuccessful.

"Good morning, Mrs. Caldwell," Marianne called out with a smile. "How are you today?"

"Miss Singleton." She gave Marianne a curt nod, dour expression intact.

"I need to look at the back issues of the Maple Hill Register."

"You know where they are. Please take only a few at time."

"I will. Thank you."

The last year and a half of issues were stacked in a pile of paper copies. The hitchhiker seemed like a contemporary soul. Marianne spread each issue out on her table and scanned the pages carefully. Compared to New York City with its daily litany of crimes and death, this little Hudson Valley town was pretty peaceful. Most crimes were minor and often attributed to malcontents coming up from the city to cause trouble. After an hour, she had the impression there was a spike in incidents during the summer, and wintertime brought a lull except for the occasional car accident connected with icy weather. Most importantly, there were no reports of deaths on the road outside of Maple Hill in the last year. Perhaps it was farther back. She checked the microfilm catalog and found a gap of about a year between the paper issues and those on film.

She approached the librarian's desk. "Excuse me, Mrs. Caldwell?"

"Yes?" The woman looked up from her task, pencil poised.

"Where might I find the back issues for last year?"

"They are still out being converted to a long-term storage format. They're due back by the end of the month."

"Rats. Thanks anyway." She frowned and half turned away.

"You're very keen on local doings." Mrs. Caldwell gave her a frankly curious look.

Marianne turned back. "Yes." She didn't think the librarian would understand needing to discover the identities of dead residents. "I'm new to Maple Hill and wanted to get a feel for the area." Not the best excuse, but the only one she could think of.

"I see." Mrs. C. didn't seem fully convinced, but her work seemed more compelling than questioning Marianne further.

If Marianne wanted to keep going, she had to switch to the microfilm reader and hope her ghost hadn't died during the missing year. She glanced at her phone. It was coming on to noon. She needed to get back to her class lecture writing soon.

She sat at the reader and threaded a reel of images. Now that she'd seen the rhythm of a year in the *Maple Hill Register,* she moved more quickly, looking for accidents or events on the roads near town. Despite that, it was hard not to pause and read things that caught her eye. At last, four years back, she found an article that jumped off the microfilmed page.

LOCAL TEEN KILLED BY DRUNK DRIVER

Samuel Naismith, 35, driving a Ford SUV, struck and killed a local teen from Beacon, Jason Fargate, 19, as he stood by the side of the road hitching for a ride. Naismith was arrested for driving under the influence and charged with vehicular manslaughter.

The accompanying photo of Jason showed a smiling young man with shaggy, dark blonde hair. There was no specific location for the actual accident listed, but it was the only one of its kind that she'd seen. The article listed his parents' names, Gretta and Tony Fargate, and a funeral home in Beacon. Marianne wondered if they still lived in Beacon and how they might take a visit from a complete stranger claiming to have talked to their dead son. *Yeah, that might not work out too well.* She hit the copy button and tucked the printout into her bag.

While she stretched the kinks out of her back, the film rewound itself, and she put it carefully away. It was mid-afternoon, and her stomach grumbled.

"Thank you," she called out to Mrs. Caldwell.

The woman looked up. "You're welcome."

She walked home in a light drizzle. Poor Jason, going home from a concert in the city when his ride dropped him nowhere near his home. She couldn't help imagining his moment of terror when he realized a car was about to hit him. The impact would have flung his soul right out of his body. Maybe that's why it got stuck there.

How do ghosts remember anything? She wondered. The popular science she'd read suggested that memory lay in the brain's hardware, the chemicals, and neurons, and such. Souls, essences, or spirits would be non-corporeal. How would they remember anything, much less converse with people, or do new things? She was no neuroscientist. Maybe there was more to life than what the body held.

That night, as she stood on the stoop to call Oscar, Marianne caught a hint of movement among the trees on the empty lot next door. A glowing, indistinct figure in a hooded jacket leaned out from behind a tree and looked toward her house. Her heart sped up, and the hairs on the back of her neck prickled.

Oscar bounded up the steps, ready for his dinner. She picked him up and cuddled him. "Hey mister, I know you're hungry, but I need a little help. We have to talk to the local ghost and see what's going on. Will you keep me company?"

He gave a 'mrrup.' Too bad he couldn't talk in the waking world. "I'll take that as a yes."

Summoning her courage, she sat on the front stoop. The big orange tabby sat next to her, crooked tail curled around his front paws. A quick look at the cul-de-sac showed no other people around, so she called out softly, "I know you're there. Let's talk."

She stared into the darkness under the trees until an indistinct figure detached itself and half floated, half paced toward her with remembered leg movements. He passed through her front fence unimpeded to stand at the bottom of her steps. His upper body was more solid than his lower, which faded away.

"You followed me the other night and now you're hanging around looking at my house. What's going on?" she inquired, surprising herself by sounding so normal. Oscar's solid, warm presence seated next to her boosted her confidence.

The young man glanced at the two of them nervously. *+I couldn't get a ride after you dropped me in town. When I saw you again, I followed you here. I couldn't come inside, so I waited for you.+* His mouth moved, but she heard the voice in her head without the benefit of her ears.

"What's your name?" she asked.

+Jason.+

She let out a breath she didn't realize she'd been holding. "Jason, I'm Marianne, it's nice to meet you. Do you mind taking your hood off? Thanks." Jason's face was paler than his clothing and glowed a little in the darkness. He looked young and vulnerable and a lot like the picture she'd seen in the paper. "What is it you want?"

He shifted uncomfortably and said, *+I tried to bum a ride in town, but everybody ignored me like I wasn't even there. You were the first person to offer me a ride in a long time, and the only person who talked to me. I didn't know where else to go.+*

"Yeah, Jason, about that," she said, not sure how to break the news to him. "What do you remember about the night you were hitching?"

He looked past her. +*The driver totally pissed me off. He wanted to come up this way to visit his girlfriend. I just wanted to get home, you know? He kept telling me it wouldn't take long. Finally, I was so mad I got out. I was walking on the road toward town when I heard a car behind me.*+ Jason turned, reliving the moment, and put out his thumb. +*It must've been a big SUV 'cause the lights were really bright.*+ He put his arm up to shield his eyes. +*Then something knocked me over. I thought maybe the guy was a really bad driver. When I got up, he was gone.*+

Her heart went out to him. "Jason, I have some bad news. He was more than just a bad driver. He was drunk, and he killed you."

+*What? That's not true!*+ He looked shocked.

"Think about it," she said gently. "You've been waiting a long time for a ride, right? According to the newspaper, you died four years ago. I'm really sorry." She felt bad for him.

+*But that's impossible! I just fell over the guardrail or something. I must've hit my head. When I woke up, he was gone. It was just a couple of nights ago!*+ He drifted back and forth across her walkway in his agitation.

She waited patiently for him to process the information. Oscar sat next to her, like an orange and white version of Bast, crooked tail tapping slowly up and down.

Finally, Jason stopped, his expression resigned. +*Well, if I'm dead, it explains a lot. Guess I should've stayed in the car and visited the girlfriend, huh?*+

She thought for a moment. "I'd be willing to take you to your parents' place in Beacon. Will that work for you?"

He nodded slowly. +*I'd really appreciate that. Guess you're my 'Death Cab,' right?*+ He said with an endearing, wry grin.

She shrugged and said, "I don't know what that is, sorry."

+*It's a band. You know, 'Death Cab for Cutie.' You're the cab, and I'm the dead cutie, get it?*+

She grinned back. In life, he must have been quite the

charmer with the ladies. "If you say so. I'll be here at ten tomorrow morning to take you, okay?"

+*Could I stay on your couch, please?*+ He asked, looking hopeful and winsome at the same time.

That felt like a terrible idea. She didn't want an invisible guy watching her get ready for bed, much less prowling around inside while she slept. "No. You'll be okay out here."

+*I won't be any trouble, I promise. It's cold and lonely out here.*+

"You'll be fine."

He nodded resignedly and turned away. By the time he reached the fence, he'd faded into the night. Marianne wondered if he did that consciously or not. She petted Oscar, still sitting tall at her side. "Thanks for the backup, mister." He butted her hand and meowed.

"Sure, I better live up to your designation as Food Goddess."

After dinner, she surfed the internet for information on hitchhiking ghosts. Unfortunately, none of those stories fit her situation. According to the lore, the driver picked up the person on the side of the road, took them to their destination, whereupon they disappeared. The theory was that the ghost was stuck in an endless loop of roadside death, unable to get home. Jason had come home with her and not disappeared. Hopefully, if she took him to his parents' place in Beacon, he'd be able to reunite with them or at least get some personal closure and be able to cross over to heaven or some kind of afterlife.

She came across the subject of possession and wandered down a rabbit hole of fascinating articles about angels and demons and, weirdly, the Victorian notion of possession by fairies. Supposedly, fairies took over people who had offended them, causing fevers, headaches, nightmares, and marked changes in behavior. She chuckled and made a note of that reference in her research notebook for later. If she had time to do a lecture on some of the more esoteric Victorian beliefs, she could include it.

CHAPTER 8

$\mathcal{M}$onday morning, SueAnn Talmadge called Ruari into her office as soon as he arrived. The weekend had been peaceful compared to the previous one. What was she on about this time? Alyssa spared him a worried look as she spoke to a client on the phone.

Talmadge gestured for him to close the door behind him and offered him a chair. Warily, he sat on the edge of the seat. She bared her teeth in a predatory smile. "Allen, I found you an assistant to help with the repair and maintenance schedule."

Stunned, Ruari said, "Really? Who is it? When would he start?"

"Casey Hopper'll be here in a little while, and you can take him out with you on your rounds today. Now, you won't have any excuses not to get all your work done." She gave him a smug look.

His brain clicked furiously, rolling the name around like a grain of sand in an oyster. "Casey Hopper? Is he related to Gloria?"

SueAnn gave him a sly look. "Yes, he's her son. So, he'd better work out."

"Does he know anything about fixing things? Or dealing with people?" Ruari asked, feeling uneasy.

"He took metal shop in high school and is taking a year off before going to college. You asked for an assistant. He needs something to do." She narrowed her eyes and tapped a red taloned finger on her desk. "Make it work."

Ruari closed his eyes and took a deep breath. "Fine."

"Leave the door open," she ordered as he left.

Full of foreboding, he tried to be optimistic. *Hey, she actually listened to me and got me help. Maybe it won't be so bad.*

He lowered his voice and said, "Alyssa, are there any new listings? A small apartment, a month by month, anything? My sister's looking."

She scrolled through her computer and shook her head. "Nothing like that at the moment, but I'll keep you posted."

"Thanks."

Ruari perused the daily list of work orders gloomily as he waited for the new guy to show up. He saw Gloria Hopper only a couple of times a year when she came to town to deal with her business in person. She lived in Cold Spring and generally ran things from there. As far as he knew, she and SueAnn were birds of a feather. Racking his brain, he tried to recall what Casey looked like. All he could remember was a chunky, ten-year-old kid with a mop of dark curls.

At quarter past nine, there were footsteps down the back hallway. A young man in a bright Kelly green polo shirt and new jeans entered the reception area and scanned the room. He nodded absently to Alyssa and fixed on Ruari. He smiled and strode forward, his hand outstretched. Casey had grown since Ruari had last seen him but hadn't lost his chunky look. Built like a fireplug, he radiated smugness. Ruari kicked himself for not insisting on being part of the hiring process. He just hadn't believed Talmadge would take his request seriously.

Trying to give him the benefit of the doubt, Ruari shook his hand. "Hi, I'm Ruari Allen."

Casey grinned and squeezed firmly. "Casey Hopper. My mom owns this place."

Ruari's faint hopes foundered on an iceberg. He kept his expression neutral. "Right. Well, I keep it running. Our job is to make sure the clients are happy. We do repairs, respond to emergencies, and do long-term maintenance on more than thirty properties. If you work for me, you'll learn how to do that too."

"I'm only taking a gap year between high school and college. I'm going to study engineering."

As they walked out together, Ruari said, "Tell me a little about your qualifications for this job." In the back parking lot, a huge, shiny red pickup dwarfed his old white truck. *Who owns that monstrosity?*

"I took metal shop in high school and a class in electronics in eighth grade," Casey said proudly.

"Okay, that's a good start. Have you ever fixed anything before?"

A crease appeared on the young forehead. "You're supposed to teach me that. Besides, I was told I didn't have to interview for this job! You have to take me."

Ruari's hackles rose. "I'm willing to give you a chance. You still have to learn how to do stuff on the job."

"Fair enough," he replied grudgingly. "Is this your car? Kind of old and messy, isn't it?" Casey slid into the passenger seat, distastefully pushing a handful of tools, parts, and receipts out of the way to find the seatbelt lock.

"It does the job." His hope upended like the Titanic and sank.

Marianne went out to The Flea mid-morning. She was a little nervous. *I'm just getting him some closure. He needs to go home. If his parents don't believe me, I can let him out anyway, and he can stay there.*

Opening the back door of the little Escort, she said quietly,

"Okay, Jason, time to go." She couldn't see anyone, but sensed a presence, and hoped it was him.

She drove toward Route 9. Jason was silent, except for a faint sense of his proximity, like a tickle in her ear, and the odd sensation of coolness inside the car. The Flea didn't have A/C. George Rutherford's ghost had possessed a distinct chill about him and perhaps Jason did as well.

To fill the uncertain silence she said, "So I Googled The Melvins and Death Cab for Cutie."

+Yeah? What did you think?+ He sounded interested.

"The Melvins sounded like classic headbanger heavy metal rock to me. Death Cab for Cutie seemed very different. Their lead singer made me think more of Neil Young."

Jason snorted, and his laugh whispered across her mind. +Yeah, I like the Melvins more, but some of Death Cab is okay. I like their name mostly.+

"It is pretty catchy."

+What kind of music do you like?+

"I like some folk and classic rock. I'm learning to like classical piano."

+Really?+ He sounded genuinely puzzled.

"There was a ghost in my house when I first got there. She was a classically trained pianist and taught piano in Maple Hill." She'd briefly gone back to playing the piano for the first time since she was a kid, but practicing hadn't been any more enticing now than it had been then, and the enthusiasm had worn off.

He paused for a beat and then said, +What happened to her?+

"She moved on, but I hope she'll come play my piano sometime."

+Must be nice,+ he murmured almost too softly for her to hear.

Marianne sensed his sorrow and confusion. "Don't worry. You'll figure something out."

He was silent for some miles, then said, +Are my parents going to be able to see me?+

She jumped a little. It was easy to forget he was there. A glance in the rearview showed his faint outline.

"I don't know," she said honestly. "Maybe not. I only know two other people who can see spirits."

+What should I say to them?+

Marianne didn't know what she would say to them, let alone how to advise him. "What do you want to say? Were you on good terms with them?"

She felt a mixture of anger, pain, and sadness. *+Sometimes. My dad can be kind of a jerk. He lost his job and is on disability. I think it makes him crazy not to work. Mom keeps trying to get me into community college. It's really annoying. Was.+*

"Sounds like home was hard for you. Even if they can't see you, they might be able to feel you somehow. I'm sure they were very sad when you...didn't come home."

He thought for a while. *+I guess I'll tell them I'm sorry. They just want the best for me. All I did with my life was go to concerts and get killed on the side of the road.+*

He was silent again for a time. Marianne angled over to Route 9D. She hoped that seeing his parents would help him. What was she going to say? She played around with variations on: "Hi, you don't know me, but I picked up your son's ghost out where he was killed. He just wanted to come home. Here he is." None of them sounded good.

+Do you know what happens next?+ He broke into her thoughts.

"What do you mean?"

+Like, am I supposed to go towards the light or something? I don't know what to do next.+

"I don't know either. I'm new to helping out dead people. No offense meant."

+Is there someone who knows more? No offense to you+.

"Yeah, but she's busy." *You're stuck with the second string, kid, sorry.*

The car was quiet until they crossed the turnoff for Route 84 and the Newburgh-Beacon Bridge.

+Go left at the first light,+ he told her.

She followed his directions all the way to his house. It was in a well-kept neighborhood of clapboard homes, built fairly close to one another, but each had a little postage stamp yard in front or along the side. He told her to stop front of a cream colored, two-story structure with a little porch. There was a car in the driveway.

She took a deep breath and rang the doorbell, hoping Jason was nearby. While she waited, she fretted about what she would say to the Fargates.

The door opened, and the moment of truth was on her. A middle-aged man said, "Yes, can I help you?" His hair was thinning, and his pudgy face was wary but polite. Was this the difficult father? He looked like he could be retired or on disability.

She put on a friendly smile. "I'm sorry to bother you. Are you Mr. Fargate?"

He shook his head. "No, sorry. They moved away a couple of years ago. My wife and I bought the house from them."

Marianne's exhale of surprise was echoed by the sense of shock next to her. "Um, do you happen to know where they moved?" she asked, trying to rescue the situation. "I mean, do you know if they're still in the area?"

He shook his head. "They moved to Connecticut, I think."

"Oh." Marianne's shoulders slumped.

"Why are you looking for them?" The man gave her a curious look.

She gave him her fall back story. "I'm a historian, and I'm doing a follow-up story on their son Jason."

"They told us a drunk driver killed him up near Maple Hill, and they didn't want to stay in the area any longer. He was their only child."

"I see. Do you happen to know where he's buried?" It was a long shot.

The man looked uncomfortable with the entire conversation and shook his head as he retreated. "No idea."

"Sorry to bother you. Thank you for your time, sir."

He closed the door with a snap.

Marianne murmured, "I'm so sorry, Jason." There was no answer.

The drive back to Maple Hill was even more silent than the trip down, and Marianne had trouble detecting any emotion from the backseat. She wondered if her passenger had elected to remain in his old home. It was possible that the unknown man would now be living in a haunted house. Well, she'd done what she could for Jason, and that would have to be that. Maybe people didn't always find their happy ending.

Pulling the Flea into her driveway, she put the gearshift into park.

+*What do we do now?*+ He spoke from the seat next to her, and she nearly jumped out of her skin.

"Geez, Jason, you scared me!" She held her pounding chest with one hand. Her other hand gripped the steering wheel.

+*Sorry,*+ he said morosely. +*I just don't know what I'm supposed to do. I didn't see any lights or tunnels or anything.*+

Marianne let her heart slow down to a semblance of normal before she said, "We'll figure something out. I need time to think and maybe do some research."

+*What about the person who knows more than you?*+

"I'll ask her. I promise I'll do what I can to help you. Just be patient."

+*Can I come inside?*+ He sounded so small and lost that she almost relented.

"I don't think so. You could hang out in my garage, if you want. Or go back to the trees across the street."

+*Okay.*+

And he vanished, like a switch turning off. She went inside, wondering how she was going to solve this.

· · ·

The first place on the list was a rambling old house that Gloria's had turned into a duplex. One side held a family of four, the other was a summer rental. Ruari knocked on the door of the family side. A woman came to the door with a toddler trailing behind and a baby in her arms.

Ruari smiled. "Hi, Jeanette. We're going to be working on the other side today. I just wanted to let you know."

She looked harried, her dark hair coming loose from its ponytail. "Thanks. Do you know if anyone is planning to rent the other side anytime soon? The people who were here this summer were up at all hours and kind of loud. We were really enjoying the quiet."

He replied, "I don't know. You could put in a request for another family or a quiet person."

Hitching the baby up on her hip, she said, "We did that, and we ended up with the trendy twosome from the city who invited their friends up every weekend to party. Jack, no!" She reached down and restrained the toddler from dashing out the door.

"Well, it's worth a try, anyway."

"Gloria's has to fill all the rentals," Casey piped up. "Or it doesn't make money."

"I get that," Jeanette said with some asperity. "It would be nice if they were a little more considerate."

"We'll try to be quiet," Ruari assured her.

"Thanks, I try to put Carrie down at ten-thirty."

He led Casey across the porch to a side door that opened onto the other half of the house. "How about you let me do the talking until you get the hang of things."

Casey threw up his hands. "Fine. It's true, though. We have to fill all the units."

Ruari stopped outside the door. "It's not about true or not true. It's about making our current renters happy. She wasn't happy, so I was listening to her. It's part of being in this job."

Casey barely suppressed an eye-roll and followed him inside. The cleaning crew had been through, so everything was spotless.

Ruari set him up in the living room and showed him how to fill in gouges and cracks. When his new assistant complained that this wasn't what he'd expected, Ruari told him this was part of the job and did some basic repairs in the kitchen.

Around twelve-thirty, he finished the last turn of his screwdriver on the loose handle of the fridge. Putting his tools away, he found the front room empty. Casey was sitting on the porch, listening to music on his phone.

"Did you finish everything?" Ruari frowned, disbelieving.

Casey pulled one earbud and looked up. "Yup. I finished everything I could reach."

Ruari returned to the living room and inspected the work. It was just as Casey had said. He'd patched everything up to shoulder height and completely ignored the space up to the nine-foot ceiling. He'd done nothing at all in the other rooms.

"Casey, come here, please," he called. There was no response, so he went out to the porch and tapped him on the shoulder. "Hey! Come here."

Casey pulled the earbuds and got to his feet, looking put upon. "What? I did what you asked me to. I did a good job too! Look how smooth everything is."

Where did he begin? Ruari wondered. This kid had clearly never learned how to work. Granda had sometimes softened his criticism with positive words. "Your work looks good—as far as it goes. There's a ladder on the truck. Use it to reach the higher places. And, when you're done with one room, you move on to the next one and do the same thing. If you finish something, you come ask me what to do next. You don't take a long break."

"You didn't say that when I started," Casey griped.

Ruari bit back a sharp reply. *Owner's son. Make it work.* "True. I didn't. Now you know. We'll come back and finish the rest of the house after lunch."

"And I know my rights," Casey added sullenly. "I get a fifteen minute break every two hours. If I don't take it, I can combine it at the end."

"You get a break, but you have to do all the work by the end of the day, 'cause it just builds up. Whatever you don't finish, you have to do tomorrow plus any new stuff."

Casey looked perturbed. *Welcome to the working world.*

"Let's go eat something." The kid was a bit of a twit, but maybe he'd learn and mature a little. "Did you bring food?"

"Um. No. I thought we'd be eating out." He looked a little alarmed at the prospect of missing lunch.

"Don't you know? If you always eat out, you'll never be able to save much of your paycheck. Tomorrow, bring your own lunch. Today, we can get a couple of slices at the pizza place."

They drove back down the hill to Main, and Ruari found a parking place on a side street. He ate his sack lunch and thought about working on the new muse piece after work. He gave Marianne a quick call. She was in the flow of writing but was glad of a break. They made plans for a dinner date later that week, and he hung up with a smile. The doctor's office called to tell him his bloodwork had all been normal except for some elevated markers for stress. *No kidding.* They reiterated that he should eat better and get more exercise. He snapped his old flip phone shut and sighed. At least he didn't have a horrible disease.

Ruari's relief and good mood soured as he searched for his assistant in the outdoor eating area and adjacent shop fronts. He found Casey leaning on the counter, talking to a pretty girl of the same age, wearing a visor with the pizza parlor's logo. She looked too young to be dating.

"Time to go," Ruari said unceremoniously. Casey finished a last pull at his soda can, crumpled it showily in one fist, and winked at the girl who giggled furiously.

"You're here to work, not socialize," Ruari said tersely. "Lunch is half an hour tops."

"Wow, you're a Grinch," Casey muttered.

And you're too young for this job, Ruari thought as they motored back to the duplex.

They spent the early part of the afternoon patching the rest of

the walls. Casey seemed to have settled down and worked indus-
triously until a little buzzer went off two hours later. He dropped
what he was doing and went out on the porch to mess with his
phone for fifteen minutes. Ruari bit his lip, shook his head, and
finished the job. Casey was back in time to help reload the truck.

At the next unit on the punch list, there was a tricky electrical
problem. Ruari showed Casey the fuse box and said bluntly,
"Electricity will kill you if you do it wrong, so don't mess with it.
Legally you're not allowed to do anything electrical without an
electrician's license. So, if you want to keep doing this, you'll have
to get one."

"I know that," Casey said scornfully, but he kept his hands off
the wires while Ruari showed him how to check for a live circuit.
Ruari rewired a plug and a switch that had been giving the
tenants shocks, and Casey fiddled with his phone, looking bored.
Ruari considered confiscating it and returning it at the end of the
day but decided that it would cause too much trouble.

"They should be fine now, Mr. Reynaldi," Ruari said with a
smile.

"Thank you," the old gentleman replied. "I don't suppose you
could ask Mrs. Talmadge to leave the rent alone this year?" he
asked with a hopeful look.

"I don't really have that kind of pull," Ruari answered regretfully. "You can remind her you're on a fixed income, though, and
ask her not to raise it much."

The old man shook his head.

Ruari and Casey slid back into the truck.

"I can't believe the nerve of that guy," Casey said in disgust.
"Doesn't he understand that we have to cover taxes and inflation
and everything?"

"Mr. Renaldi lives on social security. He's been in that unit for
the last thirty years. He's a good guy and takes care of the place.
Personally, I'd rather rent to a person who will take care of the
unit than a high paying client who trashes the place."

"And that's why you'll never be successful! You're not good at business," Casey stated and spent the rest of the ride texting.

Probably arranging a date with the pizza girl. Ruari was angry and tired of lugging this deadweight around. And he'd have to do it again tomorrow and the day after that. If he declared Casey unfit for work as his assistant, would Ruari lose his job?

Would that be such a bad thing?

He pulled his truck into the office lot.

"See you tomorrow!" Casey said jauntily. Then he climbed into the shiny, new, red pickup. With a throaty roar, the engine came to life, and he pulled out of the lot in a shower of gravel.

"Figures," Ruari muttered.

Once back in his workshop, he sat in front of his new inspiration, absently eating a bowl of cereal. He turned the piece this way and that, trying to recall the sense of the finished piece. He'd never attempted to do something this complex before, though he'd done leaves or animals as single elements. His pencil lines suggested small animals hidden among leaves and mushrooms.

Being ambitious and reaching past his comfort zone was something he didn't mind doing. Granda had always chided him for biting off more than he could chew and trying to run before he could walk. He saluted the black and white face across the room with an upraised mug of coffee. He picked up a chisel and, after a few minutes, slipped quietly into the zone like a seal into the ocean.

CHAPTER 9

When he closed his eyes that night, Ruari wandered through a vaguely familiar forest until he stood in a clearing dominated by a magnificent old beech tree. The foliage was in full spring regalia, its leaves a deep reddish plum color. The trunk was easily big enough for two men to wrap their arms around and just touch their fingertips. Three segments like the arms of some Herculean weight lifter supported an enormous canopy. Covered with old leaves, a mass of roots stretched like muscular tentacles in all directions. It looked like it had been there from the dawn of time.

It was the tree from Granda's pictures.

"Feasgar math." Somehow he understood her old Scots Gaelic. *Good evening.* "It is time we met, Ruari." A woman emerged from under the dark shade of the tree. She was tall and slender. Hair the color of deep red plums swept her heels and framed her austere face. It rustled like leaves when she walked. A cloak the color of silver gray bark adorned her shoulders. Her bare feet navigated the roots with unconscious grace. She approached him until she stood only a few feet away. Ruari was not a small man, but he had to look up to meet her gaze. She was seven feet tall if she was an inch. Brilliant turquoise eyes regarded him with

benevolence over a long nose and high cheekbones in a pale green face.

"Who are you?" He asked warily, forcing himself not to step back. This was a dream, he reminded himself.

"I am your muse," she said with a welcoming smile.

"My muse?"

"Yes. I am she who guides your hands when you carve or build. We made a bargain at your grandfather's funeral."

"We've never met! I would've remembered that." he scoffed. He absolutely would not have forgotten this extraordinary woman.

"I drew a veil over that memory to ease the transition. We have worked well together have we not?"

"I don't know what you're talking about!" He turned and walked away. This was his dream, and he could control it if he wanted. The leaves crunched under his feet, and a light breeze touched his cheek. Even for a dream this was getting weirder. He'd never had such a vivid one before.

She reappeared in front of him. "Ruari, it's time to remember." Her cool, hard fingers touched his forehead, and he felt a curtain open in his mind. He reeled back.

On that cold, snowy day in Scotland, in the middle of his grief and rage, Ruari heard a voice.

"Ruari," it called, "don't be sad."

He turned, expecting someone from the house, but no one was there. He looked for the source of the voice.

"I'm here," it said.

He focused on the shelf of carved wooden faces, and the wild woman made of oak opened her eyes and smiled at him. In an already unreal day, this was one more thing.

"Now I'm hallucinating," he muttered, pinching himself.

"I assure you, Ruari, you are not. I am your grandfather's muse." The voice sounded feminine.

Granda had always talked about his muse as if she were a real person who inspired him. Ruari assumed it was Nana, though she denied it the one time he made a joking comment about it. Was someone playing an elaborate trick on him?

"Erin? Seamus? Are you in here? It's not funny, you know." He walked through the shop, looking under tables and behind piles of things. He was alone.

"Ruari, look at me," the wooden face commanded. He jumped, badly startled.

"You can't be real," he protested. "You're just a carving."

"It's winter and my energy is limited. Speaking through my mother's portrait is easier for me. Your grandfather is dead, and I mourn his passing. We accomplished many great things during his lifetime. I want to offer you the same deal I gave him and his father before him. I want you to be my new creative partner. I have a wealth of knowledge about carving and woodwork to pass along to you. Your grandfather gave you much. I have more."

Granda was gone. Dad had destroyed Ruari's last gift to his mentor in a fit of jealous rage. What did he have to lose? It would be the ultimate defiance of his father's wishes. Maybe this was Granda's ghost in some weird form?

"What do I have to do? What do you want in return?" He asked cautiously.

The carved lips curved up in a stiff smile. "I need your skilled hands to work with. Your grandfather gave me the use of his hands during his lifetime, and together we made hundreds of things. The portraits of my family and ancestors on either side of me are but a few."

Ruari had his own shop in Maple Hill, but his job kept him from truly focusing on his craft. Summers with Granda had always given him new ideas and techniques. If this mystical muse could fuel his learning process, he could keep going and maybe give up his day job sooner.

"How would that work?"

"You let me enter your mind while you work, and I'll steer. It doesn't hurt," she added with a trace of amusement.

Granda's trances suddenly made sense. He hadn't just been focused on his work, this muse had literally been in charge. She was the one looking out from Granda's pale blue eyes. Ruari shivered. The memory of that blank look still made him deeply uneasy. What else could she do while she was in charge?

"Where are you when you're not in a carving?" He asked.

"I live near the farm. I cannot travel in physical form, but I can enter your mind."

"I live in America. That's a long way away."

"It would be easier if you lived here, but if you give me permission, I can work with you there."

This was so weird. He gave his wrist another sharp pinch, but he was still in Granda's shop. The carved oak face watched him with an eerie intelligence while he thought. Now that Granda was gone, where was he going to learn new techniques? He didn't have time for classes outside of work, and book learning didn't work for him. He'd apprenticed with the best, and it would be hard to change gears. If he could just up his game a little more, he could hang out his own shingle and make a name for himself. He wouldn't be a handyman with a hobby. He wouldn't have to deal with another renter-induced disaster. Or his crappy boss.

But it wasn't normal for someone to take over your mind. Where would he be while she was there? Would he be unable to respond to an emergency? Would he be helpless to intervene? What if someone found out? Would they think he was insane? Maybe he'd better n—

"Ruari," she said, "he broke your beautiful box. What better way to honor your grandfather than to carry on his legacy? I am not a harsh task master. You'll hardly know I'm with you. I have so much to show you. Please say yes. I have no one else to teach."

Something clicked. If Granda could live with her, so could he. It was a bonus that Dad would hate him continuing in wood-working.

"All right," he nodded. "Yes. What do I have to do?"

The carved mouth turned up in another stiff smile. "Just let me in when you work. You'll feel it. We'll adjust to each other over time. This is wonderful! You've made me very happy! You—"

The sound of the farmhouse back door banging and a babble of voices carried across the snowy yard.

"It's easier if you don't remember our meeting for now. But you'll be open to me. Farewell, Ruari. See you soon." The voice faded and the face stilled into the wild, beautiful visage he was familiar with. The voices outside grew fainter as they moved away.

Stunned, he blinked. "That was you?"

"Yes."

"You worked with my grandfather and great-grandfather?"

"They were long and fruitful partnerships. We created such beautiful things! I promise you will become famous among the men of your time the way they were known in their time."

He remembered Granda's trances that had scared him as a child and thought, *Holy shit, I do that. I fall into the zone. Time passes, and I don't know it.* "You enter my mind and take over!"

"We work side by side," she amended.

Your sainted Granda thought you'd never amount to anything. Dad's words floated through his mind. *Stop wasting your life trying to impress someone who's dead and didn't care, anyway.*

"Why do you want to work with me?" He said aloud. "Granda told Dad he thought I wasn't any good. My own father hates that I do woodwork."

She shook her head impatiently and waved away his objections. "The rest of your family were never suitable vessels for my needs. But you can do things your grandfather never could. You explore the boundaries of what can be done in wood with color, finish, and combinations of effects. The very idea of adding stone inlay would have been an anathema to your grandfather. I find it exhilarating." Her eyes flashed at him. "He was jealous of your creativity. That's why he stopped trying to teach you. He was angry because you exceeded his abilities long ago. I will more than make up for his missed knowledge. I promise."

That was something he hadn't considered. If Granda had been jealous, perhaps he'd masked it by acting disappointed?

"How do you like my other gifts?" She asked. "Seeing people as they truly are."

Ruari took a step back. "Wait, you're responsible for the smoke and colors around people? I thought I had a brain tumor!"

"Your family has a touch of the second sight. I merely enhanced it." She looked smug.

"I have ESP?"

She gave him another amused smile. "Your family has the ability to see beyond the veil into the stream of time, to perceive the life energies of others, and in some cases, to see lies as if they were smoke. The ability is barely a whisper in some, and in others, a powerful force. Even when they don't want to see it."

That made sense. He had a new thought. "If I made this deal with you at Granda's funeral, why are you only talking to me about it now? And why have I only been able to see lies and auras for a couple of weeks?"

"Your senses were recently opened by someone else. That allowed me to reach you more clearly. The carving you call *Sleeping Lady* was our first truly collaborative work."

He'd had inspirations to do other art pieces before *Sleeping Lady*. And, come to think of it, they were all in the last three years since Granda died. But *Sleeping Lady* had been the first one that he'd been fully focused on and obsessed by. What had happened right before that?

He racked his brain for work or family-related things. Nothing came to mind. But Marianne had come into his life about then. They'd shared a snap like static electricity the first time they'd shaken hands. She said she hadn't seen ghosts before she came to Maple Hill. Had they somehow opened up each other's abilities?

"Ruari, you've made such astonishing progress in your wood-working. You've learned by leaps and bounds in the last couple of years. The carving we're doing now is above and beyond your ability of even a few months ago. That's because we are working together. You are ten times more creative than your grandfather was. Even I am learning from you."

"You are?" It was his turn to blink.

"Yes. I watched you learn to do inlay and felt your excitement about working with stone." She gave him a radiant smile, like the sun coming out. "I want to do new things! But you are so far away it is hard for me to reach you. I want to bring you closer so we can work together more easily."

Her enthusiasm swept him along, and he smiled. Granda had always chastised him for wanting to run before he could walk. This woman loved his ideas. But impulsiveness was Erin's deal. So, instead of letting his mouth say yes, he asked, "Do lots of other artists have creative partnerships with people like you?"

Her smile faded, and she regarded him solemnly. "As far as I know, I am the last of my kind, and I am the only one to make such a partnership. This is a unique chance, Ruari, don't throw it away."

"Moving to Scotland is a huge step."

"That would be ideal," she replied, "but you don't have to move just yet. There are other means."

"I need more time to think it over."

She inclined her head graciously again. "That will give me time to make the arrangements." A smile of delight transformed her austere features, making her look younger. "Ah, Ruari, I look forward to being fully partnered with you! We will make such things together as the world has never seen."

She took his hands in hers. They were cool and hard, like living wood. "You need a token of my promise to you. Humans used to communicate in the dream world easily. Then they relegated it to their shamans and witches. Now, they don't believe in dreams at all. Lest you dismiss this as an ordinary dream or a wishful fantasy, let me give you something to remember me by." She took the palm of his hand and pressed her hard forefinger into his flesh, pricking his left palm at the base of his thumb as if he'd jabbed it with a gouge. It stung, and he jerked his hand only to find her grip as powerful as a vice.

"Ow!"

She smiled wistfully, staring at the welling orb of blood. "It will fade in a day or two, but you will remember me." When she released his hand, he grabbed it with the other. He pressed his right thumb over the sharply etched mark.

She murmured, "Farewell, Ruari, I await your decision. It is too late this night, but we will resume work on our project tomorrow night!"

The clearing faded as he held his sore hand.

He awoke in his own bed in Maple Hill.

That was the weirdest damned dream I've ever had.

He turned on the bedside lamp and looked at his palm. There was a fresh puncture at the base of his thumb, still welling a little blood. He must have stabbed himself with a splinter or a piece of wire while he was asleep and incorporated it into his dream. Gingerly, he swept his hands through his covers and looked over the edge of the bed. He could find nothing that might have given him an injury.

Did that really happen?

CHAPTER 10

Two days later, Ruari was still trying to teach Casey the handyman business. He found that the young man wasn't stupid, just reluctant to focus on the job. When he was interested in the task, he stayed off his phone and actually learned things. The moment he got bored, the device came out of his pocket. Ruari thought of it as a big electronic pacifier.

To be fair, Ruari's big date with Marianne tomorrow night occupied his own thoughts. He planned to take her to a swankier restaurant to make up for his previous blunder. The food at Crave was good, and it had only been open about a year. Long enough to get rave reviews from his friend Trevor and yet not a place he'd ever been with Jenny. He'd let Marianne know it was upscale compared to No Bones, and she sounded happy with that.

This competed with fragments of the weirdest damned dream he'd ever had as they flashed into his mind at unexpected moments. *I am your muse...*

His first inclination was to dismiss the dream as nothing more. Even though it had felt very real at the time, he couldn't possibly have been in a clearing. He'd been asleep in bed.

But parts of the dream stood out vividly. She said she'd

spoken to him at Granda's funeral and then blocked his memory. Now whenever he thought about the last visit to Scotland, the memory came more easily. He'd been distraught at the time, so he could have blocked it himself, he supposed.

Then there was the mark on his thumb. He rubbed it, feeling the little bump of scar tissue. It had healed faster than normal, but still felt sore. He'd searched again for anything that might have caused it in his bedroom and found nothing.

The muse's pale green, austere face with brilliant turquoise eyes, her antiquated and rather stilted speech, her genuine enthusiasm for his skill had made the biggest impression. It was a stark contrast to Dad's angry dismissal. If she'd been a close artistic partner to Granda, then she would know his opinions about Ruari better than Dad would, right? If Granda was angry or jealous of Ruari's curiosity and skill, that would explain Dad's words, *Your sainted Granda thought you'd never amount to anything! Stop wasting your life trying to impress someone who's dead and didn't care, anyway.* He still cringed when he remembered it.

The muse seemed to be excited at the idea of creating things with him. That was… refreshing. Carving and carpentry were essentially solitary pursuits, more so when the people around you were disparaging. Not Mom, or Erin, or Marianne. But Dad and Granda had been. Would being partnered with the muse somehow change that equation?

"Hey, Ruari, is this right?" Casey called.

He closed this train of thought and hurried to look over the young man's work before he got bored and dove into his phone again.

They finished on time, wonder of wonders. Maybe having an assistant would work out after all. After Casey pulled out in his over powered truck, Ruari dutifully filled out his paperwork and filed it. He headed home for a shower and work in his studio. On the way, his phone rang.

"Ruari Allen."

"Hey big brother, you home yet?" Erin sounded tense and frazzled.

"Just got off work. What's up with you?"

"Would you meet me at The Dutch in ten minutes?"

He could eat dinner there. It would beat another canned meal. "I guess so."

"Great, see you there."

He turned his pickup around.

They arrived within minutes of each other and got a booth. Erin's short hair had started out neatly combed but stuck out defiantly sideways. She wore a short navy blazer over a white blouse. He slid his butt across the worn upholstery.

"Where were you today?" He asked.

"Putting my resume out at local offices while I wait for a longer term job."

"Kind of dressy for waiting tables, aren't you?" He teased.

Her look would have scorched the hair off his head. "I did that in high school and college, thank you. No more bad tips and crappy customers. I was hoping for an office accountant position, but I'll settle for being a receptionist if I have to."

"How're Mom and Dad?" He asked.

She ran her fingers through her hair, further undoing the professional 'do. "They're driving me up the wall, asking me about work, making suggestions. Mom asked me to clean my room, for God's sake!"

"Now you know why I don't live there," he chuckled. "You're welcome to come stay with me if you need time away."

She snorted. "And sleep next to your bandsaw, I don't think so!"

"I could clear a table off for you right near the wood stove. You could bring a sleeping bag. It would be like camping."

"Thanks a ton. Any luck with an apartment through Gloria's?"

"Nothing so far. Alyssa knows what to look for. She'll tell me as soon as something comes up. Where's Pat tonight?"

She shrugged. "He had somewhere else to be." A trickle of

smoke accompanied her words. Ruari unfocused his eyes and looked slightly past her brightly lit shoulder and perceived a dull orange glow. Brighter colors seemed to mean more positive feelings and dull colors, more negative ones.

"Did he call it off?" He asked.

She looked up at him sharply. "No, he's just busy tonight." More smoke.

Ah, trouble in paradise. Not my business.

The server approached and set down a basket of chips made on the premises. "Hey you two, haven't seen you for a while."

Karen was in her early forties, had a couple of teenagers at home, and had known them since they were old enough to drink. Her long ponytail draped down her usual black T-shirt over black pants.

"I've been doing a lot of overtime," he answered.

She nodded. "What'll it be?"

"I'll have a half pint of the Room For Milk stout."

"Comin' right up."

Erin said, "Same."

Ruari sat for a moment gathering his thoughts. If he had the fey woman on his side, he might be able to quit Gloria's for good. "I've been thinking about starting a cabinetry business for a while, but I don't know what I need to do to set it up and keep the books straight."

Erin perked up and asked him how he was keeping his books now. He told her. Upbraiding him thoroughly for sloppy practices, she made him promise to be better in the future. "I don't know why you haven't been audited!" she scolded.

"I'm too small to bother with, I'm sure!" he replied, a little unnerved by her fierceness.

She narrowed her eyes and pursed her lips. "You can never count on that."

Her grilling about his plans and intentions helped him fine tune his ideas. She approved of the website, the photos, and the range of items he planned to offer. She asked if he wanted to include furniture restoration, which he hadn't thought about but would consider. He took her up on her offer to set prices for things based on internet research and what other carpenters and restorers in the Hudson Valley charged.

"I'll start my consulting business tonight," she said, "and you'll be my first client. With that in mind, I'm billing you for an hour and a half as of now."

A little startled, he agreed. She was worth it and probably wouldn't charge her own brother too much.

They were wrapping up when she changed topics abruptly. "So, how's Marianne?" she asked with a sly smile.

He choked slightly on the last swallow of his beer and coughed for a moment before looking at her. She had a mischievous glint in her eye.

"Are we off the clock now?" he teased, trying to regain his equilibrium. She nodded. "She's good. We have a dinner date tomorrow."

"Where are you taking her?"

"Crave."

She grinned broadly. "Good move! It's fancy. Tells her you like her. Should be a big hit." She leaned closer and said conspiratorially, "So, when can I meet her? Are you going to introduce her to Mom and Dad soon?"

Ruari hedged. "Um, I'm not sure I'm ready for that yet. You know how Mom and Dad can be."

Erin rolled her eyes and conceded the point. "Okay, fine. Can I meet her, then? If you don't introduce me, I'll just have to introduce myself!"

He put his hands up in surrender, knowing she would do just that. Preferring some control over that meeting, he said, "Okay! I'll find out from her when would be good. I'll let you know."

"Don't wait too long, big brother!" she smirked.

When he got home, he sat down at his workbench in the studio and stared at the muse's work in progress. He took a deep breath, smelling the faint scents of wood, metal, and Tung oil. He let his shoulders relax and sat still enough to hear the second hand on the shop clock tick.

...you can do things your grandfather never could...he was jealous and stopped teaching you...

"So how does this work, oh muse?" He murmured aloud, feeling a little foolish talking to the air. "Am I supposed to just trust that you know what you're doing and let you guide the chisel? I kind of like knowing where I'm going."

I can teach you everything you need to know...

An image of the completed piece flashed brilliantly into his mind. The animals and vegetation all looked so lifelike that it resembled a three-dimensional photograph. For one sizzling moment, he could see the whole thing, and he longed to make it real with a physical intensity.

"Okay then," he breathed. "I can work with that." He picked up a chisel and eased into the zone.

Marianne dreamed that she was sitting at the Co-op's street side cafe. Oscar was sitting on the table next to her, the tip of his crooked tail tapping gently. He lapped a hazelnut espresso out of a small cup while she drank tea. They watched people go by on the street, and she laughed at his pointed remarks about people's garish attire and poor taste in friends.

He narrowed his eyes and pointed with his tail. "Look at that poor guy."

Marianne followed his sidelong gaze and saw Ruari walking along the sidewalk arm in arm with a very tall woman with floor length hair the color of dark plums. She held his arm possessively, and he gazed at her with adoring eyes.

"What a handbag," Oscar sniffed contemptuously.

Marianne rose from her chair slowly, as if she were underwater. "Ruaaari!" she called out, words stretching like taffy. "Waait!"

Ruari's gaze never left the face of the statuesque, exotic beauty. Marianne called out again. The narrow, smooth face of the woman glanced in her direction, her brilliant blue eyes caught her gaze, and her lips curved up in a superior smile. Then she turned, and the couple strolled together out of sight.

"Who was that?" Marianne said.

"Psht," Oscar sniffed as he licked foam off his paw. "Old girl-friends."

She surfaced from sleep with a sense of disappointment. The dream had a sense of truthfulness. Maybe he still had a thing for his former fiancée? Was that Jenny? She felt Oscar's weight near her hip and reached out to stroke him. Her fingers met cold chill instead of warm fur.

"Oscar?"

+No, it's me.+

Her eyes snapped open, and she snatched her hand back. At first she saw nothing, but when she blinked, she saw a pale, glowing figure sitting on her bed. Oscar had vanished.

She sat up and pushed herself away from him. "Jesus, Jason! You scared the hell out of me!"

His hoody had slipped down, revealing his pale hair and morose features. *+You were asleep for like, forever.+*

"What are you doing here?"

+My parents left without me. What am I gonna do? Can you find them for me? I just wanna go home.+

"Can we talk about this in the morning?"

He looked at her forlornly. *+I guess I can wait.+* He showed no signs of moving.

"You can't stay here." She made a half-shooing motion.

+Why not? I'll be quiet. I can go sit in the living room, if you want.+ He gave her a pleading, puppy dog look.

She slipped out from under the covers on the opposite side of the bed. "No, you can't stay here." Be firm, just like Sarah said.

+Please don't make me go! You'll forget about me. My parents did. It took four years for you to find me on the side of the road!+

Her heart twisted, but there was no way she would sleep a wink if he was inside. "I promise I won't forget you. I'll work on it tomorrow. Now, out you go." She gave him her best stern teacher look and gestured toward the hallway.

He sighed, rose, and drifted out, making her skin goosebump. She escorted him to the front door, and opened it. "You'll be fine. I'll be in touch later."

He gave her a last miserable look and drifted out, fading before he reached the bottom of the front steps. She heard a barely audible, *+Don't forget me.+* She closed the door and breathed out a shaky sigh.

Either Sarah's protections were useless or Jason had somehow blown by them. Did that count as malevolent? He seemed more needy than actively spiteful or hostile. She thought Jason would respect her request to stay outside for the rest of the night, but if he could get in, who or what else could? The main emergency was past, so calling Sarah wasn't in order. She didn't have any more sage and cedar and didn't know how to recharge her gemstone protections without sunlight. Another question to ask Sarah tomorrow.

She resorted to Sarah's suggestion of imagining white light surrounding the house to ward off further invasions for tonight. To help her concentrate, Marianne went to each window including the basement and second floor ones, refilled each cat food tin with water (she'd have to buy something fancier one of these days), and lit each floating tea light. The resulting glow gave her more confidence, and she sat on the sofa crosslegged to imagine her house protected by an aura of white light. Oscar crept down the hall and joined her, needing reassuring pets.

"You weren't much help, Mister." He butted her hand and arched his back. She smoothed his ruffled fur down. "I don't blame you for wanting to hide. So, you want to help me think about white light?" He sat down next to her and began washing his flank in earnest.

"Question is: how did the wards fail? We only set them up a week ago, and Sarah said monthly recharge was enough."

Her eyes fell on the narrow face of the *Sleeping Lady* statue. In the flicker of candle light, the eyes seemed to flutter. A zing of unease flashed through her nervous system. She shivered. Leaving Oscar to his bath, she picked up the carving and put it on the top shelf of the coat closet in the front hall, pushing it behind the hats and scarves. After Jason's surprise visit, something about it gave her the creeps.

She tried to go back to bed, but she tossed and turned restlessly. She got up and retrieved the statue from the hall closet. It was Ruari's beautiful handiwork, and she didn't want to damage it, but for inexplicable reasons, she didn't want it in the house right now. Wrapping the carving in a towel, she slipped her shoes on without socks and pulled a jacket over her pajamas. She paused on the steps outside the dining room door. Looking both ways, she saw no sign of Jason. She switched on a flashlight and entered the garage two steps across a little cement path.

I'm being silly. But if it'll help me sleep, I'll do it.

The little building leaned a bit. Dirt and leaves collected in the corners. Suffice it to say, she left her little Ford Escort, the Flea, in the driveway. The beam played over the shelves at the back and she found a corner to tuck the wrapped package into. It would be safe from the rain here. If Ruari asked, she didn't know what she'd tell him. She'd think of something.

Relaxing, she snuggled under her covers again. She concentrated on the bubble of white light around her house and fell asleep.

After breakfast the next morning, Marianne dialed Sarah's cell number for ghost-related things rather than the law office line. It was kind of like the bat phone.

Sarah picked up on the third ring. "Hey, what's up? Everything okay?"

"I'm fine. Do you have a few minutes?"

"Yes, I was just changing projects. Go ahead." Marianne heard a door closing.

"I took Jason to his parents' house in Beacon. The long and short of it is that his parents moved, and I have no idea where they've gone."

"So where's Jason?"

"He came back with me."

"He's in your house?" She said sharply.

"Yeah, he showed up in my bedroom. I thought your wards would have kept him out."

"Huh, they should have."

"How did he get in?"

"He shouldn't have. Unless there was a gap somewhere…" She was quiet for a moment, thinking. "Is he still there?"

"No, I made him leave, and he's stayed out since then."

"That's good. How is he acting?"

"What do you mean?"

"If spirits are thwarted, they sometimes get really mean. Is he becoming malevolent? Threatening?"

"No, not really. He seems more depressed than anything else, so I'm kind of worried about him. Can that happen?"

"Yes, actually."

"What happens to them?"

"When spirits give up, they fade."

That sounded ominous. "What happens then? Do they move on?"

"No, they fade. They're just gone."

"They die again—more??"

"Essentially. I've heard of it happening."

"Where do they go?"

"I don't know. I've never met a spirit who came back after that."

The ghost of a ghost. Marianne was silent for a moment. "That would be a sad fate for a guy who's just trying to go home. Do you have any idea how to stop that from happening?"

"No, if I think of anything, I'll call you. By the way, I'll be out of town for a few days starting on Thursday at a law conference in Atlanta. Kelly will be here if you want company."

"How long will you be gone?" *You're leaving just when I need you?*

"I'll be back Sunday night."

I have no idea what I'm doing! "Okay."

"You'll be fine."

"What's your conference on?" Marianne had loved going to conferences as a grad student.

"Trusts and estates." Marianne heard her smile. "I can't wait!"

Ruari showered, shaved, and set an alarm on his phone. There was no way he was going to miss another date. It was still an hour till dinner, and he felt restless. The shop was as clean as he could make it. He could probably safely spend a few minutes cleaning up some of the new details that emerged last night.

The sinuous form of a pine marten, a tuft-eared red squirrel, a rabbit with its ears laid along its back, and a hedgehog were roughed in on all sides. He'd caught glimpses of these creatures when he'd played in the hillside woods behind his grandparents' farm as a kid, but never in such detail. In fact, there was no way he could have carved this kind of detail without having seen it in pictures or in person. He felt a little chill race along his spine.

...your grandfather and his father before him accepted a partnership with me...

Would that be so bad? Granda was famous. The muse was incredibly talented and promised to teach him everything. That could be okay. She liked to work the entire piece at once, putting in the larger elements as anchors around which she added other details. He marveled at her affectionate familiarity with each animal. He smoothed out the hare's ears with tiny chisel strokes and sharpened the face of the marten.

A persistent buzzing chime brought him back from a long way away. He refocused and dug out his phone from the pile of wood shavings. The alarm had been going off for five minutes already.

"Oh shit," he muttered. He was going to be late but not so bad as the last time. Grabbing a light jacket, he headed out the door. He parked half a block from Crave and half walked, half jogged to the door. The hostess showed him to a table where Marianne sat looking beautiful in a simple black dress that showed her curves and a short, sparkly black sweater. Her wavy brown hair was pulled back in a simple, loose bun held in place with a gold hair clip.

"I was starting to get worried," she said with a smile.

Not sure whether to kiss her cheek or not, he took a deep breath to cover his beating heart and smiled back. "I put an alarm on this time."

"Were you in the studio again?"

He nodded and sat down. They busied themselves with menus for a few minutes before ordering appetizers and wine.

"How is your project coming along?" She asked.

He told her about the emerging animals but said nothing about the possible involvement of the fey woman for now. He wasn't too sure about it himself still and didn't want to stretch her belief.

"Are you working on anything else?"

"I started an inlaid tabletop but haven't gotten very far with it yet."

"Did you say you wanted to start your own woodworking business?"

He half-shrugged. "I've been thinking about it, but work has been crazy. My sister Erin offered to do my books. She's a professional accountant. It's a start."

She gave him a wry smile. "Do you get along? If not, that might be problematic."

He huffed a laugh. "She's bossy, but we get along okay."

Their wine arrived, and the server poured a little in Ruari's glass for him to taste. He didn't really know much about wine, but it tasted good, and the served filled their glasses. Marianne raised her glass and clinked his in a silent toast.

"I don't know the first thing about starting a business, but do you have a website?" She asked.

"Yeah, it's on my list. Know any good photographers?"

Her eyes sparkled with a mischievous glint. "Actually, I do. Kelly told me recently that she's a photographer. She has a beautiful photo book at her salon, if you want to take a look. I bet she'd be willing to photograph some of your pieces for you."

He and Kelly had been on neutral terms through high school in spite of Erin's open hostility towards her and Sarah. As long as he kept Erin away while Kelly was there, it could work.

"Here's her number." Marianne jotted it on a piece of paper from her bag and slid it across the table. "Now I'm out of the loop."

He tucked it in his pocket and sipped his wine. "You told me about a hitchhiker last time."

"Yeah. He's been living in the trees next to my house. I tried to take him home to Beacon, but his family moved away after he died. So, he came back with me."

Ruari felt a pang of alarm. "You doing okay? He's not scaring you or anything?"

She shook her head. "No, he's more depressed than anything. Sarah told me ghosts can fade. It's like they die all over again. I feel bad for Jason. He just wants to go home. I'm not sure what I'm going to do for him."

"Is it really your problem?"

She looked indignant. "Kind of, yes. If I hadn't picked him up, I could probably keep ignoring him. Now that I know what his story is, I feel responsible. He's just a kid."

"But he's dead!"

"Yeah, so?" Her look suggested he was being callous.

Ruari felt frustrated. He worried that she was in danger, and the idea that ghosts were real and not camp fire stories made him uneasy. "Well, be careful. I'll come back you up, if you need someone and Sarah's not here." He hadn't expected to say that but realized it was true.

She gave him a warm smile. "Thanks, that means a lot."

Their dinner came and was as amazing and delicious as promised. She asked how his work was going, and he told her about his dubious assistant between bites of steak and seafood. She laughed at his description of the cell phone as a pacifier.

"You know you have access to the entire world on your phone?" She teased.

He dug his flip phone out of his pocket. "This is good enough for me. Anything less robust is likely to get broken on the job."

"They sell sturdy cases for smart phones, but I take your point."

He snuck a glance at her when she was busy with her meal. Unfocusing his eyes, he looked for her aura and glimpsed a pale pink glow around her. That seemed like her default color when she was happy, so he relaxed and enjoyed his meal.

After dinner, he asked if she wanted to see the new carving and drove her to the studio. He turned on the table lamps he used while working, and she turned it slowly all the way around.

"It's amazing. I can't believe the amount of detail you can get in wood!"

"It's a balance between the hardness and closeness of the grain and keeping my tools sharp enough to make only the cuts we—I want to."

She was absorbed in looking at the piece, and he hoped she hadn't heard his slip.

"Do you ever use power tools?" She asked.

"Granda only used hand carving tools once he got down to this level of work. He used power tools for making furniture, but not in carving. I sometimes use a Dremel tool for certain details, but mostly I stay traditional." The muse had gotten very agitated the other night when he'd used a Dremel. Now he avoided it while they worked together.

"It's really beautiful. I look forward to seeing it when you're done." She straightened. "Thanks for showing me."

She looked up at him, her lips slightly parted. He leaned down and kissed her. She put her arms around him, stepped into his embrace, and deepened their kiss. His heart beat faster, and he felt himself respond. They broke apart, panting slightly. Her face was flushed. She stepped back, and the moment slipped away.

Covering his disappointment, he asked, "May I give you a ride home?"

She nodded.

Back in his studio, he sighed. He could spend some time on the muse's carving before he fell into his clean and solitary bed.

CHAPTER 11

Ruari put in a call to Kelly who agreed to stop by after work that evening. Ruari met her at the studio door, having just gotten home himself.

"Hey, Ruari," she said.

Dressed in a navy short-sleeved shirt and long skirt with her dark blonde hair pulled back in a French braid, Kelly looked beautiful and professional. He'd harbored a crush on her in high school until it became clear that she was not interested in guys at all, and he'd let it go. He still admired her beauty and confidence. If he'd been a painter, he'd have wanted her to model for him.

While she walked around his workshop, he took the opportunity to study her with his other sight and struggled to relax and blur his vision. She seemed to be surrounded by a fuzzy glow of green whenever she stepped into the light. If she thought he was checking her out, she didn't say anything. When she'd completed her circuit, she asked to see his work.

He showed her the sketches for the inlaid table top and the new art piece. She was impressed, made notes, and took a few pictures with her phone for reference.

"Would you mind if I photographed the one you gave Marianne and maybe the lazy Susan you mentioned?"

"Not at all."

"What's your deadline?"

He hadn't really thought about it. "I'm new to this kind of self-employment," he admitted.

"I am too. Have you got a website yet?"

He shook his head. "Do you know anyone who knows how to make them?"

"Not yet. I'm keeping my ears out at work for a web designer." She considered him. "You were a decent guy in high school in spite of your sister. You've never been one of the people who spoke out against Sarah or me. That means something in my book. We're both at the beginning stages of starting small businesses. How about we help each other? If I find someone, I'll let you know, and if you find someone, call me."

Her expression was cautious but not unfriendly. There was no dark smoke accompanying her words. He stuck out his hand and said, "Deal." She shook his hand in her strong grip and nodded.

"About Marianne," she said, changing subjects completely without letting go of his hand. Nailing his startled expression with her brilliant blue eyes, she said deliberately, "She's a really sweet person who has had a lot of crap in her life. She doesn't need anymore for a while. So, if you're not serious about her, let her know up front." She released his hand.

He was nonplussed. All of the complicated things in his life rolled around like marbles in his mind. "I would never want to hurt her."

Kelly's expression grew opaque. She was clearly dissatisfied with his answer. "What ever happens, be honest with her. You both deserve that."

He nodded. After she left, he changed out of his work shirt and warmed some canned soup in the microwave. He absently rubbed his fingers over the scab at the base of his thumb as the bowl rotated slowly. He felt a stirring of restlessness to get back to work on the carving down below. Instead, he called Marianne.

"Hey, Ruari!" She said happily. "What's up?"

"Just wanted to say hi and see how you're doing." *Should I tell her about my dream? No, too awkward. I have to find the right time.*

"Pretty good. Making headway on the third lecture."

"Would you like to have dinner again?" *Maybe then.*

"Sure. Crave was lovely, but how about something a little simpler? I passed by Gertie's Burgers the other day. How is it?"

"It's 50s themed. They make a good shake."

"Let's go there. How about Friday?"

"I'll see you there."

After his uninspiring can of soup, he sat in front of his carving, turning it this way and that, until he got drawn into the miracle of the smaller animals, birds, and insects emerging from a growing texture of leaves, flowers, toadstools, and bark. The muse liked to work the whole piece at once which was a new approach for him. He picked up a chisel and slipped into the zone as the world around him vanished.

Much later, he turned off the light and threw the cover over the project. He staggered up the stairs and barely had time to undress before falling into bed.

He dreamed he was sitting on a log in a familiar forest clearing. The red-haired muse was pacing back and forth in front of him. She stopped and fixed him with an exasperated look.

"You waste so much time outside of the studio. Time we could use working together."

"I have a job," he protested. "I have to eat, pay my bills."

She waved her hand dismissively. "Yes, yes. If you trusted me and spent all your time building and carving, we could create pieces people would pay lots of money for and you wouldn't have to think about that anymore. I know you've wanted to create your own business. You have to just do it!"

"I'm working on it," he said testily.

"And you spend too much of your evenings out and about. You are holding us back."

"I have friends. Family."

She stopped and gave him a narrow-eyed look. "And that

woman you spend time with. You have feelings for her, don't you?"

He was taken aback. How much did she know about his life? Did she read his mind? Was Marianne in danger?

"My personal life is my own," he said shortly.

"Not when it impinges on our work together." She resumed pacing. "Your grandfather lived close to me, and it was easy to work with him. You are much farther away, and it's exhausting to reach out to you so we can connect." She stopped and gave him a look. "When are you going to live here?"

"I'm not moving to Scotland!" He protested again. "My family and my life is here."

She threw up her hands. "You like working with me. I can feel your pleasure and satisfaction at our work together."

Reluctantly, he nodded.

She made up her mind. "Good. I have enough power to make a stronger connection. Then I will be able to work with you much more easily."

"What does that mean?"

She smiled, her pale green lips curving up slightly. "I will take care of everything. See you soon, Ruari."

The clearing faded. He had other dreams after that, but a sense of unease carried over through all of them.

On Friday, Ruari spent most of the day repairing a porch on an old Victorian home. Casey seemed interested in rebuilding until he realized how long it was going to take and then spent the rest of his time complaining or trying to take short cuts. Ruari kept his temper, but it was a near thing. They knocked off at five, and his assistant disappeared with alacrity. A shower removed dust, dirt and at least some of his annoyance.

The humble burger beckoned.

Marianne met him just inside Gertie's. She fairly radiated a pinkish-purple halo, and he had to blink quickly or risk staring.

"You look really happy," he said with a smile as he hugged her.

"I finished my third lecture and mailed all of it off to Dr. Plank today! I've got a good feeling about it."

He leaned down and kissed her cheek, letting her good mood wash over him. "Congratulations."

They got a booth and perused their menus. They were discussing the selections when a familiar voice said brightly, "Hello, Ruari!"

Ruari looked up and saw Erin with Pat Whelan standing slightly behind her. Erin's hair was moussed back in an elegant wave, and an irrepressible, mischievous grin lit her face. Pat stood a little behind her, looking slightly uncomfortable.

"Erin!" Ruari said in surprise and consternation.

"Pat and I were just passing by and saw you come in here. We haven't eaten yet, so we followed you. Mind if we join you?" she asked with a glance at Marianne.

Ruari looked at his date and saw her brows quirk in amusement. She shrugged slightly which he took to be assent. "Sure."

They both scooted over, making room for the new arrivals. Erin sat next to her sibling, and Pat sat next to Marianne.

Erin immediately stuck her hand out across the table and introduced herself. "Hi, I'm Erin Allen, Ruari's sister. You must be Marianne! Ruari's told me so much about you. I wanted to meet you for myself. This is Pat Whelan; we've known each other since high school."

Marianne shook the proffered hand. "Nice to meet you, Erin. I've heard a little about you from Ruari. He said you're a financial wizard, among other things."

After they ordered burgers, fries, and shakes, Erin chatted ebulliently about setting the books up for her brother's new business. Ruari listened, more than a little annoyed at having his evening with Marianne hijacked by his sister. Erin had threatened to introduce herself if he wasn't fast enough. Marianne didn't seem perturbed by the interruption, so he tamped down his irritation. She shared her good news with Erin and Pat who murmured congratulations.

Ruari sat back and watched the interaction. With some effort he shifted his vision. Erin had an energetic orange glow. Pat, by comparison, had no apparent halo at all. Ruari still didn't know what that meant. At any rate, things seemed to be going well enough between them. Pat watched Erin's cheerful countenance with bemusement, as if he couldn't quite believe he was in her company. Ruari remembered they'd graduated from high school in the same year, and now he worked at the Chamber of Commerce or something.

Dinner came, and Ruari ate his Hawaiian burger and seasoned fries hungrily. Marianne seemed to be enjoying her food and snuck him a little wink when Erin was looking away. After they'd eaten, Erin excused herself to the ladies room, and Ruari had a chance to ask Pat whether they had post-dinner plans.

"We thought we'd catch a movie at the Avery," he said. "You're welcome to join us if you like." Ruari thought he detected a hint of hope that they would join him. No smoke though, so he was sincere about his offer.

Ruari glanced at Marianne who shrugged noncommittally, and he said smoothly, "Thanks for the invite. We had other plans."

Pat nodded and paid his and Erin's tab. When she returned, she turned to Marianne and said, "It was really nice to meet you, Marianne. This was fun! We should double date again some time!"

After they were gone, Ruari said with some embarrassment, "I hope you don't mind my sister crashing our dinner date? She's kind of hard to say no to."

Marianne smiled graciously. "I can see that. No worries. It was nice to meet her. Thank you for declining the movie though. I was hoping to have some time just with you."

His heart warmed at that. "Want to go walking?"

They split the bill and departed.

"Where to?" She asked.

"Have you been to the park yet?"

She shook her head and slipped her hand into his. "Let's go."

They walked in silence for a few blocks. Ruari enjoyed the feel of her warm hand in his and wondered how to bring up his troubles. When they'd first met, she'd confessed to him that her house was haunted and that she'd actually seen the ghosts. Maybe she wouldn't find his new vision strange, much less his dilemma with the sylvan fey. He still hadn't found any casual way to broach the subject by the time they'd reached the little park. *My artistic muse doesn't like you and wants me all to herself,* seemed overly melodramatic.

The green space one block back from Main Street had been created when a block of houses had been demolished about forty years ago. It contained a basketball court, a play area with slides, swings, and a climbing structure, a few picnic tables under some old trees, and a little fountain. The sun had set, but the late summer twilight lingered. The air was cool, and Marianne pulled her sweater closer around her.

He drew her to a picnic table and sat down. She sat opposite him and looked expectant. "You're very quiet," she said. "Is there something on your mind?"

He nodded and glanced around. There were people at the play area at the other end of the park, but no one was close by. "I've been going through some stuff lately, and I really need someone to talk to about it." She looked curious, so he took a deep breath and said, "Do you ever see haloes around people?"

Her brows lifted in surprise. "Haloes? You mean like auras? No, never. Do you?"

He nodded uncomfortably. "Recently, if people are in the right light, and I unfocus my eyes a bit, they're sometimes outlined with a glow. Not everybody, and not all the time. And sometimes when people are talking, I see black smoke coming out of their mouths."

She considered for a moment before replying. "Seeing auras is often associated with spiritualism. It was very popular in the Victorian era for people to claim to see auras, foretell the future, and speak with the dead. I've never heard of seeing black smoke though." She looked intrigued. "How does that work?"

"I think it happens when people are lying to me."

"That's wild!" Her eyes were alight with interest as she leaned forward. "So, if I told you I was a hundred years old, you would see smoke coming out of my mouth?"

Her words were so incongruous that he laughed. "The light isn't good, so I can't see anything right now. Besides, I know you're not a hundred years old."

"Does the smoke look different if you already think the other person is lying?"

Frowning, he thought about it. "I don't know. I haven't thought about it that way. I don't think so. I'll have to check." She was taking this all so calmly. Maybe she wouldn't freak out if he told her everything. "You don't think that I'm weird?" he said anxiously.

She shook her head with a smile. "It sounds interesting and kind of cool. It's no weirder than my seeing ghosts." She folded her hands together. "How did this happen? You said it was recent."

Twilight had faded, and there was only the cold light of the lamps on the street and along the park paths. Her face was shadowed, but she sounded calm, like a researcher asking someone to explain a point in history. He relaxed a little more.

"Well, it started a couple of weeks ago. At first my eyes were all blurry most of the time, and it gave me headaches. I wondered if I had a brain tumor or something."

"Was this when you were sick?"

He nodded.

"Just in case, did you see a doctor?"

"He did some bloodwork and told me I was overworked and not eating right."

"Probably true."

He agreed. "So, I worked with the screwy vision, and now I can more or less turn it on and off at will."

"Okay, let's assume you've suddenly acquired the ability to see auras. Any ideas on where this came from or why it started? Have you had a near death experience or something and didn't tell me?" She kept her words light but her gaze was sharp.

"Well, I haven't hit my head or connected myself to live wires recently. But, when we first met and shook hands, did you feel a zap or spark?"

She nodded. "It was like static electricity. I was a little afraid to touch you again," she admitted, "but I haven't felt it since then. Have you?"

He shook his head. "I think that might be the connection. Maybe once was all it took."

"I've sometimes wondered if that's why I could suddenly sense ghosts."

She fell silent. Ruari watched her. She'd taken the news about the auras and smoke well. Perhaps she'd be open to the rest of it? He really needed to talk about the fey woman with someone.

He opened his mouth. "I—"

She said at the same time, "I don't know—" and broke off with an apologetic smile. "Sorry, go ahead."

"No, you first."

"Okay. Um, I don't know how to ask you this, so I'm just going to say it. I heard through the grapevine that you were on the verge of getting married and then called it off." She looked up at him a little anxiously.

Not what he was expecting. It derailed his tentative thoughts, and he cleared his throat. He was going to have to share this story with her if they wanted to move forward, and this was as good a time as any. "I was engaged to a woman named Jenny. I guess I got cold feet, and I backed out a day before the wedding."

"Well, you must have had your reasons?" she said tentatively, leaving him room to expand.

He stared down and rubbed his forefinger on the rough surface of the picnic table. "That's just it. We had a few issues between us, but they weren't deal-breakers. I just suddenly felt like I couldn't go through with it," he finished.

"She must've been really upset."

He nodded. "She stayed on the phone long enough for me to apologize and then hung up without a word."

"Does she still live here?" She asked with a half-flinch as if expecting bad news.

He shook his head. "She moved back to New York, and I haven't seen her since."

She let out a breath, then cocked her head. "By any chance, is she tall with long red hair and kind of austere features?"

"No, she's tall and blonde." *Long red hair?*

"Do you have any other old girlfriends with long red hair?"

"Not…exactly. Why do you ask?"

"You remember I have clairvoyant or 'true' dreams, right? I dreamed you were walking with a tall, red-haired woman. I called out to you, but you didn't hear me. She did though, and gave me a look like she owned you. Oscar thought it was one of your old girlfriends." She ducked her head. "My cat can talk in my dreams."

He stared at her. *The fey woman had invaded her dreams as well?* He cleared his throat. "She seems to be my muse. My creative self takes the form of a sylvan woman."

"Sylvan? Like in trees and fairies?"

"I guess."

"Huh." She gave him a look like she was adding things up. "Did you know the Victorians believed in possession by fairies? I don't know if they meant it metaphorically or literally. You were 'sick' with a headache and fever and blurry vision, and now you can see auras and lies. That checks the boxes for Victorian possession by fairies. What do you think?"

And the conversation had swung around again. Did he dare tell her everything? Well, she brought it up…

"I think you may be right. When I was sick, I started having these unusually vivid dreams. Like I was someplace else."

He told her about the fey woman, the forgotten 'memory,' and her unspecified, vaguely threatening desire to make a stronger connection with him. It was such a relief to lay it all out there, even though it sounded slightly absurd as well.

She was quiet for a few moments before saying, "Now, that's way weirder than ghosts." She took a deep breath and let it out. "So, your question is what to do about all of it?"

He nodded.

"Assuming it's all true, not the product of a fevered or tumored mind," he looked so alarmed that she added, "and it seems true to me from what you said, what do *you* want?"

He ran a hand through his short hair and let out a breath. "I can make things with her help that I couldn't make without it."

"Could you learn it on your own?"

"Maybe. But she's a master craftsman willing to teach me, like Granda was, and that's worth something."

"What does she want from you?"

"She gets to make things. I don't think she does much else."

"Is there a downside? Like, did your grandfather do well?"

"He was world famous in some circles. People came from all over to buy his things." *He left his family twisting in the wind… But it doesn't have to be that way for me, though.*

"Then why are you worried?"

He hesitated, then said, "I don't think she likes you."

Marianne tilted her head. "I got that impression from my own dream."

He reached out and took her hands. They were cold in his. "You're freezing."

"A little cold."

"You want to walk again?"

She got up and tucked her arm into his. They were quiet

while they made a half circuit around the park. The kids had gone home, and there were only a few others, crossing from one side to the other.

She stopped him under a light and looked up in all seriousness. "Ruari, this sounds like an incredible opportunity for you. One that doesn't come along more than once in a lifetime. If you want to take her up on it, I can respect that. If that gives you cold feet about us, then please tell me."

He could feel her withdrawing like the sun going behind the clouds, and he felt cold. "Mahri, I don't want to lose you. You make me happier than I've been in longer than I care to think about. Please don't go."

She took a deep breath and let it out. "I really like you a lot. I just need you to be honest with me. My ex wasn't, so I'm kind of hyper sensitive about that. I want to be here. If you want me to fight by your side, I can do that."

He wrapped his arms around her, and she hugged him just as hard. "Yes," he breathed into her hair.

They broke apart and she looked up. "Okay. What's the next step?"

The relief of having her understanding left him feeling limp in mind and body. "I'm going to have to talk to her about the deal. Once she sees that I can work with her and still be with you, she'll come around. Granda had Nana his whole life and that was okay."

"Are you sure?"

"I can handle this," he said with more confidence than he felt. He didn't want her to be in danger or worry about him.

He walked her back to her house on Violet Lane and kissed her on the front step.

"Before you go, here." She pushed something into his hand. It felt like a little cloth bag with stones or marbles inside. There was a faint whiff of something floral.

"What's this?"

"It's my protection charm. It's worked for me against ghosts so far. Maybe it will give you protection."

"Your charm?"

"I can make another. Please take it."

His buddies at the Dutch, including Trevor, would make some rude joke about his girlfriend giving him the stones to protect himself. *No need for them to know.* He smiled and slid the bag into his pocket. "Thank you, Mahri."

"Let me know how things go."

CHAPTER 12

Ruari fell asleep like a stone sinking through dark water. Gradually, he became aware of lying on his back, looking up through a tangle of branches at the night sky. The branches seemed to be swaying in a high wind, but the sound was on mute. His limbs and body felt heavy as he stared at the mesmerizing motion. Gradually he became aware of another movement at ground level and turned his head with some effort. A familiar tall, red-haired figure walked past his field of vision. Her arms were upraised, and she appeared to be chanting or speaking to the tree and the air around her. Sound returned to his perception with a roar of wind and voice. Her words sounded like snatches of Old Scots and a hissing, whispering that sounded like wind in the leaves.

She disappeared and reappeared again a few moments later, and he realized she was circling the tree. The hard bed of roots he lay on shifted under him like snakes made of wood and wire, slowly creeping over him.

"What are you doing?" His voice came out in a whisper.

She heard him and paused to gaze at him from her considerable height. "You leave me no choice. I will bind you to me, and you will forget her. I must have hands." A faint smile curved her thin lips. She seemed to think she was being kind. "You will see that this is a good thing. We will create extraordinary things together. Your hands have more skill than your grandfather's did, and your ideas complement my own. You will become famous among the men of your time."

"You don't have to do this. I can work with you like Granda did. Marianne won't be in your way." He tried to sit up and only managed to twitch his hands.

She shook her head. "She is a passing infatuation like the other one. As far as I can tell, you haven't even bedded her."

"That's not important. I need her. I can learn woodworking on my own. Or I'll do something else." He concentrated on trying to move his hands, managing to slide one up over his pocket. A burst of lavender and mint scented the air as the little gemstones ground over the herbs. His head cleared and his strength began to return. He pushed at the twining roots.

"Your pitiful charm cannot protect you." She raised her hands again and called out, "I invoke thee, o spirits of forest and air and storm, bind this human to me that we may glorify and remember you to the world of men. Old Man of the Forest, you are the one we look to for guidance. You have no love of humans. If you can hear me, help me bind this human to my service."

Managing to pull free of the roots holding his arms, he sat up and tried to loosen the ones holding his legs in place. "Let me go," he said through gritted teeth. Something tickled his face, and he brushed small tendrils away. In that moment, an enterprising stem circled his arm, preventing him from reaching his legs and another wound around his other arm, holding him immobile.

A small swarm of golden insects emerged from the dark woods beyond the clearing. They glittered, making a high buzzing sound like bees. The fey woman curled her fingers, beckoning them to her. In a sweeping gesture, she sent them flying toward him. He thrashed and tried to turn away, but they surrounded him. One landed, piercing his shoulder with a sharp pain. His scream was drowned by her triumphant cry.

"You are—"

The world exploded in light and sound. Ruari was flung out of the tree's grip and bowled end over end. A hail of sharp little needles peppered him as he flew. He fetched up against a rocky outcrop. Deafened and dazed, his head spun. Freezing rain pelted down, slapping his face. Soon it plastered his hair and clothes to his skin as a storm sliced through the clearing. Jagged lightning forked dangerously near, and he instinctively cowered and covered his head. He had to get off this exposed outcrop to where it was safer. He struggled to crawl away, but before he could move, another sizzling bolt ripped through the black sky, blasting the tree. A searing pain shot down his arm, setting it on fire. He screamed again and flung himself away.

Landing with a thud on the floor, he fell out of bed, thrashing and clutching his right arm. The sickening smell of singed flesh and burnt wood stung his nose. Heart beating irregularly, he turned on the bedside light and saw to his horror that his right arm was smoking slightly. His hand tingled and throbbed as if he'd grabbed high voltage wires. Opening and closing his fingers experimentally, he watched them barely move as though they'd forgotten how.

"What the hell?!" he whispered to himself.

The dial on his bedside clock showed it was a little after midnight. The fey woman had tried to put a spell on him, but something happened. A storm. Lightning. He picked up has phone to call Marianne and felt a static shock. The little screen went black. Out of juice. The last thing he wanted was to fall asleep again. Cradling his arm, he headed down to his truck.

Ruari knocked on her door until she opened it. She looked sleep frazzled and wore a long T-shirt and sweatpants.

"Ruari!" She stepped aside. "Come in!"

He felt like he might break into a thousand pieces. The ride over had been nightmarish. He'd struggled into a jacket, then the truck had balked at starting. His vision had come and gone, and he'd had to wait for a spell of faintness to pass, resting his head on the steering wheel for several minutes before he could continue. His right arm was useless, so he'd driven one-handed. He'd pulled over for more dizzy spells. Twice he'd woken with his mind a jumble of images that made no sense and wondered where he was. He'd barely been able to park at the curb and make it up her front walk.

"Oh my god you're bleeding! What happened?" She looked shocked.

Feeling at his wit's end, he stepped over the threshold, and she wrapped her arms around him. The moment she touched his bare skin, he felt a sharp static snap, and she leapt back as if she'd contacted a live wire.

"What happened?" she exclaimed again.

"You're not going to believe it," he said, feeling his vision blur again.

"You need to sit down," she said firmly. She put his good arm over her shoulder and helped him to the couch. "It's like four in the morning. Were you on an emergency call?"

He shook his head, sinking down on the cushions. Four? Had it really taken him almost four hours to drive a few blocks to here? His head felt stuffed with sawdust. He closed his eyes and leaned his head back. She'd painted recently. The smell of latex paint was oddly soothing. He heard her doing something in the kitchen. As he sat, the ache in his arm and shoulder eased, making way for tingling as if pricked by dozens of needles.

She returned and put several things on the coffee table. "Okay," she said gently, "I need you to sit up if you can." He hunched forward, curling around his injured arm. She slid the jacket off and hissed. "You'll have to take your shirt off too. You look like you jumped in front of a wood chipper. Maybe I should take you to the ER or urgent care?"

He shook his head once and regretted it as it pounded sharply. "Don't think they could help."

She pressed her lips together disapprovingly but helped him get his shirt off. There was the sound of water splashing in a bowl, and she began dabbing at his shoulders and back with a warm wet washcloth. "Most of it looks okay, and it'll stop bleeding on its own. But this," she gingerly moved his right arm, "is something else. What stabbed you?" She cleaned the place on the front of his shoulder and taped some gauze over it.

He sat for her ministrations quietly, not yet trusting himself to speak. Waves of dizziness passed over him, and he fought to stay conscious. His brain felt muzzy as images flashed like movie stills through his mind. Finally, she finished and helped him lie down with a blanket over him. She slipped her hand into his left hand.

"When I fell asleep, I was in her clearing. I think she was casting some kind of spell to make me forget you. I couldn't get away. I tried." She squeezed his hand. "She called a swarm of gold insects, and one of them stung me. I think she would have won, but there was a storm, and her tree was hit by lightning. I was thrown free. All her bark was blown off. I don't know what happened to her. I woke up when I fell out of bed."

"Do you think she's dead?"

"I don't know. Maybe?"

"Were you wearing the charm I gave you?"

"In my pocket."

She reached into his jeans pocket to retrieve it and emptied it into her hand. Crushed, blackened leaves and coarse fragments of tumbled black stones littered her palm.

"Maybe this kept you from being killed." Her voice was tinged with awe.

A noise from the kitchen startled her. "I put water on for tea. Be right back." She poured the pile onto the top paper lying on the coffee table, scrambled up, and left. The warmth of the blanket seeped through him, and he felt his muscles relax. His arm still prickled madly.

She returned with a mug of something that smelled sweet and

herbal. He managed to sit up and take a sip. Not usually his favorite, it tasted surprisingly good.

He cleared his throat. "How is it possible? Mahri, I was asleep in my own house. How could I feel things that happened in a dream? That wasn't real."

She tucked her legs under her in the arm chair nearby, cradling her own mug in her hands. "When George Rutherford was here, I dreamed about him several times. Whenever he manhandled me I woke up with bruises. Sarah told me I existed in my dreams more solidly than most people do. From what you've told me, you do too when the tree woman is involved."

"It's completely crazy."

She nodded. "I knew a person who was struck by lightning through her computer. She said it was like the motherlode of all electrical jolts and just made her want to cry. She was okay, but felt like her entire insides had been rearranged. When she went to her friend who did Reiki massage, the masseuse could tell immediately that something major had happened. I think she was able to calm her system down eventually. I don't know anyone who does Reiki. Hopefully your system will calm down on its own. I think you'll be safe here. Try and get some sleep, if you can."

He closed his eyes and felt her pull the blanket up under his chin as he gingerly shifted to his side. He fell asleep.

Marianne woke as the early dawn light crept into her bedroom. Oscar slept warm and heavy against her side. She gave his fur a sleepy pat, and he tightened his curl. She'd checked on Ruari twice during the night, hovering in the doorway to the living room to be sure she could hear him breathing.

I've got to set up a guest room. The couch is no place for anyone except Oscar to sleep.

She'd mulled over everything that had happened last night from their walk in the park to his sudden arrival at her door. She was sure he was telling the truth as far as he knew it, and the dream damage in the waking world was too familiar to dismiss.

Remembering her hands roaming over his muscular back and the feel of his smooth skin under her fingertips made the heat rise in her face and a gave her a deep tingle in her belly.

He finally takes his shirt off, and I get to play nurse, that's classic, she thought with a smile. *If he stays more than a day or two, my resolve is going to take a beating. I promised I wouldn't jump into bed with the next hot guy I dated until I was sure he really wanted to stick around, but...*

What to do now? Sarah could help her protect Ruari against unwanted fey intrusions most likely, but she was away at a conference. If the fey woman was trying to coerce Ruari against his will, then Marianne couldn't feel too much sympathy for her being hit by lightning.

Ruari wasn't the only worry in her life. She was still waiting on Dr. Plank's response to her lectures. Was she going to have a job or not? And Jason was still out there among the trees waiting for her to come up with a solution for him. She sighed. It never rained but it poured.

She got out of bed and pulled on her bathrobe. In the kitchen, she put water on for tea and got a bag of coffee out of the freezer. She had a French press pot to make it in. She sliced a couple of bagels, hoping Ruari liked onion flavored ones, and made scrambled eggs.

"You're up early," he said.

She jumped. She'd been so intent on not being too noisy that she hadn't heard him approach. He stood in the doorway to the pantry pass through from the front hall, looking wan and tired.

"Hey, how are you feeling?" She asked.

"Like I stood in front of a wood chipper," he said with a wry smile. "That smells good."

"I made coffee." She poured him a mug and offered him milk.

He took a sip and his eyes went wide, and he coughed.

"Too strong? Sorry. I always heard that was better than too

weak." Geoffrey was a coffee man and derided any of her attempts to make it. She'd given up early on and let him brew his own.

"Really, it's fine!" He took another swallow and turned a cough into a hearty throat-clearing.

She laughed. "You're a terrible liar. Breakfast?"

"I could eat enough for an army."

They sat in the dining room and ate. Ruari moved gingerly as if his back still hurt, and the fork looked awkward in his grip. At least it was the weekend, and he had a couple of days to rest up. Oscar wandered through, waving and curling his crooked-tipped tail on his way to the litter box. She heard a distant crunching of kibble in the pantry.

"Looks like your arm still hurts," she observed.

He flexed his hand and grimaced. "Still tingles and prickles, but I have some strength back."

"That's a good sign. You're welcome to hang out here as long as you want."

"Thanks, I might take you up on that."

"I don't have anything to fit you, but I could wash your shirt if you like."

"You don't have to."

"It's no trouble, I have to do a load anyway."

After breakfast dishes were cleared off the table, he looked tired. "I've got these," she scolded. "Go lay down."

It was a measure of his fatigue that he let her steer him back to the sofa. After she got everything tucked away, she peeked into the living room. He lay with his feet tucked up asleep. Oscar had claimed the high spot and was curled up on Ruari's hip. Marianne smiled. Oscar was making sure Ruari stayed put, and the orange tabby was getting the first of several naps in.

She got through a shower and started a load of laundry. She'd planned to tackle Jason Fargate's problem today before Ruari had turned up. Maybe she still could. At least thinking about Jason and Ruari took her mind off whether Dr. Plank had looked at her lectures or not.

The chime of her cell phone caught her bringing the dry laundry up from the basement.

"Hello, is this Marianne?" The cemetery caretaker's warm voice made her smile.

"Hi, John. Thanks for getting back to me." The day after Jason's unexpected nighttime visit, she'd called the Maple Hill Community Cemetery with an idea.

"I got your message. I'm sorry to make you wait. We had a couple of burials. What can I do for you?"

"I'm hoping you can help me." She explained Jason's situation and concluded, "Neither of us knows what to do next. I don't think he should live in the woods at the end of the street forever, and he showed up in my room a couple of night ago. I think he'd like to move on, but I don't know how to help him. Is there anything you can suggest?"

"It can sometimes happen. Would he be willing to come here?"

"I don't know. I can ask him."

"I'll see if Jesse has any suggestions. Maybe Jason would talk to him?"

"It's worth a try. Any chance I can come today?"

"I'm here all day."

"Perfect. I'll find him, and we'll be out later. Thank you so much."

She folded the laundry and put Ruari's T-shirt on the table where he'd see it when he woke up. He was still sleeping soundly, though he was twitching the way Oscar did when he had a dream. It didn't look like a nightmare at least. Marianne picked the tabby up from his perch and gave him a snuggle. "Let's let him sleep. How about you go out for a while, hmm?" She kissed him, and he rubbed his head on her cheek. She let him out quietly.

Time to find Jason. She left Ruari a note on top of his clean shirt and slipped out the front door. The sun was playing hide and seek with the clouds, and she glanced up the street. No one was out on the block at the moment, so she felt confident searching for an invisible person without her neighbors thinking she was crazy.

"Jason? Are you there?" She prowled through the garage and under the trees at the end of the block, calling quietly. "I've got an idea about how to help you, if you want to try it." She'd been walking for a good fifteen minutes before she heard a soft voice nearby.

+I thought you'd forgotten me. I could hear you, but it took me a bit to find you.+ His voice was fainter than it had been.

She stopped under a tree with a pang of guilt. "I didn't forget you. Are you okay? You're very quiet."

+I guess.+ He sounded really down.

"I found someone to help you, I think. Are you willing to try?"

+I guess.+ She imagined his uninspired shrug.

"Come with me. Please?" She held out her hand and closed her eyes, listening with another part of her. The lightest of touches brushed against her palm, and through her closed eyelids, she thought she could see the faintest glimmer of something man-sized. Trusting that Jason was with her, she opened her eyes and strolled back to her car. Pulling the handle on the back door of the Flea, she mimed letting him in, then got into the driver's seat. The car should have been sun warmed, but it was subtly cool with Jason's presence. She shivered. *I'm driving around with a ghost in my car.*

As she drove up Violet Lane toward Main Street, one of her elderly neighbors stared at her as she passed by. *Too late to worry about that now,* she thought.

"Jason, are you there?" He didn't respond for so long that she thought about turning back.

A wave of sadness washed over her with a soft, +*Uh huh.*+

"Hang in there, buddy. I have a friend who might help you."

It took about twenty minutes to reach the cemetery, and she fought the urge to cry the whole way. Jason's feelings of abandonment threw her empathy into overdrive. Finally, she turned through the wrought-iron gates and parked by the machine shed near the little cottage where John lived. "Jason, we're here," she whispered. There was no answer.

She swallowed the lump in her throat and called, "John?" as she approached the machine shop. The dark space smelled of cut grass, oil, and gasoline. The bulky mower and maintenance vehicle he used were both parked inside. "Jesse?" she called more tentatively. *Please let him be here*, she thought. *I don't want to have to take this poor kid back home.*

There was a slight movement toward the back of the shop by the workbench. Focusing in the gloom, she could just make out the shadowy bulk of a person larger than John. She had a sense of canvas overalls. "Jesse, is that you? It's me, Marianne."

+*Yes.*+ His voice was deeper than John's.

"I brought a friend of mine to see you. His name is Jason, and he's kind of stuck here." Briefly she explained the situation. "I'm worried about him. He's getting very faint, and I don't know what to do to help him. Do you think you could talk to him, maybe?"

+*Sure.*+

"Thank you! I'll be right back." The backseat of her car was ostensibly empty, but she said, "Jason, I want to introduce you to Jesse Carlton. I think he can help you. Take my hand." She reached into the car and felt a cool hand touch hers. Tears pricked her closed eyes as she felt a wave of despair. His hood had fallen back, silvery blond hair framing a bleak expression as he stood like a pale watery outline in the sunlight. She smiled encouragingly at him and led him to the doorway of the shop. Later, when she remembered this moment, she wasn't sure if her eyes had been open or closed as she walked.

Inside the cool shed, a deep, comforting voice said, *+Hi, son, I'm Jesse. Come on in. I used to work here. I guess I'm retired now. I heard you lived in Beacon. I had a friend there. Do you know... +*

Marianne could just make out Jesse's heavier figure putting an arm around Jason's thin shoulders before the darkness of the space swallowed them up. The burden of sadness lifted, and she felt lighter.

"Marianne? I'm sorry. I was on the phone," John Irving said as he approached from his stone cottage. He was lean and tan, his lined face sporting the best white Mark Twain mustache she'd ever seen. Her tension released.

"Hi, John. Thanks for seeing us. I introduced Jason to Jesse. I'm hoping he'll be alright now." She wiped her eyes with one hand.

John nodded. "I'm sure he will. Would you like to come in for a minute? You look like you could use a cup of coffee."

Feeling utterly wrung out, she took a shaky breath and said, "I'd love that."

CHAPTER 13

Ruari dreamed. A jumble of images twined themselves in an unruly tangle: walking in a forest, Erin's infectious grin, Marianne laughing. He walked his darkened Maple Hill studio, making his way between the tables to open the huge rolling doors to get some light. Outside there was no street, only a wide, rolling landscape of tall grasses and small flowering plants blooming in front of a cliff of dirty ice. Stepping out, he felt a chill wind ruffle his hair. Everything around him seemed brighter, more colorful, and more real with sharply defined outlines.

In the distance, a herd of large red deer grazed bathed in a steady reddish glow of life and health. One stood a little apart with a duller aura and seemed to be favoring a hind leg. As Ruari watched in fascination, three stocky men carrying spears crept up on them, using a low rise for cover. Their auras were a bright orange. At an unseen signal, they rushed the herd, casting their spears. The deer scattered, their red auras flaring brightly in their panic. Struck in the flank, the slower deer fled. The men shouted, trying to separate it from the others, but it slipped past them, adrenaline fueling its stride.

Suddenly a tall, slender woman rose out of the grass in a flare of bright yellow. She flung her arms around the fleeing deer, and he felt her fierce triumph as she broke the deer's neck with her powerful arms. Its dull aura faded with its life force. Her friends would eat well tonight. The men converged and began the messy process of butchering their prey. Ruari hadn't realized it was possible to see all living things so full of the pulse of life. When he'd first started seeing it in Maple Hill, he'd been confused. Here it seemed natural to be fully aware of it all the time, and he tried to let it flow through him.

Later that night around the fire, men and women with dusky, bronze skin, long matted brown hair, and heavy browed features celebrated with songs and stories. Their voices were mellifluous, and they laughed often. Ruari tried to join them, but was unable to get closer. Disappointed, he resigned himself to watching them.

Their auric colors were mostly the red and orange of physicality, energy and adventurousness. Mixed in with them were several of the taller, more slender people, her own family whose auras were more yellow and green. Ruari sensed they were strongly connected to primal life energy, intelligence, and creativity. Children of both groups wrestled and played together.

Ruari watched the memories flow by, realizing he was seeing them through the eyes of the tall, slender woman he'd first seen. She felt vaguely familiar, like the sister of someone he knew.

Seasons of snow and warmth passed in a blink as the ice retreated. They worked with the bronze-skinned people, sometimes arguing and separating, but always coming back together. When the humans were off hunting on their own, she exulted in running fleet-footed across the steppe grasses, her tall friends running next to her, for the sheer joy of speed. They followed the paths of hunting hawks and long-toothed cats, racing alongside horses and deer. When they grew tired, they lay in the sun on the grass to recover their energy, watching the ants and beetles make their homes in the earth.

She lived with her people for a very long time. They subsisted on air and sunlight, wind and rain, and the occasional animal body. Although her people's lives were long, sometimes an accident, a falling boulder, a cliff that broke away underfoot, took the life of one of them. Older members of the family sometimes curled up and fell asleep, never to waken again. A few walked into the mist and were never heard of again.

They traveled far and wide. The tall, slender people who lived near deep lakes or on the shore greeted them by touching hands and singing to each other, exchanging news and stories. The mountain people lived among the stony cliffs and were wilder. They growled their greetings and challenged their visitors to feats of strength and speed, which she loved just as much.

Over time, the landscape changed, and the weather warmed. Lakes and rivers grew and receded. One day, a mixed group of women and children of her people and their darker-skinned friends walked into the hills, following a narrow stream out of the wind. She carried a pouch of woven grasses over one shoulder. At a suitable spot, she drew seeds from her pouch, little pearls carrying the power of life within them. She cupped one in her hands and poured her power of sunlight, water, air, and life into it.

The human women and children gathered around her and gasped as a tiny root grew, followed by a small green shoot. Gently, she took the seedling, poked a hole in the mud near the stream, and planted it. As they watched, the sprout took hold and grew into a foot-tall sapling in a matter of minutes on the sheer momentum of life she'd given it. She and her people planted many more trees from seeds gotten from their relatives across the great valley to the south. Forests grew where they walked. They nurtured the trees and lived in them when the seasons changed.

There came a day when new people arrived. They were lighter skinned, taller than the brown-skinned humans, though not as tall as she. Their faces were sharper, bodies leaner, and their language was different. The old humans gave them food and showed them where good hunting was. But something was wrong with these new people. Their auras were duller in color, bordering on muddy. Among her people that meant sickness. They also carried a darkness with them. They were more aggressive, and sometimes they fought, not only with each other but with her friends.

One day, when she was on the other side of a little valley, she observed a fair-haired man visit her friends' camp. The couple offered the newcomer food which he took and ate. The longer she watched the more uneasy she became, and she began walking back to camp. The newcomer seemed to have a dark blob of something attached to his head. She began running. Without warning the newcomer stabbed her friend with a spear, pinning him to the ground. He threw the woman on the ground, climbed on top of her and held her down while he thrust himself into her as she screamed.

The woman Ruari followed closed the gap, running like the wind, filled with a fury she'd never felt before. As she ran, she scooped up a rock and threw it at the invader. Struck squarely on the the head, he fell over. She leaped upon him and gouged every part of him with her long fingered hands until he lay still. The dark blob emerged from his head as he died, and she reared back instinctively. It drifted along the ground toward her friend and touched her thigh as she wept inconsolably by the side of her mate. The tall woman watched in horror as it suckled at her friend's aura feeding on her life energy. Disgusted she swatted at the thing and drove it away.

The sound of others approaching drew her gaze. The attacker's friends were coming. Still furious, she wanted to kill them all, but there were too many. Instead, she picked up her friend and ran away, outpacing the men in no time. Later that night, she returned with her own family, and they dealt out justice as the men camped on the bones of the dead.

More time passed, and there were fewer and fewer of her old friends and more of the fair-skinned people. Some of the new people were artists and poets with bright, clean auras, who showed her beautiful carvings and drawings on hides, and taught her people new songs. She learned their language, but they did not trouble to learn hers. And there was conflict. They invaded the places where she and her family had lived for centuries. When the newcomers fought, it was to maim and kill and take the land. If her people had a victory, the invaders came back in greater numbers. Worse yet, they cut trees to make buildings and burn as firewood. Sometimes they cut the tree homes of her people. When that happened, her people died.

Finally, her people held a counsel in a hidden valley. Hundreds of voices echoed like wind in the leaves as they talked about what to do. After much discussion, they agreed to move south. They had relatives beyond the great valley who would take them in. Runners went to the mountain people and the lake people, inviting them to leave with them.

When the emissaries returned several days later, it was with devastating news: the fair-skinned people had driven the lake people into the ocean where they had changed into seals and vanished. The mountain people had been pushed into hiding in the most desolate places in the highlands and hills. The runners had only been safe traveling at night when the strangers' eyes were not as keen. In the wake of this news, The Old Man of the Forest talked about all out war. Even if it meant extinction, at least they would take many invaders with them. Those who wanted to be left alone disagreed. They would go south. Those who wanted to fight for their land stayed.

Having seen the light-skinned people commit murder and possess the land, she wanted to stay and fight, but her family urged her to go south with them and let go of the past. They parted from the fighters one misty morning with a great host of their kin, striding swiftly south. A handful of humans saw them go and told stories of the exodus of a great host of tree-like people.

Along the way, the ground trembled faintly as if it, too, sensed the end of an era. When they arrived at the edge of the great valley, lush and green, stretching as far as the eye could see between the rising sun and the setting sun, they camped for the last time on their land. Heartsick and weary, they gathered their strength for a final push south.

A few intrepid travelers, eager to go, started down the slope. Then everyone felt the ground shake again, this time a sustained vibration that grew into a sound. Confused, she looked in the rising sunward direction and saw a strange thing moving in the distance. It was tall and broad with small flecks of movement on its surface like insects on the face of a dead thing too long in the sun. She pointed it out to the others. They rose and watched it gather speed as it approach. At last they perceived a vast wall of water, carrying a churning maelstrom of stones and trees, brown from the earth it had torn up. It bore down on the animals and people in the valley and swept them away in a flash, rushing onward. The water did not stay within the confines of the valley. It lapped over the edge in a deadly sweep. She grabbed her nearest kin and pulled them away from the lip as fast as they could move. Those who made it above the waterline stood in shock and horror as churning, muddy water covered everything they could see to the south.

Waiting to see if the water would recede, they stayed for a time. After a week, it grew smaller so it only occupied the valley, but it never went away. It formed a chill, steely gray barrier between them and their escape. Resigned, they turned north-ward, retracing their steps to the hidden valley, to join their kin for war.

More time passed in an eye blink. A landscape of gently rolling hills covered with stands of thick forest grew around Ruari. He recognized oak, beech, elm, and linden. Time slowed again as a beautiful scarlet sunset spread across the sky, fading into twilight. The air was warm and thick with the scents of summer and hummed with insects. Slowly, the tall people emerged from their trees, stretching and greeting one another.

There were perhaps two dozen of them. Each one had hair that reflected the tree they lived in. His gaze was drawn to a woman with wine red hair, like the leaves of the beech tree she favored. This was the person he'd been following. With a tantalizing sense of familiarity, Ruari thought he'd seen these faces before outside of the dream, but he couldn't remember where.

Someone brought a flute, another a tabor, a third brought an instrument made of cattail leaves and willow withes, and together they began to play. The music started out slow and stately as people joined them. They formed a long line that wove in and through itself as they stepped and swayed in time to the music. The full moon rose above the trees, painting silver across everything with its cold, bright light.

At last, a huge, gnarled, ancient figure stepped into the clearing. He was half again as tall as the rest of the crowd. His oak brown beard was shaggy with lichen and moss, and his aura was a deep, wise purple. The face beneath was craggy and stern. Everyone stopped and bowed as one. When he spoke his voice was like slow summer thunder or water pouring into a deep ravine.

"Welcome, my children, on midsummer night. Although there are fewer of us this year than there were last year, take heart. Many of the soldiers have left the isle. Humans are moving together into their stone forts and villages, leaving the countryside and forests to us. This is a time for us to grow in strength and numbers. Does anyone have a union or offspring to be blessed?"

Two couples stepped forward, their arms intertwined with one another, and the Old Man smiled for the first time. He placed his stiff, gnarled hands over each pair and said, "May your union bear fruit. May you live in harmony for many summers." People from the company brought forth flowered wreaths and placed them on their heads.

The copper beech-haired woman stepped forward and said, "I have a daughter who is twig of my twig, bark of my bark, sap of my sap." She opened her cupped hands and showed a tiny, roughly formed, two-legged figure that resembled nothing so much as a splinter of wood. She leaned down and blew her breath upon it, whereupon it opened its eyes and yawned. Two arms pulled free and stretched as she stood up on her mother's palm. The Old Man leaned down and blew upon her as well, and she grew several inches. The others took turns giving her a breath of their own life. As she grew straight and strong, she resembled her mother but carried the thoughts and memories of everyone there. When they were done, she was five feet tall. The Old Man said, "I name you Hhthfehrtessen, after your mother. Be your own person, but remember the words and history of your people. Never trust humans."

"I shall," she said.

Ruari felt a shock of recognition. This was Granda's fey woman as a child. He suddenly understood that he was seeing her very long life and that of her ancestors.

Hhthfehrtessen and her mother walked more freely on the land for a time, residing in a carefully chosen tree in a secluded forest each winter but emerging as the sap flowed in spring. She delighted in all living creatures, from the smallest woodlice to the deer and wolves that roamed the land, and she spent hours watching them. She avoided the humans who occasionally strayed through the woods. Curiosity sometimes brought her to the edge of human habitation, and she watched them grow their crops, tend their animals, and squabble amongst themselves. Their auras were dull and sickly, and they showed only fear of the woods beyond their clearings, and that was good.

One spring morning, a human child strayed deep into the woods. Feeling lonely, Hhthfehrtessen watched the bright little person play with stones, sticks, and acorns. When she got bored or perhaps realized how far she was from home, the girl ran off. Hhthfehrtessen followed at a safe distance, knowing the girl was going farther from the village. She cooed like the pigeons she'd seen on the roofs of the village, trying to lead the girl in the right direction. Whether she was too frightened to notice or didn't understand, the girl continued deeper into the woods.

Finally, Hhthfehrtessen stepped out from behind a tree and spoke to her. Startled, the girl uttered a little shriek. Although the girl didn't understand the words, Hhthfehrtessen did her best to soothe her. Finally, she offered her hand and led her back to the village. At the edge of the trees, late in the day, Hhthfehrtessen pushed her toward the houses and retreated into the forest. From a safe distance, she watched the little girl's mother hug and scold her.

Hhthfehrtessen returned to the place where she'd first seen the little girl and found a small wooden mannikin wearing a simple cloth skirt. It had been badly made with no proper attention to detail, so she fashioned a new one from twigs, grass, and flowers. Stealing back to the village under cover of darkness, she left it with the old doll on a tree stump.

The little girl returned to the woods on several more occasions, bringing little offerings of flowers and broken implements each time. Hhthfehrtessen transformed them from broken human things into little figures of animals and birds, making the girl laugh when she found them. Furious, Hhthfehrtessen's mother forbade her from speaking to the girl, so the fey girl watched her from a distance.

One day, a man followed the little girl all the way to their clearing. He watched her playing with several of the little figures before stepping into the clearing to snatch the girl by her arm. Yelling and making her cry, he broke all the things Hhthfehrtessen had made before dragging her back to the village. Afraid for her friend, she followed, flitting from tree to tree. She watched as he beat the girl with a willow switch, shouting all the while.

When her mother found out, Hhthfehrtessen suffered much the same fate of shouting and slaps from her mother's hard hands.

At the annual gathering of the local tree kin on midsummer

night, they danced to the tabor, flute, and cattails as they always did. Caught up in their revels, they didn't see the human men creep up on them. Suddenly, the men rushed into the clearing, sowing panic among the tree people. A man holding a tall, rough cross shouted, and the men set fire to the trees, cutting and burning everything they could reach. Her people tried to flee but were cut down. Her mother stood between her and a group of three men wielding scythes and axes as Hhthfehrtessen ran blindly into the woods. She ran until the stench of fire and smoke and the sounds of shouts and screams were far behind her.

She hid for several days, but her mother didn't find her. Finally, she crept back and wept at the scorched and blackened bodies of her mother, her kin, and their trees. A slow rage emerged from the ashes as she remembered every bad thing that had been done to her people in her own life and those of her ancestors. All the wars and murders and petty hurts and hates. When the Old Man had been younger, he'd led his people in battle against the invaders, but he was far away, and her family was gone. It was up to her.

Carefully, she scouted the small village and its surroundings. She noted when the villagers came and went. One night a mist rose from the land, and she went to work. Channeling her anger, she killed every tame cow, pig, goat, and chicken she found, snapping their necks or piercing them with her sharp fingers. Tendrils grew from her body, and she silenced the barking dogs. The men who came outside to investigate the disturbance were strangled and torn to pieces. She grew in height with each death, and her cold fury swelled. How could something this weak and small have killed her mother and destroyed her people? Then she swiftly entered each house and killed every inhabitant with ruthless, blind rage. When dawn came, nothing was left alive. She came back to herself and mourned the loss of the little girl.

After that she walked, passing into places she'd never been before. She carried a heavy burden of death and avoided humans and forest people alike. Winters passed as she shunned all company. In her grief and loneliness, she fashioned a little figure of her mother out of wood and decorated it with flowers and moss. Then she made a likeness of everyone from her family and placed them in a circle in a clearing.

It was difficult at first to shape the wood with nothing but her own hard fingers, but she made sharper tools from flint. When a tinker carrying his pack of wares crossed her path, she pierced his heart with a tendril and took his tools. With them, her work became more precise, more detailed, and she made new likenesses of her mother and the others, leaving them in a stone circle on a remote hillside.

One day, another of her kind approached her. She'd become so wild, she'd almost forgotten how to speak. He stayed with her until she remembered. She learned that humans had multiplied again, pushing their people into more remote areas and cutting trees to make room for their livestock and crops. He urged her to go with him further north. Having no particular attachment to this bit of land, she followed him.

On midsummer's eve, they entered a grove far from human habitation. She danced for the first time in many years. The steps brought memories that she couldn't contain, and she fell to the ground. The others gathered around and heard her story, weeping with her.

For a time, she lived among them, sharing her life with Ausillanithes, who had found her. Humans encroached deeper into the wilderness. The tree kin she lived with drifted away as the years passed, and fewer and fewer of her people danced at midsummer. One spring, Ausillanithes did not wake, leaving her bereft. She began making little dolls of flowers, wood, and grass to remember her people again, leaving them like memories or offerings. When she was the only one left to dance, she walked away, drifting across the landscape like a ghost in her own world, hoping she would just drift away like mist.

At last, she took refuge in an old copper beech tree near the top of a craggy hill. Winters came and went, and she made her figures out of beech and flowers and moss, remembering her people. She never strayed far, even on midsummer nights. The tree grew around her until she became too stiff to carve on her own any longer. Through the network of trees, she felt the edges of this forest dying as humans cut the trees to make way for yet more pasture. If she could have walked into the mist and dispersed, she would have, but her body had merged with the tree. If it died, she shared its fate.

One bitterly raw day, as her consciousness was slipping from wakeful to hibernating, the sound of crying roused her. Extending her awareness, she saw a young girl enter her clearing. Lost and cold, the little girl hunched down at the base of the old beech tree. A memory of a long ago little girl made Hhth-fehrtessen extend her energy enough to envelop the child in a pocket of slightly warmer air. The night passed and the girl slept. Hhthfehrtessen felt the human life ebbing slowly. Then a man emerged from the trees. She would have ignored him, but he caught her attention. Dressed in ill fitting clothing, he wore a knit cap and heavy boots. His aura shone with a bright, clean yellow-green.

When he looked at her tree, he saw not just her body, but her. When he touched her bark, she felt the power of his creative being, and she spoke to a human for the first time in centuries. She offered him a bargain. He offered her a renewal of life and purpose.

In a rush, Ruari saw his great-grandfather's life, then his grandfather's life shared with this fey being, and he understood.

When Marianne returned from the cemetery, Ruari was awake. He looked better, if not well rested.

"Hey, how are you feeling?" She asked, happy to see he'd put his clean shirt on..

He flexed his right arm absently, opening and closing his fist.

"Better. The tingling is mostly gone." He gave her a wondering look. "I had the most incredible dream."

He looked happy about it rather than worried, so she relaxed a little. She tucked her feet under her in the easy chair across from him. "Did you dream of the tree woman again?"

He nodded. "Last night, when this first happened, it was a little after midnight, but you said it was four in the morning when you let me in. I've been trying to figure out what happened to the time in between. I remember pulling over a couple of times on the way over, and I think I dreamed of her then. But it was on high speed, and I couldn't process it. When I fell asleep this morning, it was like my brain unpacked it and showed me again at normal speed."

"What was it about?"

He chose his words carefully. "It was like a National Geographic special about the last ten-thousand years woven into a very personal movie. I'm guessing she and her ancestors have been alive since the end of the glaciers."

"The fey woman is 14,000 years old?" Marianne goggled.

"Her mother certainly was. The one I know was born—made? —some time after that." He made an impatient gesture. "You're a historian, I wish you could have seen it! You'd know exactly when things happened."

"Maybe. Tell me from the beginning."

He backed up to when he'd walked out of the studio and into the cold breeze of the last glacial times. She listened raptly, asking occasional questions for clarification. As far as she could tell, the tree woman's people had befriended the Neanderthals, planted the forests of Britain, and witnessed the arrival of the Cro-Magnon people. They'd seen the last flooding of the English Channel, cutting them off from the continent, and died at the hands of fearful settlers in the Neolithic. The fey woman herself had come into being some time in the last 1,500 years.

"That is amazing," she said with a sigh, sitting back in the chair and feeling a little envious. "What do you think it means?"

"I think she's dying," he said slowly.

"If her tree was hit by lightning, that would make sense."

He looked down, fiddled with the edge of the blanket, and then looked back at her. "I want to go to Scotland and find her."

Surprised, she burst out, "Why? You remember she was trying to put a spell on you, right?"

He winced. "Yes, I've thought about this since I woke up. I don't have all the pieces, but I think I understand her better."

Recalling something he'd said to her not too long ago, she said, "Is this really your job?"

He stared at her with a wry twitch of his lips. "Yes, I think so. My Granda pushed his family away because she demanded so much from him. He became her family. Now, she's dying after such a long life. If he were there, he wouldn't let her die alone. She has no one else."

"Are you sure? She would have enslaved you without a second thought."

"I know. But she can't now. I'm pretty sure."

Marianne felt a deep chill. "That mark she gave you," she gestured at his shoulder, "it made your connection strong enough to let you see her memories. What will happen to you, if she dies? Can she take you with her?"

He looked startled. Clearly that hadn't occurred to him. "I don't know. I sure hope not." He gave her a wan smile. "I guess that's another reason to go. See if I can get free, maybe?"

She gave a short nod. "Okay, then I'm in. I'm coming with you."

His eyes widened. "You don't have to."

She set her jaw, feeling her new stubbornness rise up. "You stood by me when my ex came back."

"This is way more than that."

"If you think I'm going to sit around, wondering if you're dead or not, you're wrong." She fixed him with a bright, slightly manic smile. "I've always wanted to go to Scotland. Now's as good a time as any. Maybe I'll even get to meet a person who's 1,500 years old!"

He gave her an answering smile, and let out a breath. "I look forward to showing you Cold Burn Farm, then."

"Cold Burn? That sounds like an oxymoron."

He grinned. " 'Burn' means stream. It's named after the cold stream that brought water to the farm when my great-granda built the house."

CHAPTER 14

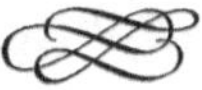

The following day was Sunday, and Ruari went back to his own apartment to take care of some things before their trip. Marianne had offered to book the tickets and arrange for them to get to the airport. It was a bonus that he would sleep in his own bed. Two nights on Marianne's couch had given him a crick in his back.

His cell phone rang while he was cleaning up the studio. He glanced at the ID and saw his parents' number. Tempted to let it go to voice mail, he answered to get it over with. "Ruari Allen."

"Ruari, it's Dad."

"Hi, Dad," he answered cautiously. It had been several weeks since the argument on Labor Day, and Ruari had been glad of the distance with everything else going on in his life. Was he calling to apologize?

"Son, I was wondering if you could come to dinner tomorrow night. Your mother is baking a chicken and putting on all the trimmings, and we'd like to have you come by."

So, they were pretending nothing had happened. Okay. They'd been doing that for long enough that he could manage. "Is this about a job or something?"

"No. There have been some developments on the family farm in Scotland."

Ruari felt his stomach lurch. This couldn't be a coincidence. Had the tree woman somehow affected his family? "Is everything okay there? Is everyone alright?"

"They're all fine. They want to have a family meeting as soon as possible, and I wanted to ask if you would be willing to go and represent our branch of the family. Work is very hectic for me right now, and I can't go."

Maybe the universe was giving him the break he needed. "Yeah, Dad," he said slowly. "I can do that. What's this all about?"

"We can talk tomorrow. See you at dinner around six."

"I'll be there." He considered asking if Marianne could join them, but decided against it. This sounded like an Allen family thing.

Ruari's thoughts jumped from one set of tracks onto another. No one from his family had been to Scotland since Granda died. It must be serious if they were asking Dad to join a family meeting. Were they going to sell the farm to people who would cut the trees down and develop it? What if the fey woman's tree was cut down? That would accelerate her fate from its slow, natural death.

He went upstairs to pack. As he threw things into a duffel, he called Marianne.

"Hey, there," she answered on the second ring. "I got two tickets for the red-eye flight on Tuesday to Edinburgh. We'll get there early on Wednesday morning. That was the soonest I could get us there."

"That's perfect. There's been a new development." He told her about the call from Dad.

"That's an odd coincidence."

"No kidding. I'll find out what's going on. I hope you don't mind meeting my relatives?"

"Don't worry about me, I'll be fine."

Something in her tone made him hesitate. "They're nice people. You'll like them," he assured her.

"I look forward to meeting them, then."

He hung up after a couple more minutes and wondered what he was going to tell Talmadge.

Monday, Marianne put the plane tickets on the dining room table where all the things she wanted to take were slowly accumulating. She made arrangements with the next door neighbors to feed Oscar while she was away for ten days and tried to straighten all her research piles into something less chaotic.

That threw her into fretful worry about Dr. Plank. What if he tried to call her while she was away? Maybe she should be brave and send Dr. Plank another polite follow up email? No, it was time for decisive action.

She dialed the history department at Park University and left a message with the administrative assistant. Hands shaking slightly, she put the phone down and directed her attention to packing.

Some thirty minutes later, her phone rang. It was an unfamiliar New York number but the exchange was Park University. Heart thudding again, she answered.

"Hello?"

"Is this Dr. Singleton?" The voice was male, educated, unfamiliar.

"Yes, this is she."

"This is Dr. Plank."

"Hello! Thank you for getting back to me."

"Yes. Thank you for your sample lectures."

"Of course. I can fill them out and expand on them further if you need me to. I have a full list of the topics I plan to cover and..."

"No, this is quite enough for me to see your thinking." There was no hesitancy in his voice. She held her breath. "Dr. Singleton," he emphasized her title slightly, "you must know that Park University is dedicated to a tradition of rigorous intellectual education."

"Of course, your history department is highly respected."

"I'm afraid that the material you sent me would be better suited to a community college level where the students were… less serious. Your slide shows are a bit too high school."

Her heart sank. "But this is a 200-level class that needs to be accessible both to majors and to people who are only taking history to fulfill a requirement. The slides are for the visual learners in the class."

"At the college level, students need to learn how to take notes from lectures. This is not the History Channel. I'm surprised Dr. Braithwaite submitted your class topic."

"These are only the opening three lectures. I could make the rest more challenging. I really want to teach. Please give me another chance." She hated the pleading tone in her voice. *Did you mean you were surprised Gillian suggested me as a teacher?*

He paused, then said coolly, "If you want to resubmit them for reevaluation, you have two weeks." She heard his unspoken skepticism.

Feeling awful, she said woodenly, "Thank you for getting back to me, Dr. Plank. I'll consider it."

"Good bye."

That was that. She stared at her half-full suitcase, unseeing. She could scramble to restructure the lectures and resubmit them, but he was already predisposed to say no. It would likely be a lot of wasted effort on her part. If she got in, she'd have to work every minute to please him. Did she really want to teach in his department that badly? Why had Gillian told her to dumb her material down?

She wrote her colleague an email, explaining the situation and hit send. She didn't accuse her of anything and stayed polite.

The lump in her throat was part humiliation and part panic. Teaching history had been her best hope for a steady income. Her ex had hidden a majority of his six-figure income with the help of a savvy lawyer, and she hadn't gotten that much in the divorce settlement. If she didn't teach in the city, where would she go? Her rent was deeply discounted in exchange for painting the interior and getting the yard in shape. But she still had to eat and pay utilities. Those tickets to Scotland suddenly felt very expensive.

She gulped. There would be plenty of time to worry about that when she got back. Ruari's situation was more pressing and, besides, maybe something would turn up in the meantime.

Ruari arrived early at work the day after Dad's call and informed his boss that there had been a family emergency in Scotland, and he had to go as soon as possible. He'd spent part of the night thinking of how he was going to do it before falling into an uneasy sleep.

Talmadge wasn't pleased at all, but he explained, "Casey's been a decent student and has a grasp of the basics. I think he can manage for a week or ten days if you just give him a chance. Save all the hard stuff for me when I get back, and I'll take care of it then." He was sure he'd be belching black smoke if he were able to see it. Assuming she couldn't, he spun his tale with as much conviction as he could.

She narrowed her eyes, and her aura flared and swirled. "Ten days?!"

He tried to remain dignified. "I have a lot of unused vacation time, and this is really important to my family. Besides, it'll be a chance for the kid to spread his wings and see how well he handles things. He'll be able to tell his parents he was in charge of the job." Appealing to her business sense had been his one stroke of brilliance in the middle of the night.

After several tense moments, she straightened some papers on her desk and told him he was going to owe her. He had known that would be the price and nodded.

When Ruari told Casey he would be handling the daily work orders solo, the young man's normally ruddy face turned pale, and he backed up a few steps. If he hadn't been up a creek, Ruari would have enjoyed Casey's sudden recognition that he was unsuited for the job.

"I can't do all this stuff by myself!" Casey blurted.

Ruari spread his fingers in a soothing gesture. "Mrs. Talmadge told me she would lighten the load and save all the hard stuff for when I get back. We can tackle it together then. You've done basic plumbing, repairs, and painting. Don't do any electricals, and you'll be fine. Besides, you'll be in charge, and your parents will be happy about that, right?"

Casey considered, his enormous ego reasserting itself like a buoy temporarily rolled by a wave, and he grinned. "Yeah, they will be! I can do this."

Ruari gave him a short list of people whom he could call as backup if needed. Then they spent the day getting the to-do list under control. Somehow, with the impending transfer of responsibility, Casey was more attentive.

Ruari arrived at his parents' place later that night feeling apprehensive. He'd spent the day wondering what the mysterious family meeting was about. It couldn't be about the fey woman because Granda had been so quiet about it no one else knew. Unless everyone but Ruari knew about her? *That was crazy.* He rubbed his shoulder absently. It had to be about the farm, but what about it?

On top of his worries about Scotland, he was hesitant about seeing Mom and Dad. Though Dad hadn't said a word about the fight on Labor Day, it had been ugly, and Ruari felt guilty about that pointed middle finger.

He walked into the delicious smells of a roasting chicken. Mom was the only one in the kitchen, and he gave her a big hug. "Hey, Mom."

She hugged him back. "Glad you could come."

He stepped back and said, "I'm sorry I haven't been by recently. And, well, just sorry."

"It's okay," she said, hugging him again. She seemed to understand what he meant.

"Thanks." Relief washed through him.

"When you get out of your jacket, will you take these things in to the table?"

Dad was in the living room watching a football game. A quick glance told Ruari neither team was his Dad's. Mom called dinner a few minutes later. Erin emerged from her room in a subdued blue sweatshirt and jeans. Her short, red hair lay flat. They all sat, and Ruari had an odd moment of familiarity. They'd all sat in the same seats since he was a kid. It struck him as weird: they were all adults, and his parents' hair was graying. *It won't be like this forever. There will come a day when we won't be able to sit like this, ever again. Like Granda.* He took a serving of meat and potatoes and let the odd mood go.

After everyone had enough, Dad announced that he'd made a second call to his brother Fergus. "After you and I talked yesterday, Ruari, I let them know you would be there in my place."

Ruari's anxiety returned in a rush. "Do you know what they want to talk about?"

"The farmhouse is empty at the moment. Your uncles Fergus and Reggie have been doing the basic maintenance and paying the taxes, and your mother and I have chipped in financially each year, but they're having a hard time. They've been talking about selling some of our parents' land and using the money to pay the bills."

"That's a bummer," Erin said. "I really miss going."

"I'll grant it was fun for you all to visit as kids, but what with the bills and repairs and long distance, I'd just as soon sell the whole thing. I think Reggie is of the same opinion."

"What do the cousins say?" Erin asked.

"They're more inclined to keep it," he acknowledged reluctantly. "Mary's in real estate and mentioned turning it into a bed and breakfast."

"What about a limited liability corporation? I could help with that," she offered eagerly.

"I don't know the first thing about how to do that in the UK," Dad admitted.

She grinned. "That's what Google's for! I'll work on it."

"Either way, I don't want it to continue to be a drain financially. If you and Ruari want to keep it, you're welcome to the bills." He looked at them pointedly.

Erin nodded, and Ruari said, "Understood."

Ruari would have to act fast. Find the fey's tree, if it existed, find her, and then deal with her. If the family sold the land, it would be that much harder. And if they sold it, there was a chance it would be developed. But who knew if or when that might happen. "When exactly is the meeting?"

"This coming weekend. Your mother and I can help with the plane ticket since it's such short notice and family business."

"Thanks for the offer. I went ahead and got a ticket after we talked. I've been wanting to see the old place again. I got some time off at work. No worries, Dad. I'll go to the meeting. I'm glad to do it." He caught Mom's pointed look across the table to Dad. It held a whole silent conversation. Dad cleared his throat, looking a little uncomfortable.

Ruari tensed. *Now what?*

"In his will, Da gave Reggie, Fergus, and me the land. The house and barn and a couple of acres around it are jointly owned, but each of us got some acreage. Reggie and Fergus both got acreage next to the farm that included pasture and woods. Da gave me a parcel that was way up the hill on a rocky, wooded slope. I guess it was understandable, since they live near the farm and are more likely to have use of it." He sounded unhappy about it.

Ruari's mouthful of potato suddenly felt tasteless. *Where are you going with this?*

"What didn't make sense," Dad continued, "was in a separate, sealed letter Da asked me to give you the wooded parcel. I meant to give it to you when he died, but kind of forgot in all the shuffle." He pulled a worn envelope out of his pocket and laid it on the table before passing it to Ruari.

You mean after you smashed the box? The thought flashed across Ruari's mind, jostling the lid on his old anger. He tamped it firmly down and slid his finger under the flap. There was a single sheet of paper inside. It was typed up on an Edinburgh barrister's letterhead stationery, signed and dated just weeks before Ruari and family had visited him that summer for the last time.

Dear Ruari,

I, Coll Allen, being of sound mind and body, give to you the parcel of land at the top of the hill in perpetuity. It is for you to keep and care for as long as you may.

Erin burst out, "What? Why would Granda do that? Did he leave me something?"

Dad shook his head. "I don't know why. I'm pretty sure he didn't ask Fergus or Reggie to give their parcels to their children. And, no, there was nothing for you."

Ruari let out his breath. "Did he tell you why?" His voice came out surprisingly calm.

"I wondered if you could enlighten me." Dad gave him a sharp look.

Ruari shook his head. "I don't know." But he had his suspicions. Had Granda been planning for Ruari to make a new bargain with the fey? Had he known the fey woman would want to take over Ruari's life? Had he set Ruari up? He cleared his throat. "Have you been up there?"

A muscle twitched in Dad's jaw as he clenched and unclenched it. "Just trees and rocks. I don't think you can build on it, particularly if there's no access. I'm pretty sure there is nothing of value on it."

"Maybe it's a wood carver thing," Erin offered.

"Aye, maybe that's it." Dad muttered, "Da was a daft old bugger at the end of his life." He cleared his throat and said more clearly. "Take that paper with you when you go. You might need it."

Ruari tucked it into his shirt pocket and felt the paper crinkle.

"Lucky you." Erin eyed him enviously.

"If it were mine," Dad resumed after Erin and Mom rose to clear the dishes, "I'd sell it. I've been paying taxes on it, and even though they aren't a lot, you probably don't want to be spending your money on something you're not likely to need or use."

Ruari felt an unexpected rush of gratitude. "Thanks for doing that, Dad. Do you want me to pay you back?"

"No. I didn't tell you it was yours, so that wouldn't very be fair." He smiled faintly. "They're yours from now on, though."

Mom quietly brought out a tray with cups of coffee, cream, and sugar. Erin must have retreated to her room.

Ruari stirred a generous dollop of cream into his cup. This was the best time he could think of to broach the subject. He cleared his throat.

"Mom, Dad, I want to tell you that I have a girlfriend, and she's coming with me on this trip. Her name is Marianne."

Mom smiled. "Oh, you should have brought her tonight. We'd love to meet her."

A crease appeared between Dad's brows, and he said, "Son, this is a family meeting. It isn't the best time to be introducing a new girlfriend. Why didn't you tell us before?"

Because I didn't want to deal with your reaction. "I didn't think it was appropriate to invite her to dinner tonight for just that reason. She'll be fine on her own while the meeting is going. I just wanted to show her around, see the farm. Particularly if it's the last time."

Mom said, "I'm glad you've found someone to spend time

with, Ruari. I worry about you, not finding a special someone, particularly after, you know…" she trailed off. "Be sure to bring her by when you get back!"

Dad made an effort to recover. "Yes, bring her around."

They talked further about the disposition of the family farm. Ruari caught up on some of the behind-the-scenes conversations his father and uncles had had over the last few years, and the family politics he'd missed now that he wasn't living at home. They also touched on what his parents were willing and not willing to spend money on vis-a-vis the farm.

Ruari drained the last couple of drops from his cup. "Thanks again, Dad. I'll do my best to represent our branch of the family at the meeting."

CHAPTER 15

Ruari rubbed his gritty eyes and tried to relax in the seat. The white noise of the plane's flight and the dim lights should have lulled him to sleep, but it wasn't working. Marianne had fallen asleep after take off. She looked sweet and peaceful in the twilight of the cabin. They had caught each other up on things on the ride to the airport, and he felt bad for her. Even so, it sounded like she was better off without the Plank guy anyway. He sounded like Talmadge's soul mate.

He still couldn't believe that she'd insisted on coming with him. He didn't know what would happen when he got to Scotland, or how things would play out, but he was glad she would be there. At least they wouldn't have to rent a car and drive themselves. Dad had asked Uncle Fergus to meet them.

Casey had already called in a panic earlier in the evening, and Ruari had talked him through a relatively simple repair. "But it's after five," he whined. "I'm supposed to go home at five!" *Welcome to responsibility, kiddo. Maybe Talmadge will be kinder to you than she is to me. After this, Talmadge will either beg me to come back or fire me.* He was too tired to care at the moment.

He'd done Erin a last-minute favor by checking out a small apartment over the florist shop on Main. It was a new acquisition by Gloria's Valley Homes and Properties, and Ruari knew nothing about it. He did a quick walk-through and determined that it was recently renovated and in good condition. The rent was within Erin's budget, so he gave her the thumb's up.

"Thank you!" She'd said, giving him a hug. "We're even." He smiled. "You want to pay me a finder's fee?" She laughed. "Fine, you get a free consultation next time!"

He packed lightly but warmly, placing a handful of his favorite carving tools, including his whittling knife, in his checked luggage out of habit. He'd always traveled with those essential tools, so he could work side by side when Granda showed him something new. It was more of a reflex, a security blanket, at this point. They probably would just get shuffled to the bottom of the bag with all the family stuff he had to do. He'd also tucked the blue apron-wrapped bundle of fragments from the box at the bottom of his carryon. He didn't know why. Maybe he would bury them at Granda's grave or next to the barn in Nana's garden. Maybe he'd try to glue them back together. He didn't know.

Would he be able to find the fey's tree? A part of him still wondered if it actually existed. Granda had all those photos of it, so it must be somewhere, likely on the parcel he'd willed to Ruari. The family meeting was on Saturday and Sunday, so they would have three days to find the tree, meet the fey, and figure something out. The mark on his inner right shoulder had healed to a dime-sized spiral, within a patch of reddened skin. It twinged randomly, reminding him of the link between him and the fey. Would he die or suffer some horrible fate if she died? His brain had made up all kinds of wild scenarios since Marianne had brought up that possibility. He'd shut his panic down, telling himself sternly not to borrow trouble until he knew the shape and size of it.

Ruari's brain hurt, and he finally relaxed enough to doze.

His uncle met them at the curb. Fergus' shock of dark red hair and ruddy face stood out sharply. His father, Douglas, had been less markedly Scots, and his mother's Kenny blood had softened Ruari's appearance even more. Fergus smiled widely, exposing crooked white teeth, and said, "Glad you could come, Ruari. Good to see you." He shook Marianne's hand and said, "Welcome to Scotland, Marianne."

"I'm so glad to be here." In spite of her expressed concern at meeting unknown relatives, she was gracious. She'd woken looking rested, and he envied her. His own sleep had been shallow and unsatisfying.

"Aye, thank you for getting us, Uncle Fergus. I would have been an accident on wheels if I had to drive." It was easy to slip back into the sounds of his youth.

Fergus laughed. "Rest and I'll catch you up on all the doings."

The buildings and traffic of Edinburgh give way to green countryside as Ruari listened to all the news about the cousins and their young families. Part of him slipped back into memories of this drive when he was little with Granda at the wheel. The towns they passed through were a little more built up since then, but much of the drive featured the same beautiful countryside. Marianne looked out the window with interest and made polite conversation.

Fergus apologized for not being able to put them up at his house, but his youngest son still lived at home, and his other two children had come home for the family meeting. Aunt Maura had filled the old farm fridge with breakfast items and invited them to have dinners with them. Uncle Reggie and Aunt Maggie lived a little farther away but also had a full house. Ruari assured him they didn't mind and looked forward to spending time at the old place again.

They finally pulled into the gravel drive a little before eleven. Ruari pulled his duffel and carryon out of the trunk and set them on the gravel drive. Together, he and Fergus pulled Marianne's considerably larger suitcase out.

"Thank you, Uncle Fergus. It's grand to see you again." Ruari gave him another hug.

"Likewise. I'll come for you around five. Maura'll have dinner for us all."

The farmhouse nestled at the base of a forested hillside, stretching up toward a blue sky. The white paint on the clapboard walls and stone foundation needed a fresh coat, but the peaked slate roof still looked tight to Ruari's eye. The building's squat, sturdy presence had stood for generations and outlasted many storms. To the left of the house, a stacked stone fence blotched with lichen enclosed a grassy yard. It looked empty without a couple of shaggy red cows and the old horse. To the right, the gravel drive led past the house to the looming shape of a two-story, weathered wooden barn.

"Ruari, it's beautiful!" Marianne said delightedly.

He smiled. "Welcome to Cold Burn Farm."

Ruari picked up his bags, and she pulled out the extendable handle on hers. Fergus had reminded him where the key was hidden, so the lock yielded to his touch.

Stepping into the old farmhouse was like stepping back in time. Little had changed. He half expected to see his sturdy Nana at the kitchen sink in her old boots, trimming flowers to put around the house. At this time of day, Granda worked in his wood shop or did chores around the place to keep it running. Remembered shouts and laughter of his cousins made it feel even quieter. Faint smells of cooking, old carpet, wool, wood, and Nana's dusty, sweet perfume brought a lump to his throat. He swallowed hard.

Nana, Granda, I'm home.

Marianne glanced at him and squeezed his hand. Her stomach growled audibly in the silence. "I think my peanuts and pretzels ran out," she said with a laugh.

"Let's stay in the little room off the kitchen. That way we don't have to haul your bag up the stairs to the attic."

"Sounds good. Do you mind if I look for the food your Aunt and Uncle left?"

"Not at all."

The kitchen was spotlessly clean. The counter tops, sink, and stove lined the back wall of the house under a long set of windows. Wooden cupboards built by Granda and his father supported the counter and filled the adjacent wall next to the old refrigerator. The passage of feet had worn the floor slates smooth in front of the sink and by the backdoor. A single small room lay behind a door next to the fridge. The full-sized bed practically filled it, leaving just enough room for a tiny side table, a chair, and a wardrobe. It hadn't changed a bit since he'd been there last.

He dropped his bags on the bed and left hers standing near the door.

The fridge contained a small package of sausages wrapped in brown paper, a quart of milk, butter, and a loaf of bread. Marianne fell on them like a starving wolf and put a couple of sausages on to fry. The cupboards were largely empty except for mouse and insect repellent tucked here and there. No coffee, but they found a half empty box of Brodie's tea bags and put the kettle on.

"Go look around," she said. "I'll take care of this."

Wordlessly he hugged her and indulged the pull of the past. Next to the back door, Granda's old plaid work shirt and a faded yellow apron hung on a short row of pegs. The slate floor transitioned to wide wood planks in the living room. A couple of old couches with a faded orange, gold, and green floral print brought back memories of sitting tucked against Nana's ample side or playing cards and checkers with Erin.

A large stone fireplace and chimney with a raised hearthstone dominated the room. Granda had painstakingly fitted shelves beside the irregular stone chimney on both sides. They held a collection of dusty books interspersed with shells, stones, pieces of curiously shaped wood, carvings of animals, and small, inlaid boxes. A beautiful wooden chest stood to one side, and Ruari felt a jolt when he saw the intricately carved motif of animals and leaves. He'd never registered on it before. The muse had been carving animals for a very long time. She'd refined her ideas and technique, though. The designs on the box were more like bas relief and less like the three-dimensional picture he'd created.

I wish you'd said something, Granda. Mentioned her. Anything.

He walked through the living room and out into the foyer. Across the hall from the living room the door to Granda's and Nana's bedroom stood open. Two closed doors faced the front door. One led to a small basement that had once been a root cellar but now housed the huge, ancient boiler and a small water heater. Modern conveniences Granda had installed for Nana's benefit when their children were young. The other hid the stairs to the attic. That space had been redone to house three rambunctious boys in their youth and later a passel of cousins when they came to visit. Everywhere he looked were signs of age and neglect. He couldn't help making lists of repairs in his head.

A powerful aroma of burning bread permeated the air along with a string of muffled curses. He'd forgotten to tell Marianne you had to watch the treacherous old toaster like a hawk or it would take its toll in blackened bread.

"Everything okay?" He called.

"As long as you like your toast really dark."

He laughed. "Sorry, I forgot to tell you about Old Scorch."

She made a noise of exasperation, and he heard the frying pan scrape across the stove burner. "No, no, it's all good."

He opened the door to the attic and walked up the narrow stairs that were so steep they were more like a ladder. At the top, the attic room was dim under the sloped roof. A trio of metal framed twin beds lined up under the two dormer windows on the south side. They had bright handmade quilts on them. He and Erin had vied for who got to sleep under the one with the sheep or the one with the chickens. He crossed the floor and looked out the window over the back yard.

Nana's flower and vegetable gardens were all overgrown.

Someone had tried to tidy the worst of it up, maybe cousin Mary or Aunt Maura in her spare time. The paths between the beds were a mixture of pebbles and bits of seashells. Granda's big old barn loomed silently over everything.

Ruari's body felt heavy with fatigue. The trip and anxiety were taking their toll. He descended the stairs and joined Marianne at the wooden kitchen table. She'd put together a good meal, and he ate hungrily.

"You look like you could use a nap," she observed when he was done.

"Yeah. I'm sorry. I feel like I'm abandoning you."

She smiled. "Don't worry. I'd love a tour later. Go get some sleep."

He lay down on the spare bed fully clothed, his body gravitating toward the divot in the middle. Sleep overwhelmed him.

Ruari surfaced groggily from a sound sleep. He felt a warm weight behind him. Was that—? A soft noise of protest greeted his roll onto his back.

"Mmm, sorry," Marianne said. Her tousled brown hair tickled his cheek. "You looked so comfortable. I only meant to close my eyes for a moment."

"No, it's fine. How long have I been out?" He was aware of her hips and breasts resting against his body and felt a nudge of desire send a warm pulse through his own body. Maybe they had some time to explore the possibilities.

"I don't know," she murmured. "An hour maybe. It's dark out."

Suddenly the light turned on, making them blink. A jovial voice said, "Ruari! Oh damn! Sorry, sorry! Da didn't tell me you'd brought someone."

"Donal?" Ruari peered up, identifying the voice. A tall man about his age with a thick head of auburn hair peered in at him from the doorway. His crooked grin pegged him as Fergus' son.

"Donal!" Ruari scooted to the foot of the bed and stood up to give his cousin a bear hug. "So good to see you!"

Donal had seemed so much older when they were kids. Being invited to go out with Donal and his friends had been Ruari's greatest desire. Now Donal had a wife and two kids. He was still way ahead of Ruari.

He held out his hand. "Um, this is Marianne, my girlfriend. Marianne, this is my cousin Donal, Fergus' son."

Marianne stood and offered her hand, and Donal shook it enthusiastically. "Nice to meet you, Donal."

Donal grinned again. "A pleasure. Tatties and neeps time. Mam'll be mad if we let it get cold."

"Give me a sec." Marianne disappeared around the corner.

"She's a bonnie lass," Donal commented. "Sorry about interrupting your wee coorie," he added.

"No worries. We're both jet lagged and trying to get into the right time zone."

Marianne came back with her hair neatly brushed and her clothes straightened. They grabbed their jackets and got into the little green Mini parked in the drive. Donal chatted happily about his family on the way to Uncle Fergus' house. The drive passed quickly, and the car soon pulled into a suburban neighborhood of identical detached and semi-detached homes with small lawns.

The house was full of people, and the large forms of two border collie mixes added to the noise and chaos. Ruari greeted his Aunt Maura, Donal's wife Alleen, and two young children. Newly married and pregnant, Donal's sister Mary stood with her husband Tomas, a short, fair-haired, soft-spoken man. Donal's younger brother Gerald still lived at home while he completed his schooling. Chewie and Leia, the dogs, swirled around everyone's legs.

Marianne hung back feeling shy. He put his arm around her waist and pulled her close to him, introducing her to everyone. She smiled and shook hands, staying close to him.

Soon after their arrival, everyone sat down at the table. A big ham with three side dishes, rolls, and salad graced the table. Uncle Fergus asked Ruari if he'd gotten a rest that afternoon.

"Aye, slept like a log."

"Excellent. How's your family?"

Ruari gave them an update on everyone. Food and drink flowed around the table as everyone noisily talked about work and events of the day. The children were in the Scots equivalent of kindergarten and first grade. They gave the newcomers shy glances and said little.

After dinner, Ruari offered to help clear the table.

"Get along with you, Ruari," Aunt Maura said. "We'll get that. Fergus wants to see you."

"I'll help," Marianne offered.

He gave her a look that asked, *you'll be okay?* And she nodded slightly. Aloud he said to Maura, "Thank you for stocking the fridge. We'd have starved if you hadn't!"

She gave him a pat on the shoulder and smiled. "Can't be having that."

Uncle Fergus invited Ruari into the den to have a little scotch.

"Ruari, it's been a while since you were here last. I didn't ask you before: how have you been?"

"Can't complain. I'm still making repairs and fixing leaks for the realty agency, but it pays the bills."

"Are you still single-handed then?"

"Nay, I got an assistant recently. Now, both my hands are tied behind my back 'cause both of his feet might as well be in a bucket."

His uncle chuckled. "Well, mayhap he'll learn something in time. I'm sorry Douglas couldn't come, but I'm not surprised." He sounded regretful. Fergus proceeded to confirm most of Ruari's family scuttlebutt and filled in the gaps in Dad's knowledge.

When the clock on the mantlepiece chimed ten, Ruari couldn't stifle his yawns any longer. He made his farewells to each of his cousins, aunt, and uncle. He loved seeing them all again, but it felt very strange to be part of making such momentous decisions. Such matters had always been left to Dad and his generation. He was honored they'd included him and hoped the letter he carried would not wrong-foot them too badly. Somehow, he hadn't gotten around to sharing it with them, even though it lay in his breast pocket. He told himself he wanted to see the parcel first.

He stepped into the living room and saw Marianne reading a book. She rose and put it back on the shelf. Aunt Maura had to teach in the morning and had already excused herself.

"You going to be alright before then?" Donal asked as they drove back to the farm through the dark. "You're both welcome to spend the day with the family if you want. Get to know your little cousins."

It was tempting. It would certainly be more fun than confronting a powerful fey being on her own turf, but he couldn't enjoy the family until that was settled. "I appreciate the offer, but we need a little time at the farm. Another time?"

"Sure."

After the noise and fuss at Fergus and Maura's, the silence of the farmhouse was heavy. Ruari roamed from room to room, unable to settle.

"I know it's late, but do you want to give me a tour?" Marianne asked, watching him. "My nap earlier kind of wrecked my ability to sleep for now."

"Sure." He showed her all the rooms inside.

"Your grandmother was an amazing quilter," she said, running her hand over the fine stitching on the comforter in the main bedroom. The design was one of interlocking Celtic rings in blue, white, and gold scraps. It reminded him of the pattern he'd done for the lazy Susan. "I don't really craft anything," she added. "Too busy reading books, I guess. But I appreciate other people's handiwork."

"Nana sewed, crocheted, knitted, gardened, and I don't know what else. She was as creative as Granda was, in her own way."

The tour took all of half an hour, and Ruari still felt restless. "I'm going to go look in the barn. You want to come?"

"Sure." She shrugged into her warm jacket again while he got the big flashlight out of the kitchen drawer and searched the other drawers until he found the old fashioned key to the barn.

They walked up in the cold darkness, feet crunching on the gravel and shell path. The air smelled like rain was coming. He could see his breath in the beam of light as he fumbled the lock open and slipped inside.

The master switch flipped with a heavy clunk. The lights came on, and he stood looking around. Very little had changed since the wake three years ago. There were now some boxes of random things on the work bench nearest the door. Someone had put a couple of broken chairs on a table in the middle of the room awaiting repair or the trash. Granda's tools hung neatly on their pegs, and a couple of rows of pale, photo-sized rectangles graced the wall near the old wood stove.

He remembered his furious effort to put all of Granda's materials away neatly into the loft. He looked at the rows of carved faces on the shelves and had a shock.

"Oh," he breathed. That's where he'd seen the fey's family before. Granda had carved all of them. Her mother, her aunts and uncles and kin, for want of a better word for the people who had breathed life into her. The Old Man of the Forest who still looked fierce even though Ruari was no longer five. She remembered them all and still grieved them. His throat felt strangely tight.

"What's the matter?" Marianne asked.

He gestured at the carved portraits and swallowed hard. "That's her family."

She looked at them with a keener interest. "The fey woman's? Are they the ones who died?"

He nodded. Their names were on the tip of his tongue even if he couldn't pronounce them. At least Mary and Maura hadn't followed through on their threat to put them on Etsy or Ebay yet. He couldn't let them be sold, though he didn't know what to do with them instead.

He tore his gaze away and continued walking through the old studio. Everything brought some kind of memory. Marianne believed in ghosts. She'd said the spirits of relatives hovered over their living kin or lingered if they had unfinished business. Maybe Granda was still around.

"Granda, are you here?" He said into the thick silence. "Dad finally gave me your letter. Any chance you could show me where that land is?"

There was no answer. He glanced at Marianne, but she shook her head.

"I'm cold. I'll see you back in the house," she said. She squeezed his arm and left.

Ruari roamed the shop restlessly. "Why did you never tell me about her?" He asked the empty space. He tried a different tack. "I'm sorry about the box, Granda. I haven't been able to fix it yet. Maybe I can do that while I'm here."

Again, there was no answer. He sighed. The farm was thirty plus acres of hilly, forested land with a handful of grassy pastures near the road and house. The rest of it was pretty wild. He'd thought he'd been over every inch of it as a kid, but he'd never seen a massive old copper beech in a clearing. Disappointed that Granda hadn't given him a sign, he murmured, "Well, wish me luck finding it tomorrow."

He went to the odds and sods box of wood scraps. They were often destined to stoke the firebox in the workshop, but sometimes served as scraps to test ideas on. He found a dusty piece of maple the size of two fists and tucked it into his jacket pocket, then turned the lights out and returned to the house.

Marianne had crawled under the covers in the little full-sized bed they'd napped on earlier. She looked up sleepily.

"I'm going to stay up for a bit longer," he told her. "Go back to sleep."

She murmured assent and put her head down again.

He sat on the end of the couch near the fireplace and idly whittled.

We have to talk, Lady Muse. How do I find you? What happened to you? What's going to happen to me?

He let his mind wander as his hands shaved bits of wood off with his knife, trying to get into the zone and invite her into his head. But he remained stubbornly alert, aware of his surroundings. After an hour, he gave up and set the wood aside. He contemplated joining Marianne in the little side room. She had joined him earlier. But she had been so clear about her boundaries in Maple Hill that he didn't want to presume. It was clear that her ex had been horrible to her, and she needed to make up her own mind in her own time. Anyway, he was too exhausted to pursue a simple hug much less hanky-panky.

He pulled a quilt over him and lay his head on the arm of the couch.

CHAPTER 16

Ruari awoke to the smell of cooking food. He opened his eyes muzzily and saw Marianne standing in the kitchen wearing a long green sweater over thick leggings. Her hair was pulled out of her face with a big clip, leaving little bits sticking up in all directions. He smiled and rubbed his face.

"Hey, there," she called. "I'm glad you got some sleep. Breakfast is nearly ready. You're stuck with tea again until we find some coffee."

He pushed the blanket back and stretched the kinks out of his neck and back before joining her.

"You sleep okay?" He asked.

She nodded. "I figured you needed space."

"I tried reaching her last night, but no go."

She served up sausages and toast with two mugs of tea. "Do you think she's gone already?"

"I don't know. I think we should try and find her tree and the mysterious parcel today."

"I brought good shoes for that."

"I hope you brought rain gear too. It smelled like rain last night."

"I hate being cold, so I brought lots of warm things. By the way," she pulled a little cloth bag out of her pocket. A long ribbon cinched the top closed. "You used up the last charm I gave you, so I made another. Just in case." She put it over his head and straightened it so it lay on his chest.

"I hope I won't need it," he said, though he was grateful to have it.

After breakfast, he pulled on a flannel shirt over his T-shirt and found the sweater in the cedar-lined wardrobe that he used when he visited. Thankfully, no one had cleared it out. Made of rough, dark brown wool, nubbly with cables, it was like wearing a heavy old bear skin and was about as impervious to the cold. It smelled faintly of mothballs, sheep, and wood smoke. Marianne looked like she was ready for a mountain trek in winter with a puffy jacket and a wool hat. She smiled gamely and followed him out of the little farm yard and up the hillside into the trees.

It was a dreich day. The leaden gray sky didn't lighten much, and the air smelled heavy with moisture. Wind fluttered the grass and fallen leaves fitfully. Good old Scots weather. Dinner conversation the previous night had included comments about the recent wild storm that had knocked power out and downed trees in heavy winds. A smaller storm was threatening to follow up today and tomorrow though it wasn't supposed to be as damaging.

They rambled through the fields, following the old stone boundary walls into the oak and birch trees, and up the slope of the big ridge behind the farmhouse. Memories of summertime exploration with Seamus and Donal made him smile.

He regaled her with stories when they stopped to catch their breath. Here was the outcrop where Seamus, younger and wilder than Donal, had jumped them. Here was the little stream where they'd cooled off. It had a pool heavy with decayed leaves that they'd flung at each other in wild abandon. Here was the upper pasture where the old red bull had chased them.

Marianne laughed and said wistfully, "I wish I'd had cousins to knock about with. You're lucky you have such a nice extended family. I'm an only child and both my parents were only children. Makes for a pretty thin family tree. By the way, I really enjoyed meeting your aunt and uncle last night." She sounded pleasantly surprised.

"I'm glad you like them."

"They're nothing like Geoffrey's family who, quite frankly, never liked me or my mom. Strangely enough, I don't think they liked each other very much either. Always suspicious, wondering what was going on behind their backs. A pretty miserable lot."

Ruari couldn't imagine being part of a family that actively distrusted and disliked each other. He had his disagreements with Dad. Except for the broken box, he felt like Dad cared for him but just didn't know how to express it. He pulled the tartan cap off and ran his fingers through his hair. He hoped he would make a better dad some day.

"I'm sorry you had to deal with that," he said.

She shrugged. "I didn't realize how bad it was until I divorced Geoffrey and got out from under them. I could never go back to something like that."

"I hope you never have to."

They continued their climb through oak, rowan, birch, and hazel in their fall colors of yellow, gold, orange, and red, following the stone wall. They paused at the boundary of the neighbor's farm. The wooden staircase stile over the top had badly rotted steps. Round bales of hay lay stacked in the distance. The old field building at the far end had finally fallen in. He recalled sneaking over the fence to play in the abandoned structure. Out in the open, the wind had a cutting edge to it and carried a splatter of rain. Between the impenetrable sweater and the cap, he was over heating. The cold rain felt good on his cheeks. Marianne's face was flushed with exertion, and she'd unzipped her coat. She grinned at him.

The stone border ran up the hill into the trees again, and they climbed, grateful for shelter under the oaks. After another hour of criss-crossing the slope, they reached the crest and walked along the spine with no sign of the mysterious parcel. He'd seen beech trees but none like the photos in his studio. They followed a boundary fence that was a newer combination of field stone and wooden posts, and he guessed they were at the farthest end of the Allen property. He hoped they hadn't strayed into the neighbor's. Not that they'd care or be likely to be wandering about on a day like today. After a hundred paces, they encountered an older, more dilapidated stone wall.

"The weather seems to be turning worse, Ruari," Marianne said. "How much farther do we have to go? I also hope you know where we are because I have no idea." She looked a little worried.

He said with more confidence than he felt, "I'm pretty sure I've been up here before, but I always thought this wall belonged to someone else. What if it's the right one?"

"I'd rather not be stuck in a storm far from home."

"Let's give it one more try. If it doesn't pan out, we can bail out and go back."

"Okay."

The broken down wall angled toward a side of the hill, and they scrambled up a steep slope covered in flat stones and tree litter. Suddenly, the rise flattened out, and he lifted his eyes off the ground where he'd been watching his feet.

The trunks thinned out ahead of him. In the center of a clearing was a magnificent copper beech tree. There was no question it was her tree. The massive trunk was more than six feet in diameter and had three equally sturdy limbs. They supported the entire crown like giant flowers in an eight-foot high vase. At least, they would have before the last storm.

Lightning had struck, supercharging the moisture inside the tree, causing it to boil instantly, exploding the bark off in shards, and tearing one of the three huge limbs away from the body. It lay on the ground like a felled giant. The deep gash in the pale green, woody flesh of the tree made him wince. The roots resembled gnarled, arthritic fingers with swollen knuckles standing out above the uneven ground. He remembered lying among those roots and feeling them slither over his legs to hold him down.

He shivered. Marianne bumped into him and looked up to see why he'd stopped. "Oh," she breathed. "Is that her?"

He nodded and stepped up to the trunk. He ran his hands over the jagged break. The scar on the inside of his right shoulder prickled as he touched the peeling bark. He was not an arborist, so he thought in terms of board feet rather than tree health. All the same, he was sure that the lightning strike was its death knell. He felt bad for the tree which had to be a couple of hundred years old. The bark had been compromised, and the tree was open to destruction by insects and fungus. It might take a few years, but the old beech would surely die.

Its interior looked ordinary and solid. How would someone live inside it? He imagined underground chambers or hollow spaces within the trunk. What was the fey woman made of in the real world? Was she a physical person at all? Was she a being of energy, like a ghost maybe? It made his head hurt trying to wrap his mind around it.

Coppery brown leaves clinging to the canopy rattled in the wind, sounding like pebbles on a storm-tossed beach. The storm was going to break soon. They needed to get off the hill.

Marianne touched his arm. "You okay?"

"Just thinking. We're already halfway to the village. You want to walk the rest of the way and see it?"

"Love to!"

"It took us a lot longer to get here than I thought it would. We'll have to come back. Maybe after the family meeting is over, and we have a better idea of what my uncles want to do."

"Don't worry. I finally got a signal on my phone, so I bookmarked the location. We should be able to get back here more directly next time."

"You can do that?"

"You seriously need to enter the twenty-first century, Ruari Allen," she said with an affectionate smile. "I had enough signal to pull up a topo map for the surrounding area." She turned in place, using her phone as a compass. "I think, if we walk downhill that way, we'll catch up with the road a little faster."

They walked back the mile from the village in a blustering rain and were wet and shivering when they arrived at the farm. There was a scant forty minutes before Fergus or Donal was to pick them up for dinner. Marianne was shaking so badly she could barely undress herself. Ruari helped her skim out of the wet jacket and sweater. Her leggings presented a problem until he rolled them off her legs into a hard knot. In her skivvies with her brown hair plastered to her head, she looked beautiful, and he felt warmer than Nana's sweater alone could achieve. If only he had time to roll her in a duvet and warm her with his body heat.

"I n-need a h-hot sh-shower," she chattered.

He got the water going and found clean towels. It took all his willpower to chastely shut the door. She emerged twenty minutes later in a cloud of herbal scented steam with a towel around her rosy skin and another twirled into a turban on her head. She smiled. "Your turn."

He left a trail of wet clothes and dove into the last of the hot water. He had just enough to shave before it petered out and cooled off.

By the time he dressed in clean khakis, a button up shirt, and a light sweater, she had not only dressed but hung up their wet clothes. Nana's sweater dripped steadily into the kitchen sink from its limp place on the dish rack. He found her in the living room looking at the books on the shelves.

"Do I look alright?" She inquired a little anxiously. She wore a coffee colored blazer and trousers over a cream colored, soft sweater.

"You look gorgeous. I thought you were okay with my family?"

"I am, but I still get nervous around new people."

"You are a sweet, wonderful person." He tipped her chin up and kissed her thoroughly to make the point. The resting spark of desire flared, and he looked forward to fanning that flame later.

Donal arrived at six to pick them up. They drove through the dark, wind, and rain to Uncle Fergus's suburban neighborhood. The house was full of people again, and soon after their arrival, everyone took a seat at the table. Marianne sat between Ruari and Donal's wife Alleen. Hands passed roast lamb, skirlie, potatoes, and boiled greens around the table. Ruari caught up with Tomas and Mary while keeping an eye out for Marianne. She seemed to be holding her own and only hesitated a second before taking a slice of the unfamiliar dish.

Alleen leaned over and said, "You ever had skirlie before?"

"No." Marianne shook her head.

"Don't worry, it's not haggis! It's just oatmeal and onion. Try it with some of the lamb drippings."

Ruari smiled. *She'll be alright.*

"How do you like Scotland so far?" Fergus asked Marianne.

"It's beautiful. It's my first time here."

"Excellent! How long are you staying?"

She glanced at Ruari and hedged. "A few days. I'm hoping to get to London before we fly back, so I can visit the libraries there. I'm a historian."

"Are you now?" Maura looked up from her end of the table. "What kind of history?"

"Victorian era mostly, though I have a bit of background on the UK and Europe in general. I just moved to Maple Hill, so I'm getting to know a bit about local history too."

"I teach geography and history in the local secondary school. I think you call it middle school."

"That's brave! Middle school is such a rough time of life."

"Ach no, they just need a firm hand. Where do you work?"

"I'm between jobs for other people right now," Marianne said carefully. "I have several personal history projects that I'm pursuing, though."

"You must be very busy then," Maura said blandly, though she gave Marianne an intent look of curiosity.

"I am."

Ruari felt her shift uncomfortably in her seat next to him and searched for a diversion. "It's been really grand to stay at the farm for the last couple of days," he said. "Do you need help putting it to bed for the winter? The last big storm brought some branches down."

Fergus considered. "Aye, that would be very helpful, if you have the time."

"I'm sure we could do something," he said. Marianne nodded in agreement and gave him a grateful glance.

After dinner, Marianne offered again to pitch in to help with the cleanup, leaving Alleen free to tend to the two littlest Allens. Ruari paused before following the others into the living room. "Will you be okay?" He asked her.

Marianne nodded as Maura stepped up briskly. "Get along with you, Ruari." Maura waved him away. "Marianne'll be fine with us. Your uncle wants to see you."

He gave Marianne a peck on the cheek and departed. Fergus, Donal, Mary, and Gerald were in the living room. They settled into chairs and each one talked about what they wanted for the farmhouse and property, but there was no consensus. At the family meeting tomorrow, they'd hash out a clearer plan with Reggie's family in attendance.

"Just so's ye ken, Reggie's inclined to sell the place," Fergus informed them. The murmurs all around indicated no one was surprised.

Ruari added, "Aye, Dad would be fine letting it go as well."

"I, for one, hope we can find a way to keep it," Mary protested.

Gerald and Donal murmured in assent.

Fergus said, "Your mam and I are open to the idea, but it's expensive. We have to solve that problem. Ruari?"

Ruari's feelings were so mixed up with those about the fey that he wasn't sure what he wanted for the farm. He was uncomfortably aware of Granda's unexpected gift and didn't think the others knew. Should he tell them now? Wait till tomorrow? They all sat looking at him expectantly while he gathered his thoughts. If he didn't say something, they might be angry.

He retrieved the crumpled envelope from his shirt pocket. They watched him quizzically. "I don't quite know what to make of this. Dad handed it to me before I left." He turned over the envelope to Uncle Fergus, who put his glasses on and read it silently.

"This is unexpected," he said carefully, and passed the letter to Donal. He looked at Ruari. "Did you ken any of this before Granda passed?"

"Absolutely not! I only just found out myself."

In a couple of minutes, everyone had read it. Fergus looked like yet another spanner had been thrown in the works, and he wasn't happy about it.

Mary voiced everyone's question. "Why you? You don't even live here, if you don't mind me saying so." She sounded hurt.

Donal replied, "I bet it's the woodworking thing. you always were Granda's favorite for that reason." The hard look in his eye made Ruari flinch.

Gerald shrugged and said with a tinge of jealousy, "You're lucky. It would've been nice to get a little money for school."

"I swear I didn't know," Ruari protested. "I don't know what I'm supposed to do with it." He did, sort of. But that was not a thing he could explain.

Fergus's expression was shuttered. "Well, nothin' to be done about it now. We'd best get you back, so you can get some sleep. Donal?"

His oldest nodded, and Ruari, feeling miserable, put his jacket on and went to find Marianne. She was sitting in the dining room trying valiantly not to fall asleep. Aunt Maura and Alleen talked quietly together nearby. The children had gone to bed long ago. Tomas was watching a soccer match on TV with the sound turned way down. Ruari woke Marianne with a touch on her shoulder.

As he helped Marianne with her coat, Ruari wondered gloomily if he'd done the right thing or whether it would have been better to present it tomorrow to everyone at once. Uncle Reggie would likely be angry and aggrieved at being left out. Well, he'd join the rest of the family since they all seemed to be mad at him.

After a few minutes' driving in the dark, Donal broke the silence. "You have to understand, Ruari. We spent years helping him take care of the farm when he wasn't able. I spent hours rebuilding parts of the damn barn and house. Mam and Da went in the middle of the night to help get Nana and later Granda up when they fell. They took them to hospital when they needed it. Granda wasn't a particularly thankful person, ye ken. Then you and Erin and your family show up for two weeks in the summer, and you were the favorites. I think he smiled more in those two weeks than he did all year. You can understand how galling it is for you to be rewarded with a special present when you did nothing at all to earn it."

Ruari stifled the urge to apologize and said nothing. Donal fell silent. Marianne was stiff and alert beside him. When they arrived, she said, "Thank you for the lift, Donal."

He sounded tired when he replied, "Aye, you're welcome." He backed out of the drive before they'd gotten inside the door.

"I feel like I missed something," Marianne said as she hung up her coat.

"I told them about Granda's letter gifting me the parcel, and they were very upset."

She nodded. "Would you like a nightcap? Even after our walk today, I'm tired but kind of wired at the same time."

"Aye, that's a good idea." He poured them each a finger of

whisky, and they sat by the cold fireplace. He sipped, feeling the liquid burn down his throat, staring at an uninteresting point on the floor. "We never asked for it, you know. Granda's favor."

"Ruari," she put her hand on his knee, "it's not your fault. You and Erin were a welcome bit of sunshine in your grandparents' lives, and they showed it. It's not your fault they didn't appreciate all that Fergus' family did for them. Caregiver fatigue and resentment happens a lot. Your family wouldn't be the first."

"I've never seen Donal or Mary like that before." That's what had hurt the most. His cousins' bitterness.

"Hopefully, they'll realize that you didn't control your grandparents' behavior. It might take a little time."

He laid his head on her shoulder. "You're a wise woman, Mahri."

"Thanks. Geoffrey's family was an eye-opening experience after my small, calm family."

"How was the washing up?" He hoped she'd fared better than he had.

"Your Aunt Maura is a formidable woman." She shook her head ruefully. "She can detect a soft spot a mile off."

He looked up in alarm. "What did she say?"

"She asked a couple of key questions, and I found myself telling her and Alleen all about Dr. Plank and having no immediate job prospects. They were very sympathetic."

He closed his eyes. "Aye, she's like that." He sighed and felt himself skimming sleep.

She shifted, and he opened his eyes. "Stay there," she said. "Would you mind if I make a fire in the fireplace? It took forever last night for that little bed in the back to warm up."

He roused and sat up, watching her lay an expert fire in the grate from torn newspapers to twigs to small branches to a good-sized couple of logs. Satisfied by her construction, she fished around the chimney and found the lever for the flue.

She never ceased to amaze him. "Where did you learn to do that?"

"Girl Scouts. And my mom. It was one of the few things I did better than my ex did. It always ticked him off." She sounded right pleased.

The little fire grew into a cheery blaze and began throwing heat into the room. He made himself get up and find a couple more quilts and blankets. They wrapped up and cuddled close on the sofa. Her warm, soft body pressing against him jolted him out of his stupor.

She moved to sit on his lap and put her arms around him. The firelight turned her light brown eyes a tawny gold. She brought her lips to his in a tentative kiss. It was heaven. When he returned it in full measure, she abandoned caution and parted her lips to let her tongue explore. He held her close, feeling a bubble of happiness and desire well up inside.

She pulled back long enough to say, "I've wanted to kiss you like that for the longest time."

"Lassie," he whispered, "I've wanted to kiss you like that since the day we met."

She smiled and traced his mouth with one finger. "You have the nicest accent when you've been hanging out with your relatives."

"I don't have the knowin' o' the Gaelic, but I cannot help the accent when I'm here."

"I love it."

She leaned in for another kiss. One hand roamed over his chest and found his buttons, undoing them while the other twined in his hair. He leaned back and pulled his sweater off, and she took the opportunity to discard her jacket. The rest of their clothes soon followed. There was a brief pause when he panicked slightly, realizing he didn't have protection. She pulled a little foil envelope out of her discarded pants pocket.

"How did you—?" He was amazed all over again.

"Girl Scouts are also prepared," she chuckled throatily, "though I don't think our den mother would have approved." She paused, eyes unfocused for a moment. "On second thought, I think she would have," she amended.

The nest of blankets in front of the fire was the perfect place for lovemaking. He delighted in her soft skin and rounded curves. He was gratified by her appreciative gasps when he touched her sensitive places. She was more daring than he'd imagined she would be and lost all coherent thought after that.

They settled down afterwards into a drowsy, sated silence, bodies molded to each other. A stray thought passed through his mind before he fell asleep.

The family meeting would bring what it would bring. There was nothing he could do about it. In the meantime, he needed information that would tell him what to do about the parcel: keep it or jettison it. There was only one way to find out. The protection charm lay on the stone hearth, having been removed sometime earlier. He let himself sink into sleep.

Ruari stepped into the dreamscape of the hilltop clearing and gaped. He'd expected the tree to echo events from the waking world, but it was still a shock. The majestic beech no longer carried its robust summer finery. Instead, leaves rattled like dry husks on dead branches and littered the ground like flakes of peeling paint. The torn limb looked skeletal and dry, as if it had lain on the ground for years instead of days. If the tree represented the fey woman's state of mind, things were not good.

A deeper pile of wind-drifted leaves lay at the foot of the tree.

He paced toward the trunk, searching the glade for signs of life. "Lady Muse, are you here?" He called quietly.

The leaf pile moved slowly, and a pale face turned halfway into the light. "Have you come to gloat?" She asked sardonically.

She rolled towards him, scattering leaves, revealing her slender form. She lay full length, cradled by ropy, moss-covered roots.

He hissed in shock. She'd always carried herself with power and confidence, but her austere, elegant face was marred beyond belief. One jewel-like turquoise eye was gone. In its place, a jagged wound started and sliced down the side of her face, down her neck, and along the length of her body, ending in a seared gash across her hip. It was an ugly interruption in the otherwise perfect, pale green skin. White fluid like sap oozed from the wound.

"I suspect you would kill me now that I am helpless," she repeated hoarsely.

The memory of men with flames and axes washed over him. Was it his memory of seeing her experiences or her memory transmitted to him now through their link? It didn't matter. Pity welled up. He lowered himself to sit nearby. "What happened?"

"Spare me your pity." Her one good eye glared at him.

"What happened?"

"I made a mistake." Her contempt was now for herself. "I wanted to forge a stronger bond with you, but you were so far away. I thought to use the storm to augment my power. But I misjudged its strength and called down lightning on my tree instead. I deflected the energy away from its center but at a great cost." A breeze wafted through the grove like a sigh. She looked away. "My tree is dying. Maybe it is time for me to go. I have lived a long time, and I'm tired."

"Your spell or whatever it was worked Your golden bees stung me just before you were hit. I woke up with wounds from your bark, and my arm went numb from the lightning. I shared your memories like I was there."

She gave a derisive snort but he thought he saw a flicker of interest. "So you know everything. I am sick of living. It is better to go to sleep with the winter and simply not wake in the spring."

"And what will happen to me? Will I die now, if you do?"

She turned her face away.

"Will I die?" He repeated harshly.

"I don't know," she said.

"When I shared your memories, I saw what happened to you

and your people at the hands of humans. I'm sorry that happened to you, but haven't my great-grandfather, Granda, and myself made some amends to you for that? They carved your family's faces the way you made figures so long ago. I helped you carve the animals and plants you love and know so well."

She turned her face back to him slowly. "I remember them all." Her voice was barely audible.

"I know. I came to offer you a deal, a new bargain, if you will."

She stared at him bleakly.

"I would like to continue carving with you," he said, "and I would gladly help you remember them. But, I want to share my life with Marianne as long as she'll have me."

"A meaningless offer since I won't live long." She waved her long-fingered hand dismissively.

The glimmer of an idea flitted through his mind. "If that is what happens, I didn't want you to die alone. I have an idea, though. I think you have a chance at life."

The undamaged turquoise eye glinted within its pale lids. "You are no magician, Ruari. You cannot save me."

"Hear my plan." He told her his idea, and she regarded him with reluctant curiosity.

She was silent for several minutes. "You know this will work?"

"Not at all. But it's better than certain death."

She was silent for a longer time. The breeze rattled the leaves overhead, and he shivered, wondering if she'd just given up.

Finally, she said, "I'll consider your proposal. Return tomorrow night." And she closed her eye and rolled away from him, sinking beneath the leaves.

CHAPTER 17

Ruari's transition from walking through the forest to lying on the couch left him disoriented, but Marianne's warm body pressing against him brought him back. She stirred and opened her eyes.

"Mmmm, morning," she murmured with a sleepy smile.

He kissed her hair. "Morning, Mahri." The vivid dream still lay sharp in his memory. "Did you sleep okay?"

"Mmhmm. Did you know you twitch and mumble in your sleep? It's kind of cute."

"I dreamed of her."

Her sleepy eyes focused with interest. "Really? What happened?"

He recounted the conversation. "She expected me to kill her."

Marianne was quiet for a moment then said, "We don't have a very good track record as a species do we? Sounds like she has ten-thousand years of PTSD. Did she know what would happen to you if she died?"

"No, she didn't."

"That's not very helpful." Her eyes crinkled a little at the corners doubtfully. "You know, I feel kind of bad for her. What do you want to do?"

He knew full well that Mahri would stand up like a mother bear if she thought she had a reason. She was also deeply compassionate.

He said hesitantly, "I'm thinking…of rescuing her."

Her eyes widened. "What? How? Why?"

"I'm not sure. Her tree will last another few years, maybe even a decade. But the damage has opened it up to disease and rot. She will most likely die then. If she's still able to force me to carve with her, it's unlikely that she'll have changed her mind on tolerating you." He looked at her. "I don't want to wait for the tree to die before I can see you again. We might be able to move her to another tree, though."

"But if you rescue her, won't she just feel the same but in a different tree?"

"Maybe. She gave my great-grandfather and Granda room to have a wife and family because they'd done her 'a great service.' This would probably qualify as a great service. Then I could work with her and be with you too."

"Didn't you tell me she'd killed people without a second thought?"

He closed his eyes. *She's right: Don't forget. Remember everything.* "Yeah. She killed everyone in the village who'd torched her people."

"She's pretty scary. Wouldn't it be better to leave her to her fate as long as she'll let you go?"

"I thought you felt sorry for her?"

"I do, but I don't want her to hurt you or anyone else again."

"I'm with you there. Maybe I'm being selfish: she can't guarantee I won't die if she does, and I don't really want to die. And, if she lives, she can keep teaching me."

She regarded him from a hand's breadth away. "What if you have children? Won't the cycle just keep happening?"

"I'll have to cross that bridge when I come to it." He scrubbed his face with one hand. She wasn't wrong.

"Guess I'm with you, then." She kissed him chastely on a

stubbly cheek. "It's worth a try. You have nothing to lose." She sighed. "I think we have to get ready for your family meeting."

"Aye, they'll be here in a couple of hours. But we've got a little time." If he was going to die along with his muse, he'd better make the best use of the time he had. He kissed her back not so chastely, and they made love again amid the warm covers.

While she showered, he turned on the furnace and built the fire up again. His thoughts turned apprehensive as the meeting time approached. When he entered the kitchen after his own shower, she handed him toast slathered with peanut butter and jam purchased in the village the day before. She had already tidied up in the living room and whisked away all the blankets.

"We need to walk up to her tree again," he said, munching bread.

"Okay. Maybe after the meeting?"

He nodded.

She spread jam on her last piece of toast. "Is your other uncle like Fergus?"

He's a bitter, angry alcoholic according to family rumor. Not wanting to worry her, he said, "No, Uncle Reg is a little more like the reserved, stoic kind of Scotsman rather than the ebullient Scot Fergus is."

"Are you sure you want me to be here for this? I could easily go for a walk and come back later. Geoffrey's family was extremely close-mouthed when it came to money. I was excluded from any discussion about family finance."

He gathered up her hands in his and gave them each a peanut buttery kiss. "Please stay. I'll keep my cool better if you're here."

She gave him a tentative smile. "Okay."

They heard a knob rattle as someone fumbled with the front door. Finding it locked, they rang doorbell peremptorily. He wiped his mouth hastily, and she dove to swipe the counter clean and heat fresh water in the kettle.

Brushing his hands across his jeans, he composed himself. He hoped the family wasn't still angry with him. This could be a very long day, indeed, if they were. Expecting Donal or another member of his extended family, he opened the door.

Uncle Reggie stood on the front step. His dark hair and beard were neatly combed, and his florid features were set in their usual unsmiling expression.

"Fergus told me you were here," he said by way of greeting and stepped inside. Ruari stood back to let him pass.

"Hello Uncle," Ruari said.

Behind Reggie, his wife, Aunt Maggie, gave him a tired smile and a quick hug-and-kiss greeting. "Don't mind him. It's nice to see you, Ruari. I'm sorry your Da couldn't come."

Ruari stepped back again as she and Seamus carried several large platters and covered serving dishes into the kitchen. He heard Marianne introduce herself. Seamus returned to the front hall. He was wearing a respectable button-up shirt and trousers with a blazer, not a heavy metal T-shirt like Ruari was used to seeing him in.

Seamus shook his hand with a big smile and clapped him on the shoulder warmly. "Alright you wee bawbag? Been a long time." Not everything had changed.

Ruari laughed and drew him into a brief hug. He hadn't been called a 'little scrotum' in ages. Seamus had been positively dangerous when they were in their late teens, but at least Ruari didn't have to wonder how he felt. "Aye. What're you up to these days? You look like an office man wearing that kit."

"I'm studying for a psych degree." Seamus lifted his chin proudly. "I'm aiming to work in a juvie rehab center."

"No shit, Seamus? That's pure, dead brilliant!" Ruari thought it was a perfect way to turn his cousin's many youthful misadventures into help for other young offenders. He might even scare a few of them straight.

"Thanks."

"Have you met my girlfriend, Marianne?" Ruari led him into the kitchen where Aunt Maggie and Marianne were working. Actually, Marianne was standing aside, clasping her hands to keep from assisting while Maggie put some things into the fridge and others into a low warm oven. "Marianne," Ruari said, "this is my cousin Seamus. Seamus, Marianne."

Gratefully, Marianne stepped forward and shook Seamus' proffered hand. "It's nice to meet you."

"Aye, likewise. Has this old scunner taken you out and about yet?"

A faint crease appeared on her brow as she parsed this, but she nodded. "Yes, we've taken a couple of lovely walks."

He nodded and said to Ruari, "Catch you after the meeting, maybe." He stepped into the living room where Uncle Reggie was standing uncomfortably with his hands behind his back near the fireplace.

The doorbell rang again, and Ruari went to get it. Marianne caught his hand to go with him. He was glad not to face the new arrivals alone in case they were still feeling hurt. Uncle Fergus, Aunt Maura, and their family arrived with smiles and platters of food. The two children dashed into the living room, making a beeline for the toy box by the fireplace. The adults greeted Ruari and Marianne with hugs and kisses, though Ruari thought he detected a little restraint. *Maybe they're okay with it after all, and I'm just being overly sensitive.*

The Allen women bustled about, putting cold chicken and ham in the fridge, a potato casserole in the oven, and getting plates and silverware ready for a big midday meal. Marianne stood against the wall out of the way, and Ruari put his arm around her and guided her to a seat in the living room. Everyone else crowded in. Seamus, Donal, and Tomas picked up the sofa in front of the fireplace and turned it to face the rest of the room. People sat or perched on chairs as they wished.

It reminded Ruari of Granda's funeral tea. The house had been full of people paying tribute to both of his grandparents. Today, the mood was similarly subdued with an underlying edge. Ruari positioned himself so he could glimpse people's auras back lit by the windows and lamps.

. . .

As Uncle Fergus brought the meeting to order, Ruari discreetly scanned the room. He detected a yellow-orange aura around Fergus that had a thin and brittle feel to it. He was unhappy, Ruari thought. Next to him Maura's clean red glow radiated calm confidence. Hopefully, she'd help keep the meeting in order. Talmadge's angry red vortex was completely different in feel. Clearly color alone wasn't a simple indicator of personality. Mary and Tomas loosely held hands next to Maura. Ruari detected a faint white glow that sputtered in and out over her pregnant belly. He'd never seen such a thing and had to force himself to keep surveying the room rather than stare. Donal perched on the arm of one sofa out of the light. His wife Alleen sat on the hearth near the children.

"We've come here to talk about the fate of Coll and Nora Allen's farm. Our brother Douglas couldn't be here, so his son Ruari is standing in for his folk. He has the authority to speak for the Douglas branch. For those of you who haven't met his lady friend, this is Marianne Singleton," he indicated Marianne who smiled shyly from her perch on the arm of the couch. People nodded and smiled politely.

Fergus continued. "There has been talk over the last couple of years about what to do with the farm. Some of us grew up here, and all of us spent summers here. It's much loved by all." He conspicuously ignored his brother, who glowered silently and shifted his feet. "However, none of us lives here full time since we have jobs and commitments elsewhere. The yearly opening and closing of the house falls to those of us who live closest.

"We rent the pasture for hay to a local farmer, and although the income isn't much, it helps cover some of the taxes. Repairs and maintenance have fallen to my family to arrange, but everyone has helped bear the cost. Taxes and utility fees are the biggest burdens, and we have all shared our part so far. The question is, can we keep doing this indefinitely? Is there a point where the burden is too great, and we have to let the farm go? Or can we come to some other arrangement?"

The room was silent for a few moments as everyone acknowledged Fergus' summary.

Then Uncle Reggie spoke. His tone was carefully polite. "I'm sure we're all grateful for Fergus' arrangements, but I for one don't feel like we have the resources to keep the old place anymore. I think we should sell it."

Ruari leaned away and crossed his arms as he watched him speak. Reggie was attempting to be reasonable, but a dark gout of smoke accompanied his words. His genuine sentiments were much darker, and he radiated a foul, gray mood that tugged down everyone else's. Aunt Maggie sat near her husband, feet and knees drawn in, hands in her lap. Her aura was very faint, reflecting Reggie's gray.

Fergus' lips tightened. "That's one possible way," he said evenly, and Ruari had the feeling that they'd had that conversation many times, and it had gotten heated in the past.

Aunt Maura spoke up firmly. "I for one, would be sad to see the place leave the family. We've enjoyed coming here every summer, and the extra effort to keep up with it isn't a problem for us. We could keep up with it for a while longer."

Reggie spoke quickly, overriding Maura. "We live farther away and won't have a lot of extra cash to pay for a place that's unused most of the time. Seamus is going to university in the spring."

"Da, I can manage," Seamus started as his narrow yellow glow flared. "Tuition is free, and I plan to get a job to help pay for food and rent—" His mother put a hand on his arm, and he stopped.

Reggie snapped, "We have expenses of our own without carrying an empty house and a lot of land no one is using."

Fergus kept his own temper, turning to his nephew with a tight smile. "Congratulations on getting into university, Seamus. That's a grand achievement." He turned back to his brother. "We all ken, Reg, that your finances are tight. Our family could carry the expenses for another year or so. Ruari, your Mam and Da have been good about sending money to help when we've asked. Are they willing to keep doing that?"

Ruari nodded. "Dad told me they could carry on for a bit, but he's more of Uncle Reggie's mind to let it go."

Reggie's dour expression lightened, and he nodded in satisfaction. "There, it's two votes to one to let it go, Fergus. Done."

"Now wait a minute!" Donal interjected. "Not everyone thinks we should sell the farm. I can't speak for everyone in my generation, but Mary, Gerald, and I would like to hang onto it for a while yet. We all have families that would enjoy coming here. Seamus, are you in?"

Seamus lifted his chin slightly, slid a quick glance his father's way, and said, "Aye, I would."

"Ach." Reggie made a disgusted sound. "And how would you pay the expenses? It's thousands of pounds in taxes, insurance, and maintenance every year."

Donal said stubbornly, "We all have jobs and can set aside money for that."

"A load of rubbish," Reggie muttered.

Ruari interjected, "Is there some way we can rent the place out? I work for a rental agency in Maple Hill, and some of the properties we manage are family homes that are paid for by a combination of renters and family money. It's a possible model. Erin said she'd look into family partnerships."

"And who would we rent to? The farm is not exactly in town," Reggie said aggressively.

"True," Ruari acknowledged. Reggie had always been short-tempered, but this seemed more than usual. *Maybe I never noticed before?*

"What about doing it as a Bed & Breakfast? We could rent it for weekends or for weddings," Mary suggested tentatively. "It's very popular with tourists to spend the night in an old farmhouse."

"Aye, lass, and who would clean it between guests? Who would stock the food?" her father Fergus countered gently.

They talked and argued for over an hour about the merits of one model over another. Oblivious to all the deliberations, the two children played with Granda's handmade wooden toys in the middle of the floor. Uncle Reggie said he and his family wouldn't help with the upkeep of a rental property at all. However, Ruari noticed that his wife and son seemed less adamant, though they were unwilling to risk Reggie's wrath to speak up.

The main stumbling block was to how to do the renovations necessary to open the house and grounds to the public and where to get the capital and labor to accomplish them. Ruari said he could spend some time helping, and he was both surprised and pleased when Marianne jumped in and said, "I'd be glad to pitch in when I can."

"You both live in America," Reggie pointed out dismissively.

A childish cry of frustration and anger interrupted the deliberations, and the meeting broke for lunch. Everyone stretched, and the women headed to the kitchen. Marianne joined them, helping to get food and plates laid out.

"How long have you known Ruari?" Maura asked, passing her a stack of plates, while Mary and Tomas laid out a cloth on the table.

"Six weeks, I think," she answered.

"Six weeks!" Maura's broad face registered astonishment. "Lord love you! And here you are volunteering your time on someone else's family project."

"It's a beautiful place. I wish I'd spent summers here as a child. If I can help you keep it, I will."

"How did you meet?" Mary asked.

Marianne looked at Ruari with a mischievous smile. "We met over a broken dishwasher."

He chuckled. "And a couple of broken windows. I was never so glad to make house calls!"

She reached out for his hand. "And the first time we shook

hands, there was a huge spark, like static electricity, and I knew he was something special."

Maura said, "Ruari, don't lose this one! You take care of her."

He squeezed her hand and said, "She is amazing." Marianne beamed back at him, and her warmth eased the ache his family had made.

Everyone ate hungrily and spoke about things other than what to do with the farm. Relieved that the letter hadn't come up so far, Ruari hoped they were just going to overlook it for now.

After lunch, everyone reconvened in the living room with a cup of strong tea or coffee. Alleen took the little ones into the main bedroom for naps away from the grownups.

"Though it's against my wishes," Reggie said with a frown, his jaw muscles bunching, "everyone seems to want to keep the farm. It remains to be seen how you're goin' to pay for all the work that needs to be done on top of the taxes."

There was an uncomfortable silence.

He looked momentarily triumphant, and he bent his lips upward in a grimace. "Well, it just so happens I have a solution. I looked into the parcels of land Father gave us, and," he paused dramatically, "I have a buyer! He's willing to pay fair market value. We can split the cash three ways, and you'll have something to work with, and we'll have something to help with Seamus' schooling. It wouldn't be that hard to sell the rest of it after that."

There was an explosion of surprised conversation. Clearly this was the first time he'd brought up an actual sale. After the initial objections and grumbling about not alerting the family to his research, everyone admitted that the sale of the three outlying parcels would greatly help finance the farm's transition to a rental. The farm house and barn and about two acres around it were jointly held by the three sons.

"I'm sure Douglas will be more than willing to give up that rocky parcel, eh?" Reggie said to Ruari, with an attempt at a smile that was more of a painful rictus.

There was a general shifting in the rest of the room, and no one met Ruari's eye. Clearly Fergus hadn't called his brother with the information.

Ruari cleared his throat and braced himself. "Dad told me about his inherited land. He also told me that, um, Granda had added a letter, giving the parcel to me."

"Yer bum's out the window!" Reggie burst out. *You're talking absolute nonsense,* Ruari translated.

"Dad gave me the letter before I left." Ruari pulled the envelope out of his back pocket and offered it for inspection.

Reggie snatched at the letter and could not keep his tongue from spilling his thoughts. "Why would Father reward you with property?" he said in outrage. "Douglas didn't spend years taking care of our parents the way I did or Fergus! Nor did you!" His dark aura pulsed with fury. "We were the ones who took care of the place when Mam and Da couldn't. All you did was show up for two bloody weeks in summer," he finished acerbically.

"Hissht, Reggie, that's enough," Aunt Maura said sharply. "We all did our part. Douglas sent money to help pay the bills when he couldn't come himself."

Ruari hunched under his uncle's tirade, so similar to Donal's. *Does Dad even know this is how they all feel?* Would he have warned Ruari if he had? "I don't know, Uncle. I certainly didn't ask him for it. I didn't know about it 'til Dad gave me the letter a few days ago." Marianne slipped her hand into his and squeezed gently.

Reggie clamped his mouth shut. A muscle in his jaw pulsed with the effort of containing his emotions. Aunt Maura spoke sharply, "Reggie, it's not the lad's fault. He clearly didn't know anything about it."

Seamus and Aunt Maggie looked embarrassed but remained silent.

"More tea, anyone?" Mary asked while Reggie scanned the paper. There was a general murmur of no.

His uncle struggled silently for a few moments before mastering himself. He thrust the paper back at Ruari. "So, does this mean you're opposed to a sale then?" He looked like his mouth was full of bitter grapefruit rind.

Ruari said placatingly, "No, not at all. I want to go up and see it, but I don't need it. And I'm happy that the proceeds go into the support of the farm," he added, looking around the room. The unhappy faces relaxed for the most part.

Fergus nodded. "Thank you, Ruari. Reg, that sounds satisfactory...?"

Reginald grunted and gave a short nod.

"When would your buyer be willing to pay for the land?" Fergus asked.

"He's willing to pay us as early as this week," Reggie answered sullenly.

Ruari felt a surge of panic. He needed time to talk to the tree spirit. It might take several nights to implement his plan if she agreed. He thought fast. "Don't you need to get things surveyed first?"

"Aye, Reg," Fergus jumped in, looking relieved at the suggestion. "While I'm not happy you did this behind my back, I can appreciate that you've found someone who's willing to buy the parcels. Ruari is right. We should do the transfer properly. Plus, are you sure he's got the money up front and isn't just talk?"

Reginald's face darkened with anger. "My buyer is not some pub drinker! He's a local landowner who wants to expand and has the money to invest."

Fergus moved his hands in an appeasing gesture. "Fine, fine. You understand we need to know that."

Reggie turned his baleful glare on his brother. "I've been tying my own shoes longer than you have. I'm your elder, brother! Don't be telling me what to do!"

"Do you have a recent survey then?" Fergus continued stoutly, his own expression stiff.

"Fine. Do your survey then, but it comes out of your share."

Fergus set his jaw, his own face turning red. "It comes out of the sale price, and we all share it. The deal is no good if we don't do it right, and we don't get the money for every acre."

Reg clamped his jaw shut and waved his hands as if he were pushing away a cloud of annoying flies.

"Thank you, Uncle," Ruari said quietly, hoping to defuse the tension. "I'd like the chance to walk up there again and remember old times before the land belongs to someone else." It was a damn good thing no one else in the family saw lies as smoke.

Uncle Reg only grunted again in reply but said nothing more.

There was more talk about getting a surveyor hired, finding the old land maps, getting a barrister to draw up the papers and transfer the title. Ruari suggested having a local realtor come by and tell them what they needed to do to bring the place up to bed-and-breakfast standards. Mary said she knew someone in her office who might be willing to do it as a favor. She got out her phone and began texting.

Ruari asked what they would do with the barn. There was some discussion about using it as an event space for weddings or reunions. He asked if anyone had spoken for Granda's old wood-working tools.

Uncle Reggie looked at Ruari sharply. Ruari addressed the room in general. "I'm hoping to start a business making furni-ture, cabinets and the like, on commission."

"Well, I can't imagine anyone else wanting Da's tools," Fergus said. "In fact, if you want the whole lot, you can ship it to America and fill up your own shop with it!" He smiled to take the sting out of his words.

Ruari said, "I'll go through it before I leave. Then, maybe I can pack up the ones I want, and you can sell the rest and give the proceeds to the farm."

Mary looked up with a smile on her face. "Erin says she's all for a B&B and passed some links about having a family partner-ship. Do you mind if I take any tools you don't want? They'd make bonnie decorations!"

It was late afternoon by the time the meeting broke up. The

Allen women headed into the kitchen to deal with the food. Alleen encouraged the children to put the toys away. Ruari approached Uncle Fergus and asked how long it might be before the property was sold.

"If we can get all the pieces in place, maybe two weeks?" he replied.

"That would be great. That'll give me time to walk around a bit. Do you think anyone would mind if I chose some pieces of wood to take back with me?"

"How do you mean?"

"There are some beautiful old trees up there. It might be nice to harvest some wood before the sale and maybe make some things out of it to remember Granda and Nana by." It was a long shot, but Ruari took it.

His uncle considered and shrugged. "It belongs to you according to Da. So, you can do with it what you will."

"Thank you, Uncle Fergus. I'm truly sorry about this. I really didn't know."

Fergus patted him on the arm and said with a smile tinged with sadness, "We had a family talk after you left last night. It's not your fault. Da had his funny ways, so he must have had a reason. Only Mam understood him, really."

Ruari nodded. The children were bundled into coats. His aunts hugged him and told him how nice it was to meet his lady friend. Seamus caught up with him and said with a complicated look, "Sorry about Da. Don't worry about me, though. I don't care."

"Thanks."

"Do you want to go for a pint before you leave town?" Seamus asked.

Ruari smiled. "That would be grand."

"Seamus, your mam's in the motor. Time to go." Uncle Reggie scowled as he brushed by, interrupting them. His tone brooked no disobedience and Seamus hastened out the door.

CHAPTER 18

The front door shut behind the last person, leaving a ringing silence in the farmhouse. Sunlight was drawing long shadows across the yard.

Marianne let out a sigh. She flopped down on a sofa and said, "You doing alright?"

"Kind of drained." He dropped onto the cushions beside her and rubbed his eyes and face. "You have it in you to walk up to the tree?"

She stretched. "I had an attack of the sleepies midafternoon and was tempted to lie down with the children and take a nap too. I'm okay now. It would be good to get some fresh air. Do we have time to get up there and back again before dark?"

"I think so."

They dressed in warm clothes and boots. Nana's sweater had dried back into the woolly armor he'd worn yesterday. He pulled it on over his head.

"That is a powerful sweater!" Marianne said admiringly.

As they trudged down the road with a back pack carrying a few tools, a thermos of hot tea, slices of pie left over from lunch and a flashlight just in case, Marianne asked, "Why is your uncle Reggie so angry?"

He gave a slight shrug. "He wasn't this bad when I was young. If he was, I didn't notice it. It's gotten worse over time. My dad told me once that as firstborn, Granda had expectations of Reggie that he couldn't fulfill. So, Granda was disappointed and hard on him all his life. No matter what Reggie did, it wasn't good enough. I can see why he just wants to sell the place," he added sadly.

The more Ruari thought about it, Granda had been hard on all of his children. Ruari's father had escaped by moving to America. Fergus had somehow learned to let most of it roll off him. Perhaps he'd had a strong enough connection to Nana that Granda's behavior didn't push him completely away. Ruari felt a fresh wave of shame that Granda had lavished such affection on him and not on his own sons or other grandchildren.

As if she'd read his mind, she said, "It's not your fault. You have no control over other people's actions, only your own. Your grandfather was worried about having no one to pass on his woodworking to. Maybe that was one of the expectations?"

As she made the connection out loud, Ruari nodded slowly. *He left his family to twist in the wind.* "You're probably right. I'm not sure my dad understood fully what was going on, just that his father was not really there for them."

They walked another quarter mile. Marianne said, "It's strange how troubles can be passed along from generation to generation. You'd think the slate would be clean when you're born, but it isn't. Your grandfather has expectations his eldest can't fulfill. Then your uncle is hard on his son and wife. Then your cousin is a wild child. There must be a way to break the cycle. At least you turned out well."

Had he, though? He and Dad certainly had their issues. Seamus and his father. Granda had died alone, undiscovered for a couple of days, because of the rift with his family. Ruari suddenly wondered if the fey woman had been with him when he passed. He should ask her. He looked at Marianne. "You are amazingly perceptive about people, you know?"

Marianne smiled and shrugged. "Thanks."

He stopped, making her pause. "No, really. You are amazing," he repeated more tenderly.

Her smile blossomed. He'd never get tired of seeing that smile.

The climb up the steep slope through the trees prevented conversation. Ruari turned his thoughts to the idea he'd been mulling over. It all depended on what the fey thought of his proposal. He was going to have to try reaching her again via dreaming tonight. He wished speaking to her wasn't so hit or miss.

They emerged onto the shelf of land that led to the clearing and paused. Marianne held onto a slender tree trunk to catch her breath. "It was good to move after sitting still so long, but this hill's a killer!" She said.

They pushed on to the clearing and found the giant beech as they had left it the previous day. Ruari set his pack of tools down and stared at the tree, measuring and cutting blocks of wood from the downed limb in his mind's eye. Marianne sat quietly watching him. When she called him over for some tea from the thermos, he saw her big smile. "What?" he said with an answering grin.

"Nothing. I just like watching you work. It reminds me of me digging into a history problem. You get totally absorbed. I'm going up to the top of the hill for a look around, okay?"

"Okay," he said, grateful that she understood him so well.

The main trunk had survived the lightning strike at the cost of one of the main branches. This leviathan rested on its branches a couple of feet above the ground. The limb was straight for about four feet then curved and was a good two feet across. It would be ideal for his potential carving project. He took some measurements and then inspected the jagged tear on the main trunk more closely.

It was lucky that the tree had been sufficiently moist inside or it might have caught fire and smoldered for days. As he peered at the ragged edges, he glimpsed something deep in the heartwood. He hadn't seen it yesterday. He'd read that trees sometimes incorporated foreign objects like nails and wire and in one famous case, an old bicycle, growing around them and enveloping them like a slow wave. Usually, though, the wood grew smoothly around the object. Here, a pocket had formed around something.

He pushed his body between the torn limb and the trunk for a closer look. As his fingers probed, brittle flakes broke and fell away. He caught one and studied it, sniffing. It looked and smelled like burned leather. He pushed his shoulder in a little further and worked his fingers into the cavity. After a few moments of grunting and straining, he curled them around the contents of the old pouch and pulled them free. The ancient leather crumbled into dust.

At that moment, Marianne slid down the hill behind the tree. "It's a beautiful view up there," she said, brushing her hands off.

"Look what I found." He beckoned to her, and they sat down on the gnarled roots.

"What is it?" she asked, alive with curiosity.

He separated the little metal rods with a growing sense of wonder. "I think these are her old carving tools. She got them after she started wandering."

Though pitted with rust, the eight, forged iron chisels and gouges were not so different from his own set. He ran a fingertip over the working ends and shivered. They still held an edge. If his understanding of her life was correct, she'd been born somewhere around 500 AD. "These tools are at least a thousand years old," he murmured.

"Ruari," she said in a hushed tone, "didn't you tell me she killed the man who owned them?"

He nodded. "They still have an edge. I bet I could use them." *Dead man's tools. Granda's tools are like these now. Full of experience.*

Think of all the incredible things she made with these, trying to remember her family, her history.

Marianne touched his arm. "She *killed* someone for them."

"Aye, she did." He shook himself a little. *She's right: Don't forget. Remember* everything.

She leaned against him. "I wouldn't mind meeting her. Think of the history!" She narrowed her eyes. "If she threatens you with bodily harm though, all bets are off!"

He put his arm around her shoulders. "Thanks. I'm not making excuses for her, but humans haven't been very good to her or her people. Maybe this is my way of making up for some of that."

The light was fading. They were going to have to walk fast to make it down to the road before dark. Ruari wrapped the tools and their fragile wooden handles in his extra shirt and put the bundle at the top of the pack. They set out, hurrying down the slope in a barely controlled slide until they reached the open meadows and could see the road.

After a dinner of leftovers from the family meeting, Ruari and Marianne shared a nightcap in front of a fire. Jet lag and a long day had wiped her out. Tired in body, Ruari's mind was still restless. They sipped tea laced with whiskey and leaned against each other, feet up on the hearth.

"Will you try to talk to her tonight?" she asked.

"Yeah."

"I wish there was a way for me to come with you."

"Are you worried?"

She rolled her hands open in a helpless gesture. "There's not a lot I can do for you when you're off seeing her."

"Jealous?" He gave her a smile.

"Maybe a little." She returned a half-hearted smile.

"I gather that Nana was a little jealous of her too. Please don't worry."

She sipped her whiskey-tea.

"What have you been dreaming about?" He asked.

"No clairvoyant warnings, if that's what you mean."

"Have you seen any ghosts while you've been here?" He asked. He thought he'd felt Granda's presence once or twice, but he didn't know if that was an actual spirit watching over him or just the weight of memory.

She shook her head. "No, sorry. I've tried a few times to open myself up to seeing them, but I haven't."

He felt a pang of disappointment. He'd have liked to see the old man again, even for a moment.

She finished her tea and set her cup down. "If I have to share," she said with a mischievous smile, "I don't have to share this." She slipped her arms around his neck and kissed him thoroughly.

They made love on the couch again. Afterwards, Marianne lay curled against his side, one leg draped over his thigh under the blankets. "I'm so glad to be here with you," she sighed sleepily.

He kissed her hair and said, "Me too."

He fell asleep, thinking hard of the fey woman. *Lady Muse, I really need to see you tonight. Help me find a way to your tree.*

The next day, they hiked up to the glade with enough food and drink to last them all day. He hadn't reached the fey in her dreamscape glade, and he felt like time was running out. At least the weather cooperated. It was warm and sunny, one of the last sweet days of fall before gray weather drew in for the winter.

Marianne continued hiking up to the top of the ridge, leaving him to get on with it. Ruari stripped down to his T-shirt and set to work cutting the pieces he wanted. He'd brought a hand saw and wished fervently he had a chainsaw.

A few times, the back of his neck tickled with more than sweat, making him wonder if someone was watching him. He imagined the fey woman looking over his shoulder as he worked. Once, there was a sharp crack of a breaking stick back in the direction from where they'd come. Ruari stopped and looked around the trunk of the beech toward the sound.

"Hello?" he called out. "Is someone there?" No one answered, and he heard nothing more. After a few minutes he shrugged, concluding that a storm broken branch had fallen out of a tree and landed with a crash.

He went back to work, cutting the ends of the branches off the downed limb. Speaking out loud as he cut, he let her know what he was doing as if he were a surgeon performing a procedure.

At last, he detached several round logs. While he rested, he said thoughtfully, "Do you have a name? Granda never mentioned calling you anything but his muse or inspiration. That's a little awkward. You had a name among your people, but I don't remember it."

He didn't really expect an answer since she had not shown herself. "You can tell me another time."

Marianne returned a little later, saying she'd had a good signal up at the top of the knoll. She perched on the flat stone at the edge of the glade. "I looked it up. Tree spirits in ancient Greece were called hamadryads, and they were inextricably linked to their trees. If the tree died, they died. If she's a hamadryad in the classic sense, she might not be able to move."

He shook his head. "Maybe Scots tree spirits are different? She moved around independently when she was younger. Maybe she still can if we help her."

"On the off chance that we can move her," Marianne continued, "I looked into places to take her. There are a couple of big forest preserves at Dumfries and Galloway. It might be possible to drive up there and transplant her to a new tree."

He took a break, wiping his brow, and sat with her to have more tea from the thermos. Ruari had a pang of guilt at ignoring her. "I'm sorry," he said. "I'm not paying much attention to you."

She smiled. "Don't even worry about it. I can entertain myself. Do you need any help?"

He shook his head and put his arm around her in a one-armed hug. "Thanks again for coming."

They ate some lunch, and then Ruari began working on removing the outer bark and shaping the pieces he'd cut. Marianne sat nearby in a sunny place and talked about how beautiful the pictures of the forest preserve were. They made plans to drive up and look in the next few days.

"How are we going to get there?" She asked.

"Uncle Fergus and Aunt Maura might lend us a car."

"I think your grandfather would approve of what you're trying to do. He seemed to really care about her, and I think he'd be sad about her condition now." She was quiet for a bit then said, "Any ideas on how we're going to transfer her?"

His hands kept working as he replied, "I don't know. That'll be up to her."

"What if we can't help her?" She voiced his unspoken worries.

His hands stopped, and he looked up. "If it doesn't work, she said she'd probably go to sleep and not wake up in the spring. At least that doesn't sound painful."

They stayed till midafternoon. Ruari packed up and tried putting one of the pieces he'd shaped into a backpack. It barely fit. They rearranged the contents so that Marianne carried the tools and lunch leftovers, and he carried the piece of wood with the top of the pack unzipped.

Slogging their way back down the slope, they backtracked as best they could. Eventually, they turned into the farm driveway as the daylight faded.

CHAPTER 19

Uncle Fergus had left a message on the old answering machine, saying he'd be by to pick them up for supper around six. They just had enough time to shower and change. Marianne joined Ruari in the living room with her jacket over one arm.

He put his arm around her and said, "Are you sure you weren't bored this afternoon?"

She smiled with a glint in her eye. "I'll take a book next time. Other than that, I'm planning a few hours in the libraries of London on the way home. You'll have to wait for me. I think we'll be even in the 'boredom' category. Besides, I learned a lot about beech trees and some of the local sights. Could we ask about renting a car and do a little touring while we're here?"

"I'd love to. I can think of a few places I'd like to show you. I'll ask them tonight."

There was a honk from the driveway. They locked the door behind them as they left. The little Honda Civic was down the drive a ways, having already turned around.

"Traffic held me up! Maura'll have kittens if we let dinner get cold!" Fergus said with a grin. He tore off down the road, and Ruari was glad of the safety belts in the backseat.

After the tension of the meeting, the relaxed family meal was very enjoyable. Gerald was the only one in attendance. Donal and Mary and their families had gone home. Ruari told his uncle of their walk that day and "discovering" the huge old beech. He said he was pretty sure it was the tree pictured in Granda's workshop.

"Aye, Da really had a thing for that tree," Fergus said with a shake of his head.

Fergus did not allude to anything further, and Ruari was fairly certain Granda had not confided in him. "Unfortunately," Ruari said, "it was hit by lightning in the last storm, and I think it won't survive in the long run. So, I thought I might log it and send the useable lumber back to the States. It might be nice to make some things out of Granda's favorite tree."

Uncle Fergus furrowed his brow thoughtfully. "What do you have in mind?"

Ruari shared his ideas about taking it down and admitted it might be costly to do. "If you didn't mind, maybe I could use some of the sale proceeds to cover it? If not, I have a little saved up, and that might be enough. Do you know of anyone who could do the work?"

Aunt Maura handed the potatoes around again. "The father of one of the bairns at school is a forestry man. He might ken. I'll see if he's interested."

Marianne broached the idea of sightseeing. Fergus was enthusiastic. "Oh aye! I'll take a day off of work. There are some grand castles and abbeys to see—lots of history. And, of course, there are some excellent pubs!"

"I've been reading about the big forest preserve in Dumfries-Galloway and wondered if there was a place to rent a car nearby?" Marianne asked.

"I think there's an agency in town where you could hire a car for a few days. But, we could possibly loan you a car for a day, if that's all you need." Fergus looked at his wife, and she nodded.

"You could have the Civic tomorrow if that works for you," he offered.

Marianne and Ruari exchanged a glance. "That would be perfect!"

That night Ruari dreamed of the clearing. A slim figure lay between two large, moss-covered tree roots, her deep red hair draped over her body like a blanket of dead leaves. She was so still he wondered if she was dead.

"Lady?" He approached cautiously.

She stirred and opened one eye. The shattered eye and the long, raw tear along her face and body looked less fresh, but not as though it was truly healing. Her good eye followed him with a spark of turquoise blue.

"You look a little better," he said tentatively as he sat on the ground nearby.

"The sun is healing." She shifted her position slightly on the mossy cushions. "You found my tools."

"I did. May I have them?"

She shrugged listlessly. "I won't be using them again."

"I hope I didn't hurt you when I cut the limb today?"

"You did not. I pulled myself away from it after the lightning struck."

He took her slender hand in his. "I would like to try making something for you." The long fingers were cool and smooth like freshly sanded wood, and they curled around his own.

She stared at him, and he read despair and pity, but for whom he wasn't sure. What she said was, "Fine. You can keep me company while you work."

He shook his head. "I can't. I took the wood and my tools back to the farm with me. I'll work on it tomorrow."

Her thin-lipped mouth curled in a faint smile of amusement. "Stop being so limited in your thinking. This is a dream, Ruari. Many impossible things are possible in dreams." She gestured with her other hand.

Ruari looked past the spreading branches of the beech and

saw Granda's workbench and stool. They were perfect replicas. Or had she magically transported them from the barn? He got up and touched them. They felt as solid as they always did. A set of carving tools and the piece of wood he'd removed lay waiting for him. He realized the tools were hers, but here in her dream they were in pristine condition.

A ghost of her wind-in-the-leaves laugh shivered the air. "You have the most foolish expression! I believe I should get well again if only to go on seeing that."

Although the clearing was lit only by a kind of perpetual twilight, he found he could see well enough. Sitting on the familiar stool, he placed the piece in his lap. It was illogical to think he could make progress here, but perhaps he could plan out the piece and make his work tomorrow go more quickly. Picking up a small chisel, he began.

"Thank you for talking to me today while you were cutting," she said, settling back on the mossy bed. "You were the first to ask me my name in a long time. Others of my kind called me Hhthfehrtessen." The name sounded like wind in the leaves.

"Hethferson?" His clumsy pronunciation made her laugh again. "I don't think I can do it justice," he said with a wry smile. "Would you consider a human name?"

"Perhaps."

"How does 'Vivienne' sound? It means 'life' or 'lively'."

She considered. "That is acceptable, though perhaps ironic, considering." She was silent for a time and then said in a troubled voice, "When you were here today, I felt a strange foreboding; something dark lurking in the shadows beyond my clearing."

Ruari frowned, remembering the brief sensation of being watched. "I thought that was you. If it wasn't, I don't know what that might have been."

She fell silent again, and he entered the trance-like state, letting his hands work.

Some time later, Ruari heard his name being called. He had the feeling she'd been calling for some minutes. Deliberately, he laid the small chisel down and sat up, relieving the stiffness in his hands and back.

"You have complained that I never let you rest when we worked together," she said with a trace of amusement. "I am quite unable to participate at the moment, and yet I had to call you several times."

"Sorry." He stretched his cramping hands. "What is it?"

"I have been thinking. If you can build a vessel for me, and I can board it, I will need a source of energy to sustain myself. A tree goes dormant for the winter, but vital energy continues at a very low level. I tap into that to keep myself alive as well. Your carving will be of non-living wood, and I must have something."

He stared into the distance. "It would be like being set adrift in a life raft without food or water for months I suppose." His mind raced, thinking of different kinds of power. "Actual food would rot," he murmured. "Batteries would probably be too mechanical and foreign. There would be no way to rig up a little solar panel on such short notice, much less keep it hidden. What about seeds?"

The corners of her lips drew down. "Consuming the tiny new lives of trees yet to be is a crime among my people. There are stories of tree fey who thought nothing of doing that. We regarded them with as much disgust as you would a cannibal. I would prefer to avoid that even to save my own life."

"Understood." He went back to work, mulling over the new stumbling block.

Ruari awoke under the quilts in the little back bedroom with Marianne snugged along his side. He was stiff and tired, and his hands and forearms ached. He moved slightly and Marianne awoke.

" 'Morning," she kissed his rough cheek. "You were twitching a lot. I tried waking you, but I couldn't."

"I dreamed I worked on the carving all night." He still wasn't sure where he'd been.

She raised her eyebrows. "I'm pretty sure you were here with me all night."

"It felt very real to me."

"There's only one way to find out," she said, extracting herself from the tangle of blankets and putting her clothes on. "Where did you leave the wood when we came back yesterday?"

"In the pack by the back door."

He put his shirt, pants, and sweater on against the chill as her footsteps crossed the kitchen. There was some activity by the back door, and then she said in an oddly constrained voice, "Ruari, I think you'd better come look at this."

He crossed the room, pulling the edge of the sweater down around his hips against the chill. She had a very peculiar look on her face, hovering between disbelief and fear as she held the backpack out to him. Taking it from her slightly shaking fingers, he held it open and looked.

The block of wood was no longer a rough cylinder the way he'd transported it yesterday. Now it was shaped like an over-sized pea pod with a rounded bottom and flat top. The outlines of a figure were roughed in like an artist's sketch on the flat side. It would have taken hours to accomplish this much. It was exactly how he'd left it in his dream.

"How can you have been in two places at once?" she asked, looking disturbed. "I would swear that you were with me all night."

" 'Many impossible things are possible in dreams'?" he quoted, feeling stunned.

She shivered, eyebrows raised. "Somehow, this is freakier than having ghosts in my house."

"All I can say is 'magic'?" he replied, equally shaken.

"I need tea and breakfast before I can cope with this." She put the kettle on and busied herself making a meal.

A hot shower soothed some of his aches, and fresh clothing

helped lend some normalcy. By the time he'd dressed, food was ready.

"Well, if I can work on the piece at night, then maybe it will get done sooner. We don't have much time," he said as they ate.

"I've been thinking along the same lines," she replied. "Though, truthfully, if you're working all night, you aren't resting, and you can't carry that on indefinitely."

"Don't I know it."

"We were going to check out the forest preserve today as a possible new home for her. Are you still up for that?" She looked concerned.

He nodded. "Yeah. I need to walk away for a bit. Clear my head. By the way, she let me call her Vivienne."

"For Vivienne, then. If we don't take all day, you can come back and work on your carving in decent light and tell her you need your rest if she comes for you at night again."

After packing lunch and a thermos of hot tea, they headed out. It was another brilliant day that recalled the sweetness of summer. Marianne downloaded directions off the internet and navigated while Ruari drove. They both had to stay alert to be sure they remained in the left lane. Once, Ruari made a left turn into the right-hand lane and only realized his mistake when he saw the oncoming car. Veering back to the left side abruptly, they gasped in unison, "Holy shit, that was close!"

They burst out laughing like crazy for a mile, releasing some of their pent up tension.

By the time they arrived at the nearest entrance to the nature preserve, they were both feeling better. They parked the car, found a trail map, and hiked into the forest. The preserve was utterly gorgeous. The cool weather had turned the leaves bright orange, gold, and brown, which stood out like stained glass against the darker green of trees that hadn't turned yet. Shafts of sunlight illuminated the trail ahead of them, turning the bright yellow aspens into brilliant torches. They wandered the paths and scouted for specific places where they thought Vivienne might be happy. Ruari brought up the fey woman's need for an energy supply while she hibernated, and they discussed various options.

They ate overlooking a small lake, appreciating the white clouds reflected in the surface of the still water as they scudded across the bright blue sky. Returning to the car by midafternoon, they drove back, talking about places that were possible candidates.

When they got home, Marianne drove into the village on an errand, while Ruari worked on the carving at the kitchen table.

"I have an idea," was all she said as she scooped up the keys.

After a relatively quiet dinner with Uncle Fergus and Aunt Maura, they returned to the farmhouse, and Ruari resumed work on the carving. He could not sense Vivienne's presence at all and poured every ounce of his own knowledge into his effort.

They slept in the little back bedroom, cuddling skin to skin for comfort.

CHAPTER 20

That night Ruari told Vivienne they had looked for her new home. Once again, she was lying on her divan made of moss and roots. The tree looked much as it had the night before, and she moved listlessly under her blanket of leafy hair.

"I worked on the piece today," he told her. "I can't work tonight, too. When I work here, I don't get much rest. I'll do more tomorrow."

"Marianne looks after you like a mother hen," Vivienne said with a terrible mix of scorn, pity, and envy. "My time is short. There were men on my ground today with sticks and strange devices."

"Probably surveyors, measuring the land and making sure where the boundaries of the parcel are," Ruari guessed.

"Yes, that seems so. There was another man, akin to your grandfather, but I did not like him. He came into my clearing and stared at me for a long time."

Could Uncle Reggie or Fergus have been supervising the survey? But why?

Ruari vowed to work on the carving again soon and left the clearing, hoping that he'd find his way back to the farmhouse and deeper into sleep.

He awoke more rested than he had the previous day but felt uneasy. Vivienne was right, time was short, but he couldn't back out of the planned excursion. Marianne would understand, but Fergus would not. He couldn't insult his uncle after all the meals and accommodations.

Ruari relaxed a little as they drove picturesque back roads to a big, medieval castle on the coast. They stopped several times to take pictures and enjoy the windy fall day. The self-guided tour of the castle was enjoyable especially since Marianne added to the written commentary with her own knowledge. Although the Victorian era was her specialty, she put the castle and its inhabitants into the broader context of British and European history. By the end of the tour, she'd gathered several other inquisitive visitors who thanked her for her anecdotes.

They ate lunch in the sponsored cafe, and Marianne was telling them about an English castle she'd read about when Ruari felt a piercing cry tear through him, accompanied by a sharp pain on the inside of his right shoulder and a wave of fear and nausea. He jerked back from the table, nearly tipping his chair over. Swallowing, he looked up and saw the surprised looks on his companion's faces. The rest of the diners continued eating, oblivious to the sound.

Another shriek deafened him, and his vision blurred. For a split second, he was in a hilltop clearing staring at the twisted visage of a man screaming, "Die you demon spawned bitch!" as another sharp blow pierced his side. He gasped and clutched his ribs.

"Ruari, what's the matter?" Marianne said sharply, steadying the edge of the table reflexively.

"He's cutting her down," he gasped, eyes wide and unseeing for a moment.

"What's that? Who are you talking about?" Uncle Fergus said, looking puzzled.

"Uncle Reggie is cutting the tree down—with an axe!" Ruari

repeated, staring in horror at something only he could see. Nearby diners looked over curiously.

Marianne understood instantly. She turned to their host and said, "Uncle Fergus, thank you for lunch and the tour, but we have to get back to the farm right away."

Fergus looked confused. "Reg? He's at work. How do you ken what he's doing?"

Marianne lowered her voice. "Uncle Fergus, Ruari sometimes sees things that are happening far away." She looked meaning-fully at him.

The Scot swallowed and said in a shaking voice, "He has the second sight?"

She nodded.

"What do you see, Ruari?" he asked tersely.

Ruari looked aghast. "Uncle Reg found Granda's favorite tree, and he's cutting her down with an axe. He's in a rage! Please, Uncle, we have to stop him!"

Fergus paused for only a moment at the pale, stricken look on his nephew's face and nodded. Throwing his jacket on, he said, "Pay the bill. I'll get the car."

Fergus drove like a madman, traversing the distance in barely half the time it had taken them to get to the castle. Marianne sat with Ruari in the backseat holding his hand. Ruari for his part was numb with shock. He'd felt the first two blows to Vivi-enne's trunk and heard her cry of pain and fear before her voice cut off. He knew that with each passing minute his livid uncle was tearing a hole in what remained of the beech tree. If he killed her, what would happen to Ruari? The only thing that gave him any hope was that his uncle was wielding an axe not a chainsaw.

Fergus parked the car on the side of the road at the foot of the hill. Using the GPS on her phone, Marianne aimed them up the slope. They half ran, half walked through the trees, stumbling past roots and rocks, Fergus following them. It had been a little over an hour since Ruari had first felt the blows.

As they drew nearer, they could hear the thunk of an axe somewhere up ahead erratically biting into wood. Ruari put on a spurt of speed, running faster than he thought he could after their breathless climb. Bursting into the clearing, he saw Uncle Reginald, face twisted with fury, hacking away at the huge trunk. Dark red and black waves of anger and violence rolled off him in a palpable miasma.

"Stop!" Ruari cried out but his lack of breath robbed his voice of power. Reggie ignored him.

On impulse, Ruari renewed his rush forward, tackling his uncle before he could raise the axe again. His momentum bowled the man over and knocked the blade out of his grip. Reginald was puffing and blowing with his exertion, his face scarlet and purple. Ruari thought he might have a heart attack. But his uncle was sturdier than he looked and managed to get to his feet. He swung a fist wildly at his attacker. Ruari dodged aside, panting, "Stop, Uncle!"

"Get out of my way, boy!" Reggie growled.

"No! You're killing her! I won't let you!" Ruari deliberately positioned himself between his uncle and the tree's trunk, slipping a little on the tangle of roots.

Reggie looked at him clearly for the first time and said with loathing and disgust, "I heard you! You're possessed of the same madness my father was! He loved that damned tree more than he ever loved any of us! I'm doing you a favor. It deserves to die before it destroys any more. It's a shame the lightning didn't burn it to the ground." He spat, and a clot of spit smacked the leaves at Ruari's feet.

"Reg!" Fergus called from the other side of the clearing where he had just emerged, clutching a stitch in his side. Marianne was close behind, breathing hard, but she made her way across the clearing toward Ruari as fast as she could.

"Reg! What are you doing? Are you daft?" Fergus came up to

his brother, his face bright red with effort, trying to get his breath back.

Reggie said with a snarl of triumph, "I followed our nephew here two days ago and realized he'd found the demonic tree Father had so many pictures of in his shop, like some perverted pinup lover. I came back yesterday with the surveyors to be sure it was the right one, and today I came to kill the damned thing."

"Listen to yourself, man!" Fergus exclaimed, deeply alarmed at his older brother's wild look and wilder words. "Have you been drinking?"

"Shut your geggie. Maybe you never noticed Father wasn't faithful to Mam. He had more pictures of this evil thing than he did of her."

"Reg," Fergus said, trying to soothe him, "talk sense, man. Father was a woodworker. It was his passion, his life, but I ken well he loved our mam."

"That's all you know," Reggie sneered. "Our nephew seems to have caught the same fever and fallen in love with the same damned tree." He turned wildly to Marianne and said, "You mark my words, Ruari won't love you half as much as he does this thing, and your bairns will have a father that does not love them at all."

Ruari stood transfixed by the ugly expression and uglier words pouring out like sewage. But he stood gamely between his uncle and Vivienne, nevertheless. He also noted that Marianne had discreetly put the axe out of sight.

She approached the irate man. Confounded by her calm, he hesitated.

"There is no need to cut it down, Mr. Allen. The lightning killed the tree better than your axe would have. She will not live to see another spring." Her quiet tone seemed to penetrate Reggie's hate-fogged brain, and he paused. Ruari saw the same resolve with which she'd faced her ex.

"This is a tree. Who are you talking about?" Fergus asked in confusion

Marianne's eyes widened as she looked past Reggie's shoulder, behind Ruari. Reflexively, Ruari glanced behind him but saw no one. When he turned back, her eyes were closed.

Uncle Reggie snorted at her rudeness. "Get out of my way, girl." He raised his hand to push her away, and Ruari tensed ready to protect her.

Marianne's eyes flashed open, pinning the angry Scot with such a penetrating look that he halted. "Reginald, your father is deeply sorry he fostered such anger and hatred in you. He wishes he could take back all the hurtful words he ever said. He loved you and was proud of you, even though he never said so."

After momentary astonishment, Reginald scowled again. "You're talking mince. Don't presume you ken anything about my father or me, American girl. You ken nothing!"

"That's as may be. It's time to walk away, Mr. Allen. You've done what you came for. The tree is dead or dying, as sure as the sun will rise tomorrow, and any more energy spent on it would be a waste. Let your brother take you home." She stared at him steadily, pouring as much power into her words as she could.

Reggie made a move in her direction with a harsh, guttural sound, and Ruari followed, ready to grab his uncle's arm and keep him from hurting her.

She stood her ground, staring at him with determination.

"Aye, Reg," Fergus said cautiously. "The car's at the foot of the hill. I can take you back to work or to home as you wish."

Reginald Allen's face twisted into a mask of barely contained hatred and anger. He spat on the ground viciously. "I can take myself." He walked deliberately around Marianne into the woods back toward the farm. His footsteps crashed away downhill.

Fergus looked pale and agitated. "I'll follow him, see that he gets back down the hill. Maybe I can talk some sense into him. Let Maggie know, anyway, where he's been today."

Ruari nodded. "Thank you, Uncle Fergus. Call me later."

Fergus looked at him and said with some asperity, "Aye, that I will, laddie. you have some explaining to do, if you don't mind."

Ruari nodded again, and Fergus left, his footsteps fading in the distance.

"You okay, Ruari?" Marianne asked quietly.

"I think so." He took a deep, shaky breath and let it out slowly, steadying himself. "Why did you say that about Granda?"

"He was standing between your uncle and the tree the whole time. He was genuinely sorry for all the pain he'd caused his oldest son and wished he had found the courage to tell him so while he was still alive."

Ruari pulled her into a rough embrace, and she held him close. They clung to each other. Ruari turned his damp cheeks to survey the damage the axe had done. It had bitten deep on the side of the trunk opposite the torn limb. The wood was a mass of cuts from wild swings, but many of them had concentrated in one place, and Reggie had removed a sizable wedge. A thin line of milky sap was welling from the cuts. If lightning hadn't already damaged the tree, it would have struggled to recover from this fresh assault.

He put his hand on a smooth stretch of gray bark. "I'm sorry, Vivienne. We got here as soon as we could. I'll go back to the farm and work on the container to move you until I finish, no matter how long it takes. We'll try moving you as soon as it's done."

They retrieved the axe and picked their way slowly down the hill toward the road, not wishing to run into either uncle again.

Ruari spent the remainder of the afternoon working feverishly on the carving. He made gradual progress. The shape looked like a cross between a boat and a cradle, and the figure lying on her side asleep in the center took on definite shape and detail. Marianne made several cups of tea for him, but they largely went unnoticed.

Uncle Fergus called a little after six, saying that he'd seen Uncle Reggie home and advised Aunt Maggie of the trouble. She made sure he got dinner, and Fergus hoped she could keep him home. Ruari gave an abbreviated explanation, saying he'd inherited the second sight. He understood Granda's love of the big old beech and had wanted to protect the tree in his memory. He glossed over the fey woman and hoped Fergus wouldn't ask.

"I appreciate all you did for us today," he finished.

Fergus sighed deeply. "I knew Reg was unhappy, but I never imagined anything like that."

"In America, I'd suggest counseling, but here…"

Fergus blew out a breath. "Oh, aye. Reg would never consent to that. I'll do my best to keep him off the hill and away from the farm while you're here. And it would be best if you didn't contact him for a while. He's fairly angry with you and Marianne. Does she have second sight and all or just read folk well?"

"Both," Ruari said simply.

"I don't envy either of you," Fergus replied.

"We'll take dinner here tonight," Ruari said. "May we see you and Aunt Maura again before we leave?"

"Sure. I'm right sorry for all this," he apologized. "I hope Douglas isn't upset with you."

Ruari hadn't thought about that. "I don't know. I'll let him know what happened."

"Aye. When do you leave?"

"We fly out of London later this week. We thought we'd take the train from Edinburgh."

"If you can bide until Tuesday, we can have you over again. Someone can take you to the station. Donal and Mary and Gerry will be here for one more meal. Lord, I don't know what we'll tell them." It sounded like he was shaking his head.

"You could tell them the truth: that families don't always treat each other well and that they make mistakes sometimes," Ruari replied.

"Aye. That they do."

"May we keep the car another day or two? If it doesn't inconvenience you and Aunt Maura, that is."

Fergus put his hand over the mouthpiece and relayed the question before saying, "You can, but we need it back Tuesday."

"Of course," Ruari said and rang off.

They'd eaten all the leftovers from the family meeting, so they scoured the cupboards for suitable ingredients. There was half a loaf of bread, and they ate toast with peanut butter and jam again too exhausted to go down to the village for dinner. Marianne told him about her trip into the village the day before.

"You mentioned Vivienne's need for an energy source, and that got me to thinking. Remember the stones I gave you? I did some research on different gemstones, and I think they might do the trick. I remembered that the village has a couple of tourist shops. So, I went down and looked in both of them. I'm still not sure, but it's worth a try." She poured the contents of a small paper bag out on the table between them. Polished stones spilled out on the wooden surface: blue, milky white, black, pink, and orange.

"I was wondering if you could make a little compartment in the boat for Vivienne?" She continued. "We could put them in there, and maybe she could draw on them for energy." She pointed at each one. "This is agate and jasper for healing. The obsidian will connect her to the earth. The selenite recharges the other stones and provides a clear path for energy flow. And, I got turquoise also for healing, but it matches her eyes, and what lady doesn't want matching jewelry? There were other suggestions online, but I couldn't find those."

"What a great idea!" He marveled at her thoroughness and generosity.

"I thought about what you said about humans not treating her or her people well," she said.

After supper, he offered to help with cleanup, but she shooed him away so he could go back to work. The handful of stones was rather bulky, and he spent some time considering where and how to make room for them.

Marianne built a small fire in the fireplace and read a book with her feet propped on the hearthstone until she couldn't stay awake any longer. She nodded off under the old quilt on the couch, her book resting on her chest. Ruari kept working. There was no trance-like state, just his own driven focus to finish in time.

It was just graying outside as dawn approached when he put his tools down and crawled onto the couch beside Marianne to catch a few hours of sleep. She shifted and wrapped herself around his cold limbs, and he passed into oblivion.

Some time later, he awoke feeling stale and wrung out. Marianne had gotten up and put the quilt over him without his even waking. She was reading again in a separate chair with her feet up on the edge of the flagstones. She'd roused the fire, and it was small but warm. A mug of tea sat on the stones beside the chair. She looked up immediately when he moved.

"Hey, how are you doing?" she asked.

"Pretty crappy," he croaked.

"You do look awful," she agreed.

"Thanks," he said with a ghost of a smile.

"Did you finish?"

"I think so. I didn't feel her helping me at all. For all I know, she's gone already."

"Do you think you could tell?"

He scrubbed his face with his hands. "I don't know. We'll just have to try."

"Eat something first." She rose and went into the kitchen.

He lay on the sofa, phasing in and out of sleep, until she brought him a couple of sausages, a thick slab of toast and butter, and a fresh mug of strong, sweet tea.

He ate ravenously. "I thought we finished all the bread?"

"I went down to the village and did a little shopping," she replied.

He raised his brows. "I was that deeply asleep?"

She nodded.

Food and caffeine revived him. Marianne carried the work he'd done to the couch where they sat and looked at it.

It was still rough, showing the chisel marks, and was smaller than he'd intended. It reminded him of *Sleeping Lady*, but with a miniature full-length image of a woman rather than just a face and a hand. She was nude, lying on her side, her hands cushioning her cheek. Her face was austere but beautiful, and the proportions of her limbs suggested a somewhat stylized, long, narrow female figure rather than the shape of an actual human. She had emerged from the wood enough to be fully visible but not detach from the cradle she lay in.

"Ruari, is this what she really looks like?" Marianne asked.

He nodded.

"She looked more human in my dream encounter with her. Here, she makes me think of prehistoric Venus figures—but skinny rather than fat, if that makes any sense."

He traced the outlines of the figure with his fingers. "She's very old. I think humans have been making representations of her kind for a long time."

"I know it's not as finished as the piece you gave me, but it's beautifully made."

He showed her the compartment on the underside that he'd chiseled out. He'd packed the stones tightly inside just below the head and torso of the little figure. The cover fit tightly into place, and he planned to glue it shut as a precaution. The only clue to its presence was the thin seam around the edges, and the asymmetrical heaviness on that side.

"I really hope this works for her," Marianne said. "And that no one finds it before she's done with it."

He nodded and tried to see it from the perspective of a hiker stumbling upon it. "It reminds me of *Paddle to the Sea*. Did you read that as a kid?"

Smiling, she said, "I loved that book."

"I don't think I have time to make a brass plate for this, though."

She pursed her lips, thinking. "I could write a note, and we could put it with her."

"That'll have to do. Thank you, Mahri, for everything." He held her in his arms. "I promise to believe you when you tell me things, no matter how strange they might be."

She buried her face in his neck and said, "I promise the same."

It was early afternoon, and after some discussion, they walked up to Vivienne's tree, taking the carving with them. Ruari felt it would help her move during dream time.

"I don't know how I can be there to help you," Marianne said, frowning. "I've had lots of clairvoyant dreams of my own, but I don't know how to show up in someone else's dream."

"I had an idea about that." He produced two carved wooden rings from his pocket, each about an inch and a half across. "I made these from scraps of the same wood. I think if we wear them, it'll help."

"Oh Ruari, they're beautiful!" He slipped one over her thumb where it rested snugly.

Her praise and shining eyes warmed his heart. "I broke three before I finished these two. I don't know if it's even possible for two people to be in the same dream."

"I don't either, but it's worth a try." She tucked the little wooden circlet in her pocket for the time being.

He thought fleetingly of taking the broken bits of the beech wood box he'd brought and burying them at the base of the tree, but there was no room in the pack.

Even though they expected it, it was still a shock to see the fresh, deep gash in the beech's trunk and the scattering of light colored wood chips around the roots. Milky sap had oozed out of the deepest cuts like blood. Ruari put the ship-like carving at the base of the cleft where the limb had torn away. He hoped that would give Vivienne a chance to inspect her vessel and determine if it would suffice. They only had one chance at this. Uncle Fergus might not succeed in keeping his brother from returning to finish the job.

"Vivienne," Ruari said aloud as he rested his palms against the naked trunk, "this is the best I can do for you. I hope it's enough. I —we—will see you tonight and do what we can to help you. If you need anything else, let us know. We'll take you to the forest preserve in Dumfries-Galloway tomorrow, and maybe you can transplant yourself into a new tree in the spring."

They walked back down, listening to rain patter on the leaves above them. The day had become chill and dreary, and they were glad to get inside. After a little food, they went out into the barn, and Ruari selected the tools he wanted to ship to Maple Hill. Some he chose for the memories, others for purely practical purposes. Granda had several that were very old-fashioned and hard to find. Marianne located boxes, newspaper, and tape and helped package them up for mailing. Vivienne's tools went into his own luggage.

He stared at the shelf of carved portraits of Vivienne's family for a long time. Granda's family clearly didn't want them. It would be a crime to destroy them. What if they went out into the world? Should he ship them all to Maple Hill? Vivienne had left her portraits in remote circles to decay with the seasons. But Granda had made these. Finally, he packed all twelve carefully in boxes and labeled them for his studio. He tried not to think of the small fortune it was going to cost to mail them all.

They had a solemn, tired dinner at a pub in the village, then settled in front of a fire at the farm. Feeling the need for comfort, they sat close and said little, gathering their strength for the unknown. Putting on their rings, they fell asleep in each other's arms, holding their ring hands, fingers interlaced. Maybe physical closeness would be enough to bridge the gap and bring them into the same dream space.

It was a million to one long shot.

CHAPTER 21

Ruari found himself walking the now familiar path up the hill in twilight. Although it was dark, the trees were curiously luminous, providing enough light for his feet to find the way. He had a moment of disappointment that he was alone. It had been long odds that Marianne could be here. Best focus on doing what he'd come to do. As he ascended the slope, the air grew warmer and more tangible, caressing his face, like an invisible ocean. Each tree he walked past felt alive and breathing. The ground was like the skin of a huge living thing, and the leaves and branches sighed gently with his passing. It reminded him of the walk he'd taken with Marianne in Maple Hill so long ago.

The sound of hurrying footsteps behind him made him pause.

Marianne came up behind him, bathed in a faint lavender glow. "Sorry I'm late," she panted. "I don't know the way as well as you do."

"You made it!" Relief and happiness welled up in him.

He raised his hand and realized it was limned with green. When their fingers intertwined, the wooden rings clicked softly together.

She squeezed his hand with a smile of pure delight. "Come on!"

Her feet left the ground, trailing behind her, and laughing joyously, she pulled him up under the branches. He felt his heart soar.

"How are you doing this?" He asked.

"In dreams, impossible things are possible!"

Exhilarated, they half floated, half flew like birds through the warm air, arriving in the clearing faster than he expected. They flew around the bare branches of the majestic beech, surveying the damage from above. It looked as desolate as if the tree had aged a hundred years in a few days. Ruari couldn't see Vivienne anywhere. They alit and approached the place where they'd left the cradle earlier that day.

He retrieved the carving, placing it on the ground between the roots she'd used for a bed. It was held upright like a boat in a slip.

"Vivienne, we're here. Let us help you, if we can," he said aloud, casting about for any sign of her. "Vivienne! Hethferson!" Marianne stood aside and let him call.

At first, there was no answer, but then they heard a faint voice near the roots and crouched down to hear better. "I am very weak and nearly at the end," she said. "I don't know if I can do this."

"Show me how to help you," Ruari said.

"Maybe I can help," came a voice outside the circle of the tree. Ruari's heart leapt at the familiar brogue. "Granda?"

The spare, angular figure of his grandfather ducked under the branches and approached. His pale blue eyes were sorrowful under their ferocious brows. He looked much as Ruari remembered him from about ten years ago. Before arthritis swelled his joints and bitterness tinged his features.

"Ruari, 'tis good to see you. Marianne, I'm glad to meet you at last." He clasped their hands with warm, substantial fingers. She murmured a greeting.

Ruari pulled him into a hug which startled the old man at first but which he returned. Half laughing, half crying, Ruari pulled away. "I have so many questions."

"I ken that. But 'tis not the time. We must be getting about the job in front of us. I promise I will return if I can and explain."

He knelt at the base of the tree and said, "*Mo chroí*, let me help." Turning to Ruari, he said, "After I'm gone, reach into the cleft until you feel her hand, then pull like you were birthing a wee calf."

Then the old wood carver turned his big frame sideways and began pushing his way into the impossibly narrow, splintery gap like an eel. The wood reluctantly made way for him as he grunted with the effort. At last, the trunk swallowed him.

Ruari looked at Marianne who shrugged. "It's a dream. Go with it," she advised.

He knelt where Granda had just been. The ground around the trunk was loamy and springy, and the trunk tunneled into it like the entrance to a mysterious grotto. He could imagine a little room deep in the earth where Vivienne had retreated. He touched the wood tentatively, half expecting the wood to have softened somehow, but it was as hard and unyielding as it was in daylight, and he had misgivings. *This isn't possible!*

"Come now, Ruari!" Granda's voice sounded small and distant. "Put your hand in and reach hard for hers!"

Gritting his teeth, he inserted his right hand into the raw cleft as close to the center as he could. The hard wood gave a little, and his hand seemed to flow through the space. Little by little, he pushed his hand deeper into the tight, jagged opening, feeling splinters tear the tender flesh near his elbow. Blood welled up, making his arm slick. He thrust, angling downward until his entire arm was wedged in up to the shoulder. He must be reaching into the bowels of the earth, and he wondered whether he'd be able to escape or bleed out first. As he turned his face away and pressed his shoulder and chest against the bark to reach a few millimeters further, he felt a faint tug at the tip of his fingers.

"You got her, now pull like you mean it!" Granda's voice was faint.

The tugging sensation grew more definite, and he waited patiently for the fingers to get a grip on his own. When he felt the cool palm meet his own, he held tight and began slowly drawing back as if he were pulling a victim out of quicksand. His arm gradually emerged, slick and red. Marianne alternately tried to ease the lips of the wood apart and pull on his free arm.

Gradually, a pale green arm appeared, followed by a shoulder. Ruari's blood smeared her pale flesh as if she were being birthed from the bowels of the earth. A head covered in a mass of dark red fibrous hair came into view. As he and Marianne pulled gently and steadily, Vivienne's body slid from the crack, and Ruari thought he saw his grandfather's hands supporting and lifting the slender body. They laid her on a bed of leaf litter. Head lolling, Vivienne faded in and out of consciousness

Behind them, a pair of big, scarred hands reached out of the narrow gap and wrapped themselves around the roots. With an effort, Granda hauled his body free of the tree's embrace. He sat on the ground nearby, looking nearly as drained as the fey did.

The lightning had marred her features, running down the length of her cheek, neck and torso, ending in the ugly burn on her hip. But that was nothing compared to the hacking slashes that scored her torso, hip, and thigh on the other side. If she'd been human, she would have bled out hours ago. Milky sap seeped out of her wounds, but as Ruari watched, the smears of blood faded as her skin absorbed it. *She grew in strength and stature after she killed that village. I'm not sure how I feel about her consuming my blood. I suppose if it helps her live, that's okay.* He tried not to think about it.

Marianne pulled a roll of white cloth from her coat pocket and said, "Maybe this will help."

The old man knelt beside them, and together they wrapped

Vivienne's wounds in gauzy bandages, trying to staunch the flow of sap. She roused as they ministered to her injuries, and her eye fluttered open.

She whispered, "Thank you, Coll. I did not have the strength alone. Ruari, the gift of your life's blood leaves me in your debt."

"I'm sorry, *mo chroi'*, that I couldn't do more." Tears coursed silently down his lined cheeks.

"I have some well water, if you can drink a little," Ruari said. He lifted her head and poured a little into her mouth from a thermos. His questing fingers had found the container among the roots, though he didn't recall putting it there.

After she'd swallowed a few mouthfuls, she seemed a little stronger. She looked at her old companion. "Your sons grew twisted on poor, rocky soil. I am sorry for that. I forgot human offspring are not like my own."

"That's as much my fault as yours," Granda responded, squeezing her hand gently.

Vivienne turned her undamaged turquoise eye to Ruari. "Your boat is fine work but would have been more beautiful if I'd helped." He acknowledged that with a faint smile. "I will sleep inside it. I won't know until spring if I have the energy to wake again."

"Releasing me from our bond would pay that debt," Ruari said.

"I can try. Come closer."

He bent down, and she slid her fingers over the little spiral mark on his right shoulder. She closed her eyes for several long moments. The scar prickled and pinched, then he felt a faint release. She slipped away from his mind, and part of him regretted the loss.

She rolled her head slightly toward Marianne and gave a faint, sardonic smile. "There. He is all yours. Your wards kept me out for awhile, but I found a way in."

Marianne gave her a shrewd look. "You let Jason in?"

The fey woman quirked her lips. "I hoped to distract you. But you are as stubborn as a she-badger. Are you willing to be friends in spite of that?"

Marianne took the fey's hand and squeezed it. "Yes." *For now,* she thought.

"We'll take you to the Dumfries forest tomorrow and find a safe place to hide you until spring. Hopefully, that will be enough," Ruari told her.

"If I survive, I will endeavor to be more understanding of your needs. It seems I cannot escape being obliged to your family."

"Maybe because we were meant to help each other through this life, not try to do everything alone," Ruari said.

"Maybe so." The fey woman was quiet for a time, gathering her strength, and they sat with her in silence. Finally, she said, "If I am to do this, now is the time."

Granda and Ruari stood on either side and helped her stand while Marianne held the boat-shaped cradle steady. Vivienne's long, slim foot stepped up on the gunwale. Either she had shrunk or it had grown as she stepped inside and lay down on her side. She faded into the wood slowly until they could no longer tell the difference between her and the boat.

They stared at the carved vessel.

Granda said, "No doubt about it. You did a braw job."

Ruari's heart swelled with pride, but he gave a wry smile. "Aye, Granda, it is. And I know it."

The old man looked at him with a touch of his old bluster. " 'Course you do. You're my grandson."

"Would you like something to drink?" Marianne called from the flat rock at the edge of the clearing. She held up the thermos as an offering. Three cups sat on the stone next to her. Ruari appreciated the convenience of the dream world.

"Aye, don't mind if I do," Granda replied.

They sat and drank. The spring water had become something

stronger with a bite of good whiskey. Finally, Granda set his cup down and regarded them. "I promised you an explanation." He sat back and composed his thoughts, and they waited.

"I've known about the fey muse since I was a lad. My father made the first bargain with her when he found the lost girl. He offered his services as a woodcarver so that she might create things again. When I was a young man and taking up the trade, my father introduced me to his fey muse, and for a time, she worked through both of us. Da died young and passed me the partnership. For a time, everything was well. But I met my Nora and wanted to marry her. The fey muse was jealous and didn't want to share. I was lucky, though. Some neighbors wanted to convert this ground to pasture and cut the trees for firewood. I bought the land instead and put the fence around it. She was grateful and let me marry."

He smiled wistfully. "I love Nora with all my heart even though I had to share her with another. 'Twas not so difficult at first. Then our sons were born. The fey demanded more and more of my time. I was becoming famous from our work together. I never imagined people would cross the world to come to the door of a poor Scots wood carver. That was powerful.

"Nora took on more and more of the family and farm work. Da hadn't been a bad father nor a good one. I could see my own sons growing up lost and angry without me. But I couldn't stop working with my muse. That was my own fault as much as hers."

His face clouded over. "But the day she looked at my own children, looking for her next partner, I could see the coldness in her eyes. She stared them up and down and tossed them aside like they were useless scraps of wood full of knots and twisted grain." He closed his eyes and hunched his shoulders. "By then her thoughts and mine were so tangled up, I sometimes didn't ken whose they were. But my sons heard my voice when she rejected them, and I saw the hurt in their eyes.

"Part of me was glad she saw no future in them. They would be spared her influence. But we both longed to share our knowledge of wood with someone. We had a few apprentices, but she was afraid to take any of them because she was tied to the land, and they were not. She couldn't be sure her tree home would be safe with them.

"Then you came along, Ruari, son of my youngest, in America and all. You were so like me, stubborn, determined. When you were certain a woodworker's life was for you, I tried to teach you all I knew." He rubbed his ear and laughed to himself. "You were like a jackdaw, goin' from one thing to another, unable to set still and learn something. Christ, it's a wonder you learned anything at all." He shook his head.

Ruari had been following the story spellbound. Heat rose into his face. Dad had been right, Granda had been ashamed of him. "I'm sorry, Granda," he said.

Coll's face flushed, and he looked at him sharply. "Don't be a dafty! I did about six things well when it came to wood. You were never afraid to try new things, crazy things. Sometimes they worked, other times they didn't. But you were always willing to try. It's half the reason I was so mad at you."

Ruari felt whipsawed. "But Dad said you'd told him you thought I wouldn't amount to much. You told Dad to find me another profession."

Coll's shoulders slumped. He ran his hand through his hair, making it stick up in all directions. He looked ashamed. "Aye, I did say that."

Ruari was so confused. "Why?"

"That's the other half of the reason I was so mad at you. I didn't want you in the fey muse's grip. After the day she looked at my braw boys and spat them out again, I didn't want her in anyone else's life. I thought she'd die with me." He gave Ruari an agonized look. "But every summer she looked at you with such a hunger in her eyes it scared me. It's why I broke it."

"Broke it?" Ruari felt something deep bunching up inside him, like a tidal wave. It threatened to overwhelm him.

Granda looked at him with such sorrow and shame that Ruari

knew. The wave swallowed him. "The box? *You* broke it?" He whispered, his throat too tight to let anything else out. "I thought Dad did it on the day of your funeral."

"Nay, 'twas me and a harder thing I never did past telling your Da you were worthless with wood. The lie choked me, but I said it. The day I broke the box, she was with me in the barn telling me how she planned to run your life. She looked at your bonny box with them beech leaves on it and said, 'See, he is mine already, he just doesn't know it.'

"Such a rage and fear filled me, I picked up a mallet and smashed it in one blow then and there, tryin' to break her hold. She just laughed at me and wouldn't listen to a thing I said when I begged her to leave you be.

"My heart caught up with me that night, and I left this mortal world. I tried to warn you, but I haven't been strong enough for that."

Ruari was reeling. "If you hate her so much, why did you help her?"

Coll sighed heavily. "It's complicated, you ken. I don't hate her, laddie. We made some incredible things together, and she made me famous and all. I just didn't want her to tangle up someone else's life like she did mine. Poor Reginald. Fergus'll be alright. And Douglas? Tell him I'm right sorry. They're all good lads."

Marianne topped up their cups. They drank.

Ruari spoke into the silence. "I took her bargain, Granda. She marked me and all." He drew aside his shirt, baring the little spiral on his inner shoulder. "When the storm happened, I saw all her long life pass before her eyes through our bond. I realized she was dying, and I didn't want her to die alone…like you did." Granda said nothing, and he continued. "So, I made a new bargain with her: I was willing to carve with her, but I wanted to have a human partner as well. It doesn't matter now." He looked at Mahri. "As long as you'll have me, I'd like to be with you."

The slow smile that spread across her features was all the answer he needed. "I'd like to be with you, too."

Granda put his hand over their two. "Be good to each other. Ruari, lad, I needed to say all the things I should have said before I left. Now, I have to go."

Ruari stood up hastily and gave the old man another quick hug. He was reassuringly solid in his arms. "Thanks for everything, Granda."

Coll nodded wordlessly and looked across the clearing. A faintly glowing figure stood there, but Ruari couldn't make out any features.

"I'm finally coming, Nora." He strode across without looking back, becoming brighter and losing his outline. The two shapes merged and drifted up and into the night until they dissolved.

Mahri stood by his side. She was glowing faintly lavender again. "Are you ready to go home, Ruari?"

"Aye." He brushed the dampness from his cheek and picked up the carved boat with its passenger. Together they headed back to the farm.

They woke in the dim light of dawn after an exhausted sleep. Moving stiffly, they stretched and sat up. Something small tumbled down the blanket and landed on the floor.

Marianne reached down and picked up the remains of her wooden ring. "Oh, it broke!"

His wooden circlet also lay in pieces. The grain of the wood hadn't been very strong for something so small. "Did you dream last night?" he asked hesitantly.

"Yes, we were up at the tree and moved Vivienne. She called me a she-badger. Your grandfather was there. Is that what you dreamed?"

He nodded in wonderment. "I can't believe that worked—that somehow we were actually in the same place."

She looked at the little arcs on her palm. "Do you suppose we somehow got your carving down here via dream? It would be nice if it saved us a trip."

They went into the kitchen. The vessel, presumably with its passenger, rested on the wooden tabletop.

Marianne said in awe, "How did we do that? Sleepwalking? Astral projection?"

"Considering that I spent a night up there carving on something that was down here and the work got done, I won't ask too many questions," Ruari replied. "I have no idea how it worked."

She touched the carving tentatively, as if it might shock her. "Can you tell if she's in there?"

Ruari took the piece and cradled it in his big palms. Holding it in the strong light from the window, he shifted his focus to employ his other sight and stared at it, turning it this way and that. He thought he detected a faint greenish glow around the figure, but it could have been his imagination. Perhaps when Vivienne had withdrawn from him, she'd taken her gifts as well? He looked at Marianne and unfocused his gaze over her left shoulder. He was oddly relieved to see her faint lavender glow. When those abilities had first come on, he would have been happy to lose them. Now he was kind of used to them. He refocused his eyes on the carving and tried again.

He shook his head. "I can't tell. She's very weak and might not have much energy left."

"Well, it's the best we can do."

Over breakfast, they discussed how Vivienne might fare during the winter. If someone found and moved her cradle before spring, she might not be close enough to a tree to transfer safely. Marianne showed him a note she'd drafted. "What do you think?"

To whom it may concern:

Please don't remove this carving from this location. We are conducting an experiment and will return in the spring to check on its condition. If found elsewhere, please return to the coordinates listed below. Thank you.

She included Ruari's email address in case someone had questions.

They sealed it in a plastic ziplock bag and tied it to the carving with a bit of string. Ruari found an old brown shirt of Granda's and wrapped it around the piece, hoping to hide it from casual detection. They placed it in a backpack and set out in the Civic. Previously, they had scouted several locations with large trees in their prime, set back from the trail. This time they looked for a more southerly exposure with younger trees to hide Vivienne until spring.

After an hour of not seeing the right combination of elements, they returned to the parking lot and drove to another access point into the preserve and tried again. They ate a picnic lunch at a promontory overlooking a broad swath of country-side. They still hadn't found the right location and were getting discouraged. Without hiking off the trail into the forest to search for suitable trees, they were running out of options. They'd seen other people, some with dogs or small children who wove off and on the trail as they pleased, and they worried about Vivienne being found and moved.

As they descended the trail back into the trees, Ruari spotted a fine young oak some distance from the path. Something about it drew him. Seeing no one else in their vicinity, they stepped off the trail. It was secluded and quiet. The foliage was changing to autumn colors, and the air smelled pungent and earthy, full of life. They approached the tree which stood some fifty feet into the woods, and Ruari guessed it was perhaps fifty years old. It was well-formed, tall, and vigorous looking. The trees were not too dense here, and some downed giants had left holes in the canopy, letting in more light and warmth. He oriented himself based on the intermittent sunlight and thought this tree would get early spring sun.

Marianne let out a soft cry, "Ruari! Look, this is perfect!"

He hastened to her side and saw a hollow at the base of the trunk where the roots emerged from the ground. An animal had dug an extra space between them, and it was full of fallen leaves. They checked to be sure no one was watching them from the path and knelt down to remove their precious cargo from the pack. Marianne wrote the GPS coordinates at the bottom of the note and secured it to the cradle. Ruari wrapped the old brown shirt around it to protect it from the rain. Together, they tucked it between the roots and piled leaves and sticks over it to further disguise it. Undisturbed, it would decompose and return to the earth in time. Marianne took pictures of the piece both before and after they covered it up.

"Just a minute." She fumbled in her jacket pocket. "Here." She deposited several prickly beech seeds in his hands. "For luck!" Together, they planted them around the clearing.

Holding hands, they walked the rest of the way back to the car.

Seeing his pensive mood, Marianne squeezed his hand and said, "If we come back next year to work on turning the farm into a bed-and-breakfast, we can come here and see how she's doing."

He nodded morosely. After all their work, this was anticlimactic. Their efforts might come to naught, but they'd done all they could for Vivienne.

CHAPTER 22

hen they stopped at Uncle Fergus and Aunt Maura's house to return the car, Aunt Maura insisted they stay to supper. She told them Aunt Maggie had called to say Reggie had woken up the day after the big fight feeling better than he had in a long while. When she asked him what was going on, he only said that he felt fine and went to work. Maggie could not make heads or tails of his mood swing, but since that was par for the course in their marriage, she was hopeful it would last awhile.

"At least he's not full of piss and vinegar, and that's something," Aunt Maura said.

Ruari and Marianne assured them they were fine and had no hard feelings toward their uncle for his strange behavior. They described their long walk in the Dumfries-Galloway preserve that day and talked about returning the following year for a visit. Seamus texted Ruari, asking if he had time for a pint. He agreed to pick them up from Fergus' and ferry them home afterwards.

The pub was a quiet place, suitable for conversation and good stout. Marianne sat back intending to let them talk, but Seamus drew her in telling stories on Ruari. He even described the bar fights they'd gotten into. Marianne raised her eyebrows in mock alarm, and Ruari had no choice but to counter with his own tales of their wild youth. They were all laughing by the end of the second pint. Seamus drove them home. Marianne went inside first, leaving Ruari on the doorstep.

"It's good to see you, cousin," Ruari said. "I'm right glad you're getting your life together. Those juvies'll be lucky to have you when your degree is done."

He laughed. "Aye, they won't know what hit 'em. Your lass is a good one. I hope it works out for you."

"Thanks." Ruari was touched that his cousin cared.

The farmhouse seemed quieter and emptier than before. They both felt at loose ends in the alcoholic buzz from the pub and the slow eddy after all the frantic activity. Ruari made a fire in the fireplace. Without really thinking about it, he got up and retrieved the apron-wrapped bundle of wood fragments.

"Isn't that the box?" She asked.

"I'm glad I saw the old man one more time." He stroked the cloth with his fingers. "I can't believe he smashed it. After everything I put into it."

"He thought he was saving you."

"Guess I owe my dad an apology. That's going to be awkward."

"Maybe it'll be a good thing in the long run."

"With Dad, I'm never sure. At least I have a better idea of what he went through. I don't know why I brought this, but I don't think I need it anymore."

He placed the bundle on the fire and watched the flames blacken the apron and consume the wood inside.

Marianne sat with him in silence. When the last bits were only a memory in the embers, she said, "I know it's late, but you don't look tired yet. Do you play cards?"

His sadness lingered, but he appreciated her attempt to change the mood. "I haven't played cards in years. Erin and I used to play when we were kids, though. Gin rummy, Spit, things like that."

"Do you know how to play Cribbage?"

"I think Nana tried to teach me once a long time ago, but I don't remember the rules."

"Let me teach you again," she said with an impish smile. "Is there a deck of cards around? Two, preferably."

He hunted through the various side tables in the living room and came up with an old tally board and a couple of decks with songbirds on the backs. They were worn now, but he could see Nana's strong, veined hands shuffling them in his mind's eye.

The small fire warmed them against the chill of the house, and they played cards for a while. Once he recalled the rules, Ruari found he remembered more than he thought. He won two out of the three games they played. Marianne's good spirits were contagious. He watched the fall of her dark hair over her shoulders and the crinkles at the corners of her light brown eyes as she laughed and thought, *I am a lucky man.*

"Mahri," he said as they paused between games, "thank you for coming. I don't know what I would have done without you."

She stopped shuffling the latest hand. "I'm glad I came too." She tilted her head curiously. "You've called me 'Mahri' a bunch of times now. What does that mean?"

He shrugged. "It's a nickname."

"It brings out the brogue in your voice, you know."

She leaned close and kissed him. Cards were pretty much forgotten after that. He broke off their kiss long enough to put the screen across the opening to the fireplace. Then he swung her up in his arms and carried her to the bedroom where they snuggled under the cold covers, kissing until they warmed up enough to do more.

On Thursday, they woke after a long sleep, feeling rested and relaxed. They remembered they hadn't mailed the tools and carvings yet. Since they had no car and it was only misting rain, they walked the mile or so into town, pushing the five heavy boxes in an old hand cart they found in the barn. Its old wheel wobbled drunkenly, which they found hilarious.

By the time they arrived, the sun had come out for a little, and they mailed the packages for the price of a small fortune. Leaving the cart by the post office, they walked around and looked in shops. Marianne bought some postcards and jotted a few notes to her Mom, Grandmother, and Kelly and Sarah. They dropped the letters in a street side mailbox and stepped into a pub for lunch where they sampled the local beer with a basket of fish and chips.

While they were eating, the forester Aunt Maura knew called Ruari's phone, and he had a long conversation with him. When he rang off he said, "Stewart McClain said he'd be willing to oversee taking the tree down and then getting the pieces milled and dried. I'll pay the bills and give him a commission for doing the work. It'll probably take a year, but it looks possible."

She smiled. "How nice someone here will be able to oversee it for you."

"Yeah. I hope Granda won't mind."

She took his hand and swung it. "I'm sure he'll be fine. More to the point, I don't think Vivienne will mind."

They pushed the wheelbarrow back to the farm and left it in the barn. Then they took one last walk up to the beech tree. The way seemed much longer after their dream flight, and they were both winded by the time they arrived. The sun was buried deep in the clouds, and the whole clearing was gray and silent with a faint veil of mist. Leaves dripped with moisture. It was a dreich day, and no mistake. The tree with its grievous damage was flag-ging. It looked like it had aged ten years overnight.

"It feels empty now in a way it didn't before," Ruari murmured.

"I know what you mean."

They didn't stay long and returned to the farmhouse through the woods, arriving in time to get ready for their last dinner with family.

Donal came this time, all smiles and glad to see them. They'd caught up on the week's news with each other by the time they arrived at Fergus and Maura's house, though Ruari left out certain details. Dinner was jovial and comfortable with the entire family present. They talked more about plans for turning the farmhouse into a B&B. Ruari contributed what he could from his work experience, and Marianne suggested they might create a 'persona' for the house and offered to do a little historic research that might make it more appealing online. Mary promised to work with Erin to create a website since she would be on maternity leave soon, and they all exchanged Skype addresses. By the end of the evening, they'd laid out definite plans, and Mary had taken notes. She and Tomas drove them back to the farm on their way home.

The next morning, Ruari and Marianne got up early and cleaned the house, getting the laundry as far as the dryer before Donal picked them up and drove them back to Edinburgh to take the train to London.

For the next five hours, they read, napped, and watched the countryside go by. Marianne used the time to book a hotel room in the city within reasonable distance from the train station. They looked at the opportunities for sightseeing while they were there, and Marianne planned to do her research the following day. Feeling inspired, Ruari agreed to accompany her to the library to look up books on woodcraft.

Their accommodations were pleasant, if a bit snug. They had supper at a pub after walking around for a bit. London was so much more crowded and noisy with a scent of unleaded fuel in the air that they felt a little overwhelmed.

"Makes you want to rush back to the farm, doesn't it?" Ruari said.

The following day, Marianne donned her academic hat, and they saw the Tower of London and a couple of museums related to the Victorian period. "I know my class is a bust for now, but I can't resist," she said as they sat at an outside cafe'. "Is your boss going to be okay with you being gone for so long?"

He shrugged. "She told me I owed her one. Maybe she'll like Casey better and fire me. She can certainly get away with paying him less than me. If I don't have a job when I get back, I guess I won't have any more excuses not to get my woodworking studio going. I have some savings and can give it a try."

"I don't think I'll be much help to you there." She sighed. "I guess I'll go back to being a lone historian for hire."

"Something will come up, I'm sure of it."

They spent their last day at the main London library. She downloaded resources to her laptop. Ruari found several books on woodworking designs and made copies and notes for himself. At the end of the day, they treated themselves to a highly recommended restaurant and ate a traditional British Isles meal of lamb, herbed potatoes, and vegetables.

While they ate a delicious caramelized apple tart for dessert, Marianne said, "This has been the craziest and most wonderful vacation I've ever had. A year ago, I would never have imagined I could be so happy."

Ruari felt warm and contented. Mahri's soft, dark hair fell in waves over her cream-colored sweater, and her amber eyes glowed with a tenderness that he could get used to. He blurred his vision for a moment and was delighted to see a gentle halo of soft lavender and pink surrounding her. He was a lucky man. Jenny would never have understood any of this.

"I have something for you," he said, reaching into his pocket. He pressed an object into her hand. He'd finished the little carving while he waited for her to get through her research.

The figure of a cat sat on her palm. It looked as much like Oscar as he could make it, complete with a hint of stripes all the way to his crooked tipped tail. She grinned. "I love it!"

He took a swallow of his wine. "Before I met you, I was afraid I might spend the rest of my life doing the same old thing. You changed all that. After everything we did, I don't know what will happen to Vivienne, but I'm glad we tried."

"Me too."

He took a breath. "I meant what I said in the dreamworld. As long as you'll have me, I'd like to be with you."

"I'd like to be with you too."

They touched their glasses rim to rim with a faint ring.

"To the future."

EPILOGUE

Granda's conversation had been weighing on Ruari. A few days after returning to Maple Hill, Ruari braced himself and called his Dad. It had been a pretty good day at work. Talmadge had been out of the office, and Casey had been attentive. Now that Vivienne was asleep, he had no pressing urge to start a new carving project.

The phone rang several times, and Ruari fleetingly considered hanging up.

"Hello?" Dad sounded brisk, screening the evening calls.

"Hi Dad, it's me, Ruari."

"Ruari, I was planning to call you this weekend and ask you about the family meeting."

He needed to say his piece before he allowed himself to be distracted and backed out of it. "I'll tell you about it, but I need to say something first."

"Okay."

"Do you remember the box I made for Granda?"

"I had nothing to do with breaking it!" Dad said sharply.

"I know."

"You were very disrespectful to me and your mother at the picnic," he said sternly.

Ruari's hackles rose. "You weren't exactly respectful of me either."

"Your mother was very upset."

"I already apologized to her." Ruari still felt guilty.

"And so you should. You owe me—"

"Dad, stop!" Ruari took a deep breath and fought to keep his temper. "I found out some things, and I know you didn't break it. I'm trying to apologize for blaming you!"

"It's about time!" Dad snapped and fell silent.

Ruari imagined Dad staring impassively at the wall in front of him.

Dad broke the silence, his voice low as if he was confessing something embarrassing. "I think your Granda broke it. I don't know why he would have, but he was probably the last person in there. I put it aside because I didn't want you to find out."

That shocked Ruari. *What made you think Granda did it? Why not someone else? You wanted to protect me??* "You did? I thought you couldn't wait to stop me from following in his footsteps?"

"You really should do something else with your life other than work with wood. Da wasn't a very good father, and I blame that on his obsession."

"Neither were you, and you don't have that excuse!" Ruari flared.

"Maybe not," he replied.

It was Ruari's turn to be quiet, absorbing that. "I think your family life was a lot more complicated than I knew. All I saw was our two week vacations in summer, and they were pretty sweet for me."

"I'm glad you had that time with your grandparents. It was something I didn't have, and part of me is still jealous that you got it."

"There's a lot of that going around." Ruari's shoulders relaxed, and the knot of tension in his gut eased up. "So, do you want to hear about the meeting?"

"I'd like that a lot."

ACKNOWLEDGMENTS

When I first contemplated reworking *Sylvan Dreams* I thought it would take three, maybe four months. After all, I'd just had the experience of writing the second edition of Dreams of Fire. But no. Covid hit and I struggled with incorporating more background for the fey, more details, and more in-depth characterization of Ruari in particular. The story ballooned, and I couldn't find my way.

Enter some key writing help. Daniel David Wallace offered a series of on line writing courses that was better than a graduate degree at a university because they focused on the practical aspects of character-first writing. I also found help in Lisa Cron's book, *Story Genius.* She, too, is a character-first writer and showed me how one thing flows from another as long as you know the key parts of a person's background. What brought it all together was a lecture by Kris Kennedy at a Marketing Academy workshop by Brian Berni. She described a Turning Point method that crystalized everything.

I was almost done with *Sylvan Dreams* in 2021 when I had the opportunity to write book 3, *Hallowed Dreams*, with another of Daniel's courses. I set aside *Sylvan Dreams* for about a year. I learned a lot about writing and the final iteration of *Sylvan Dreams* came more easily when I picked it up again. However, I still struggled with articulating the reason for Ruari's trip to Scotland. Finally, a couple of panels on writing at Miscon 36 in Missoula, Montana where Charlaine Harris, Patty Briggs, Rhiannon Held, and others gave me the final piece, and I solved the last problem!

Books come along in the time when they're ready and no sooner. Thank you for waiting.

If you read the first edition of *Sylvan Dreams*, thank you. I have made changes in this edition. If a scene you liked is missing, I'm sorry. Please know that I miss it too. However, this version of events couldn't include everything from the old one.

For the second edition, Orion, Kelton, Austin, Mom, Penny, and Diane made helpful comments. Any errors that remain are on me. Thank you to my writer's group, Sanan, Angela, and Miles for being supportive and awesome! I also want to thank Cara F. for her amazing skill at writing jacket blurbs.

I am profoundly grateful to my family, starting with Austin for reading and re-reading endless variations and keeping them all straight, as well as for encouraging me to keep writing no matter what. I couldn't do it without you. My formidable sons Orion and Kelton also offered valuable insights and acted as a supportive cheering squad. I couldn't have done this project without you either.

I have gone back and forth several times over writing "in dialect" for the Scots in the book. Ultimately, I chose to follow the current best practices of not writing in dialect. If you want to hear Broad Scots, you can listen to Stephen Briggs' audiobook recordings of Terry Pratchett's *Wee Free Men*, or *Hat Full of Sky*. Diana Gabaldon's *Outlander* series also provides an excellent listen (and a fabulous read). Then, you can imagine Ruari and his relatives speaking in their wonderful voices.

My source material comes from all over. The ghost stories often come from real life experiences of my own or others. Many years ago, Raphael told me stories about picking up ghostly hitchhikers in Jamaica and gave me ideas. Thank you to Paul at Renaissance Woodwork in Pullman, WA and Jonathan Prince for insights on carpentry and furniture building. The internet is a wonderful place to check all kinds of things. Thank you to various websites that explained auras, their colors and how to see them, including www.in5d.com, www.reiki-for-holistic-health.com, www.witchscauldron.net and https://www.energy muse.com/about-gemstones.

I take full responsibility for any remaining mistakes or poetic license and hope you enjoy the second edition of *Sylvan Dreams*. Please leave me an honest review on Amazon or Good Reads. Simply answer these questions: why did you pick up this book? What did you like or dislike about it? How would you describe it to a friend who was considering reading it?

GLOSSARY OF SCOTS PHRASES

Awright ya wee bawbag?: how are you doing, you little scrotum? Used either to really insult someone or among close friends who won't take it amiss.

Barrister: lawyer

Bairn: small child or baby

Biscuits: cookies, not little short cakes to be eaten with gravy…

Blashie: storm

Bonny: beautiful

Braw: really nice, good looking

Da: father, Dad

Dafty: fool, idiot, stupid person

Dreich day: damp, overcast, chilling, miserable

Eldritch: weird, sinister, ghostly

Fash: worry, fret, fuss

Feasgar math: good evening (Old Scots Gaelic)

Granda: grandfather

Haggis: a dish of sheep's or calf's offal mixed with suet, oatmeal, and seasonings, boiled in a sheep's stomach. An old-fashioned way of consuming all but the baa or moo of the animal.

Haud yer weesht: be quiet!

Ken, kenned, kenning: know, knew, knowing

Mam: mother, Mom

Mo chroi: my heart (term of endearment)

Motor: car

Nana: grandmother

Pure: totally, very (used for emphasis)

Rubbish: nonsense

Scunner: person who pisses you off

Shut yer geggie: shut your mouth (Glaswegian)

Skirlie: oatmeal fried with fat, onion, and seasonings

Tatties and neeps: potatoes and turnips; dinnertime

Thig dhomhsa: come to me (Old Scots Gaelic)

Wee coorie: a little cuddle

Yer bum's out the window: you're talking absolute nonsense

You're talking mince: you're talking nonsense

Sources: Wiktionary, https://www.scottish-at-heart.com/scottish-sayings.html
https://www.highlandtitles.com/blog/scottish-slang/
https://scotlandwelcomesyou.com/scottish-sayings/

ABOUT THE AUTHOR

I have been writing all my life. My first story was in fourth grade complete with crayon illustrations. Since then, I've written fan fiction, short stories, novellas, and novels set in a variety of fantasy worlds. Getting a Masters and PhD in anthropology from Washington State University allowed me to spend summers camping and doing archaeology in Alaska and the Aleutian Islands. I spent twenty years being a taxi-mom, reading aloud, telling stories, and sneaking in a little writing when I could. My husband reads my drafts, challenges my thinking, and always makes my stories better. I currently work as a professional archaeologist in Eastern Washington. In no particular order, I love to sing, knit, garden, role play, play board games, and spend time with my family and friends.

Maple Hill is a fictional town nestled in the hills of the Hudson Valley, New York. It's a composite of several places I've lived in or visited. I loved creating this world and look forward to returning in the future to tell more stories with familiar faces and introduce new ones. Look for news about upcoming stories at palousedigitalpress.com/

If you like my work, recommend me to others!

Find me on https://www.amazon.com/ in paperback and e-books. Leave a review and help others find my work.

Contact me at ERAlix@turbonet.com if you want to say hi.

Visit my website, palousedigitalpress.com/ where I promote other local or regional authors and publications. Sign up for my occasional newsletters.

Follow me on Instagram @elizabethralix where I occasionally post pictures of the Palouse.

ALSO BY ELIZABETH R. ALIX

Maple Hill Chronicles

Dreams of Fire (book 1)

Marianne Singleton flees her obsessed ex-husband to the sleepy town of Maple Hill, hoping to start a new life. She doesn't find safe haven.

Plagued by nightmares and eerie occurrences, Marianne quickly learns the charming older home she bought is filled with a strange, spectral presence. When her ex-husband follows her to Maple Hill, she suddenly has more trouble than she can handle.

With the help of some new friends, and her cat, Oscar, Marianne attempts to unravel the mystery of who—*or what*—inhabits her home. If only her new friends could help her deal with a stalker ex-husband. As he menaces ever closer, she must find the courage to face him down.

Sadly, she's always been better at fleeing than standing her ground…

Available at Amazon in paperback and digital formats.

Maple Hill Chronicles

Sylvan Dreams (book 2)

Marianne Singleton has defeated both her horrible ex and the ghosts in her house. Her prospects for a job are promising, and her love life is back on track. Life is good.

But she's still seeing ghosts. When she picks up a hitchhiking ghost who won't leave her alone, she has her hands full. To make matters worse, her new boyfriend starts missing dates, and that may be more than her bruised heart can stand.

Ruari Allen is at a crossroad in life. His job is thankless, and he longs to start his own woodworking business. Marianne makes his heart sing, but, having broken someone's heart in the past, he's afraid of hurting her. When he starts seeing colored haloes and smoke around people, he worries about his sanity. Especially since he's also started dreaming of a mysterious red-headed woman who claims to have known his dead grandfather.

Relationships are hard enough without supernatural forces getting in the way. If Marianne and Ruari's relationship is to stand a chance, they'll need to take drastic steps. Will a desperate journey to Scotland bring them together, or forever cast them apart?

Maple Hill Chronicles

Hallowed Dreams (book 3, forthcoming)

Wake your ghostly allies, All Hallow's Eve is coming…

Marianne Singleton, a fledgling medium, embarks on a road trip with Sarah, her mentor in all things magical, to protect Canopus County from supernatural danger. As Marianne struggles to learn magic, the trip becomes more perilous. Needing to prove to herself she can stand on her own two feet, Marianne refuses to bail out and go home.

Frustrated by Marianne's stubbornness, Ruari Allen cools his heels at home in Maple Hill. When his fiercely independent sister, Erin, requests his help out of the blue, something is really wrong. A trauma has surfaced from Erin's childhood that just might hold the key to Marianne's dangerous journey.

As the clock ticks down to a showdown in the Maple Hill Cemetery on Halloween night, Marianne will have to learn magic and convince some rowdy ghosts to help her or doom Canopus County to attacks by spectral forces.

Illustrated by Andrew P. Slaughter of Pilcher Illustrate.

Maple Hill Chronicles

Legends and Dreams (book 4, forthcoming)

Everyone knows the Avery Theater in Maple Hill is haunted.

The latest production of *The Legend of Sleepy Hollow* is supposed to revive the failing old theater, but ghostly doings are disrupting rehearsals, and people are behaving strangely.

Marianne's new business as a historian for hire isn't exactly a financial success. Her first jobs are for ghosts who are notoriously short on cash. Ruari struggles to get his new woodworking venture off the ground. Separately, they are drawn into the mysterious events at the theater. Can they save the play?

As opening night draws closer, the past and the present begin to merge. The last time *Sleepy Hollow* was performed the theater burned down…

Maple Hill Chronicles

Dreams of Blood and Bone

(tentative title for book 5, forthcoming)

www.ingramcontent.com/pod-product-compliance
Lightning Source LLC
Chambersburg PA
CBHW031942110726

47902CB00001B/265